D0175275

ALSO BY RICK SPRINGFIELD

Late, Late at Night

MAGNIFICENT VIBRATION

VIBRATION

RICK SPRINGFIELD

A TOUCHSTONE BOOK
PUBLISHED BY SIMON & SCHUSTER

NEW YORK   LONDON   TORONTO   SYDNEY   NEW DELHI

Touchstone
A Division of Simon & Schuster, Inc.
1230 Avenue of the Americas
New York, NY 10020

Illustrations by Rick Springfield

First Touchstone hardcover edition May 2014

For information about special discounts for bulk purchases, please contact Simon & Schuster Special Sales at 1-866-506-1949 or business@simonandschuster.com.

The Simon & Schuster Speakers Bureau can bring authors to your live event. For more information or to book an event contact the Simon & Schuster Speakers Bureau at 1-866-248-3049 or visit our website at www.simonspeakers.com.

Designed by Ruth Lee-Mui
Jacket design by Jason Heuer
Jacket photograph © Kim Westerskov/Photographer's Choice/Getty Images

Manufactured in the United States of America

1   3   5   7   9   10   8   6   4   2

Library of Congress Cataloging-in-Publication Data

Springfield, Rick.
Magnificent vibration / Rick Springfield.
pages   cm
1. Nuns—Fiction.   2. Americans—Scotland—Fiction.
3. Fiction / Humorous.   4. Fiction / Literary.   I. Title.
PS3619.P7655 M34   2014
813'.6
2013033160

ISBN 978-1-4767-5890-9
ISBN 978-1-4767-5891-6 (ebook)

To the memory of my good friend and
boyhood bandmate:
Darryl Cotton

MAGNIFICENT
VIBRATION

M*y first memory: at the callow and impressionable-as-warm-wax age of three I'm sitting on the floor of my parents' bedroom gazing at my mother as she dolls herself up on what must have been a Sunday morning. I'm vaguely aware that her destination is a place she calls "church," but I'm too young to comprehend the judgmental, exclusionary, and ironically un-Christlike aspects of her particular tribe of Christians. So I'm enjoying watching her play dress-up.*

Strange and beautiful birds I later recognize as doves hoot plaintively just outside the window while she tricks herself out for Jesus. Translucent nylon hose crackle and sizzle with static electricity as they are drawn up over still-firm thighs. Her "good" dress seems to dance with her as she shimmies into it. She applies wine-red lipstick with stunning skill (I can't even keep my crayons inside the lines yet) and layers row upon row of faux pearls deftly around her slender throat—a throat I will eventually want to wrap my hands around and squeeze until her bouffant explodes, which I'll resist doing only with the utmost self-

restraint. She sings beguiling hymns while she primps, as my toy robots and I watch openmouthed and spellbound from the floor.

My little soul is pining for the day when I am "a big boy" and she will allow me to accompany her to "God's house." I'm thinking it must be a pretty sweet place to make her whip out her party dress. It probably has a pool. With a slide.

So this as-yet-unsullied goddess becomes my earliest paragon of sexuality and organized religion. I'm still years away from understanding the scope of its hold on me, and I don't realize I could go to Hades-for-ankle-biters just for having amorphous, erotic notions about my own mother as she ardently tarts herself up for the Lord. But it's no surprise that this powerful memory is the first one my baby brain grabs hold of. It's clearly a keeper.

The scorching intersection of sex and religion will remain a potent one for me—a mash-up that will drive me to my inevitable destiny in the years ahead . . . possibly. Did God set me up? Or did I arrive at my ultimate future under my own steam? Free will or fated? It's a tough one to call. All I can say is that at this stage of my currently imploding adult life, the last person I ever expected to have a direct line to was mom's superhero, Big "G," little "o," "d," who, until recently, has seemed content to sit out the duration of my life, ignoring my occasional eleventh-hour invocations and foxhole prayers—almost daring me to become an atheist. But one dark, lonely night, that is exactly who I find myself calling. Literally. On my cell phone.

And so it is written:

1-800-Call God

(Beep, beep, beep, beep, blippity, beep, blip, beep, blippity, blip, beep!)

"Hello?. . . . . .Helloooooooo!"

"Uh . . . yeah,. . . . *God*?"

"Yepper."

"Oh, great—God says 'yepper'? What is this? An 800 number that sells salvation for five easy payments of nine ninety-five?"

"Ixnay on the amscay."

" 'Yepper' *and* Pig Latin? You sound like a geek. I'm betting there's a bad haircut and a *Star Trek* T-shirt on your end of the line, yes?"

"You lost me."

"Ditto. So I'm supposed to believe this is God's personal line?"

3

"Probably not. But there isn't very much you believe in at this point in your life, is there?"

"That's a pretty large claim, considering you don't even know who I am."

"I know who you are."

"Well, that just sounds creepy. Like you've been spying on me or something."

"Trust me, you walking to the corner Starbucks every night to buy a ham-and-Swiss panini and a grande chai latte is hardly surveillance-worthy."

"The *fuck* . . . ?!"

"And that barista is *married,* dude. You don't stand a chance."

"Wha— Who the hell is this?"

"You should know. You called *me.*"

"How do you . . . ?"

"How do I . . . ?"

"Is this somebody I know?"

"I like to think so. Shall we move on?"

"How . . . okay . . . so, God, what's up?"

"Certainly not your prospects. Hence the call."

"What's that supposed to mean?"

"What can I do ya for?"

"Wait a second . . . Doug?"

"It's not Doug."

"That's totally the kind of thing Doug would say."

"Yeah, it is."

"And how would *you* know that?"

"I'm omniscient."

"This *is* Doug?"

"Not Doug."

"Who the hell is this?"

"You've already asked me that. Do you want something?"

"Yes, I want to know who this is. If I'm actually talking to God, prove it."

"Look, *you* called *me*, and you've just wasted a minute-eighteen of your time and mine. Do you have an actual question?"

"Yes. Prove to me you're really God."

"That's not a question. It's more like a command."

"What *is* this? What's the point of this phone number?"

"A minute twenty-six."

"This is bullshit . . . I'm hanging up."

"Okey-dokey."

"You know what's weird? I actually called with half a hope that this number was . . . real. Isn't that funny? Joke's on me."

"I'm not laughing. You've come this far. Sort of. Why not play along?"

"Play along . . . yeah, okay. I've got no one else to talk to tonight, what the hell? My life's in the crapper anyway and ready to be flushed. I'm done. I was going to off myself but I'd probably screw that up too. Wind up a vegetable. Bok choy in a bed. So I was hoping, if maybe this hotline was real, that God might be persuaded to whack me."

"Whack you?"

"*Yepper!* Whack me. Or *smite* me. His call."

"Has life gotten a bit tough for you, little buddy?"

"To put it freakin' mildly, yes."

"Boo-hoo."

"Well, whoever you are, you're doing a pretty good riff on God's general disregard for me and my life."

"Hang on, let me go get my violin."

"Yeah, I've often thought if God does exist he must be a bit of a dick, anyway."

"A dick?"

"What kind of God would sit back and let the world be as fucked up as it is?"

"Let me guess . . . a *dick*?"

"Exactly. So if God's too apathetic—"

"Too much of a dick."

"Stop interrupting. Too much of a dick to put me out of my misery for my own sake, why can't He just smite me for my sins? I understand He *loves* doing that."

"Whoa, so backing up here, you want God—who you believe is responsible for the effed-up state of your planet—to now smite you for your sins?"

"That's what God does, amigo."

"No, it's not!"

"Well, yeah it is."

"Well, no it's not."

"Then what's all that 'thunderbolt and lightning' stuff in the Old Testament?"

"Did you just quote Freddie Mercury?"

"What?"

"Skip it."

"I think we're getting off topic."

"Why don't you *try* switching your own motor off? Just give it a shot, so to speak. Thousands of unhappy customers have and done it quite successfully."

"What kind of advice is that, if you're supposed to be God?"

"Don't answer a question with a question."

"Now you just sound like my mother. This isn't my mother, is it?"

"Your mother's dead."

"How—Who the . . . ?! This *is* Doug, you bastard! How are you doing this?"

"Again, not Doug."

"Who is this? . . . How do you know me?"

"I know you."

"I don't think so."

"Yeah-ha."

"Na-ah."

"Yeah-ha."

"You sound like some kid in grade school."

"Thank you. I love kids."

"This is going nowhere. I think I'm gonna jump off."

"A building?"

"I'm afraid of heights. So, what, you write this number all over town to see how many suckers will call? You must be pretty lonely. We're just two lonely, depressed people, whadya say?"

"Is that what you think is going on here?"

"Pretty much."

"You need to widen your view. Remember when you were thirteen and you hid in the girls' locker room and watched the volleyball team while they were changing? It shifted your perspective a little, didn't it, and—"

"Holy shit! God! . . . Whoa! How do you know about *that*?!"

"Did you just say 'Holy shit' and 'God' in the same sentence?"

"How could you *possibly* know that? I never told anyone. Okay, you got my attention."

"Yippee. At last."

"Wow."

"Took you long enough."

"How could you know all this?"

"One more time: I'm omniscient."

"Okay, okay—give me a second here. But this is just some phone number I found in a . . . on a bathroom stall in a bar."

"Ah . . . no, you didn't."

"But—"

"You didn't get it at any bar. In an act of desperation, you bought—correction—you *stole* a self-help book called *Magnificent Vibration*. This number was written on the inside front cover. In pencil."

"Motherfucker!"

"I'll smite you for that!"

"This is crazy! Really? . . . GOD?"

"It takes you people a while, doesn't it?"

"Okay, see, you *do* smite. You just said so."

"That was a joke. I don't really go round eliminating folks just because they piss themselves, or me, off."

"You said, 'don't really.' That sounds a little iffy to me. Like there's some wiggle room."

"Not so much."

"Well, that *totally* sounds like there's wiggle room."

"Look, once again, I think you're focusing on the wrong thing. Anyway, I let Adolf Hitler live and he killed millions."

"But you took him out him eventually."

"No, I didn't. He killed *himself*. And not before he murdered most of the Chosen and picked a fight with half the world. What about Pol Pot and Stalin? Ivan the Terrible, Ted Bundy? So how can I justify dispatching depressed little Bunkie, just because you got up on the wrong side of the bed this morning, and leave all those other ass-clowns alone?"

" 'Ass-clowns'? . . . Is this *really* God?"

"You're kidding me."

"Well, you should know if I'm kidding you or not, right?"

"I was being facetious, and can you stop testing me now, goddamnit?!"

"God says 'goddamnit'?"

"Occasionally. When it's warranted."

"That's like me saying 'Bobdamnit!' "

"Your name's not Bob."

"I'm—"

"Horatio."

"Ahhh, I hate that name!"

"Then that would be '*Horatio*damnit.' "

"I got the crap beat out of me in junior high because of that god-awful name . . . sorry, that slipped out."

"So you changed it to '*Bob*'?"

"My mother was a European-history freak. Horatio—"

"Nelson, yes, I'm familiar with him."

"Yeah, I guess you are."

"Very famous eighteenth-century naval hero. Napoleonic wars, Battle of Trafalgar and all that."

"That's great, so let's name our only son after some old Limey sailor so he can get the daily crap kicked out of him by Steve the Jock when little Horatio joins the hormone-hell known as junior high."

"Good call on your mother's part."

"What?"

"Naming you Horatio."

"What?"

"It builds character."

"What?!"

"You might not be at the point you're at if you'd stuck with Horatio."

"WHAT?!!"

"Okay, you're gonna need to give me more back than that."

"I don't even understand why you're saying all this to me."

"We'll come back to it."

"Look, I just called—"

"—'to say . . . I love you.' Stevie Wonder, ladies and gentle-men."

"Do you have ADD? I called this number in a last-ditch hope that this was God and that you could conceivably offer a little advice or guidance. But obviously that's not what you do, so maybe you could see your way clear to offing me in a not-too-unpleasant manner . . . a quick, painless cancer possibly, or a sudden careening car . . . something short and swift that'll take me out of my sorry existence, because I'm at the end and I really don't have the balls to do it *myself!*"

" 'I just called . . . to say how much I care.' "

"Will you stop *singing?*"

"Let's go back to 'What?' I think I liked that better."

"What?"

"Exactly. Go out to a nice bar and have a drink and a pizza."

"That's all you've got to say?"

"Good night, Horatio?"

"FUCKIT!!"

(End call)

Crap! What did I just do? Did I just hang up on God? Seriously? Could it really have been *the* God, big "G," little "o," "d"? If it was, I am so screwed. No, wait; maybe it's a good thing. Maybe he'll be angry and wrathful with all that dark, festering biblical shit that I just *know* is in there and he *will* toast me. But if he's really pissed, he might do it in a vengeful, Jehovah/Old Testament kind of way . . . with serpents and locusts or raining frogs and boils, or maybe he'll kill my first-born male child, if I had a first-born male child, which I'm pretty sure I don't, but if I did and God killed the little guy, I'd never really know about it because I don't even know if I have a little guy in the first place. I realize the bizarre call has not only shaken me, it seems to have eighty-sixed my desire to leave this world. At least for now.

I'm also suddenly really hungry. And pizza's not a terrible idea. Good recommendation from the Father, Son, and Holy Ghost.

It's eleven o'clock at night. I'm thirty-two, newly divorced, I hate my job, my boss is possibly Voldemort's fatter, dumber brother, I'm alone in my new post-annulment digs at 1216 N. Detroit Ave. Apt 213, Hollywood, CA 90069, pining for someone to shave my shoulders and love me (not necessarily in that order), feeling desperately sorry for myself and thinking I just had a chat with the Almighty.

Maybe I'm a bit too baked. Since the divorce, I've somewhat fallen back into the old high school habit of lighting one up every now and then. That coupled with the mental distress of my increasingly crappy job.

My career as a sound editor at a mind-numbingly underwhelming audio/video company that has cornered the market on dubbing bad

Cambodian gangster movies into English is something I have fallen into after the rock star, Nobel prize–winning scientist, and gigolo options failed to pan out. Who watches these highly unpleasant videos in English is beyond me. Apart from the occasional kick-ass fight scene, they're awful: the acting is usually atrocious and the dialog and story lines in general suck a very large and blood-engorged Cambodian elephant dick, if you'll pardon the expression. I dislike both the product and my job. It's vapid, thankless work, made even more distasteful by my sociopath of a boss who everyone covertly calls 'The Right Whale.' And not just because he clocks in at three hundred and fifty big ones, either. He has this disgusting biological anomaly that causes tiny balls of white, cheesy stuff he apparently secretes to hang in the corners of his mouth and stick to both his lips with a surprising elasticity when he talks, causing them to look very much like the baleen of the aforementioned marine mammal. Fucking gross.

The Right Whale actually doesn't figure very heavily in my story, but for his relatively small footprint, he's managed to inject an inordinate amount of misery into my life.

I lost my dog in the divorce. *My* dog, mind you. I was okay with losing the car, the tiny house, most of the hard-earned cash (though honestly there wasn't enough left to feed the goldfish—which she also took—once the lawyers had smelled blood, gone into a feeding frenzy, and sharked down all they could chew). But Murray was mine. Why did she have to take him? Well, I know why. Because he was *mine*, and I wanted him. She doesn't even like dogs—but she apparently had squatter's rights on anything she wanted. Including Murray. I have a vague idea of stealing him back at some point, though I'm a little sketchy on the details. I think I'm hoping Murray will come up with an actual plan. He always *was* good at breaking out of the house, and

I'm trusting that with the aid of that innate global-positioning device dogs are supposed to have hardwired into their brains, he'll somehow show up on my doorstep one sweet day. I miss him.

I look at my cell phone. It looks at back me. The wacky conversation I just had replays itself in sound bites inside my head. I felt like I was talking to a really well-educated nine-year-old. I hit redial. My hand is actually trembling. Yeah, I definitely need some Taco Bell or Subway.

The dial tone sounds strange and hollow. There's a click on the other end; a pause, then a derisive, schoolmarm voice informs me that "The toll-free number you have dialed is not available from your calling area. If you feel you have reached this recording in error, please check the number and try your call again." Figures. I hit "end call," but before I do, does the voice really add "asshole" at the close of the message?

I know it's late, but I'm going out to a bar. That serves food.

I'm seven years old. I have largish ears. Some of my more aggressive schoolmates have taken to calling me "Alfred," after the Mad *magazine kid Alfred E. Neuman, who has ears like teacup handles protruding from his befreckled dome; and his prodigious auditory equipment is, if I'm honest with myself, fairly close proportionately to my own bat-ears. Damnit. Like Alfred E., I have freckles that won't quit until I'm in my twenties, teeth too big for my mouth, mouth too big for my face, a penchant for the upper-grade girls, and a persistent little boner that will not stay down no matter how much I play with my toy robots or think about baseball. My mother is driving the family to church, as is her wont every*

Sunday morning come rain, shine, bingo, flu, crying fits, or my father's infidelity.

Church is a cold, sleep-inducing, anxiety-producing, wood-and-stone edifice that smells like old ladies and is, to my seven-years-young mind, filled with losers, desperation, and people nearing death. And nothing like the super-cool church of my toddler imagination.

Mom has slicked my reluctant hair down to my little noggin (so I can make more of a statement with my ears vis-à-vis their extraordinary three-dimensional properties, I assume) and dressed me up in my good suit of clothes. The suit is stiff and unyielding (like my ever-present woody), and I will forever equate good clothes with the unpleasant experience of forced attendance at an antiquated church ceremony that was born in the middle ages when my great-great-to-the-tenth-power grandfather was probably struggling to hack a living for himself, his toothless bride, and their twelve lice-ridden children out of the frozen, harsh, and brutal sod of an English moor. And consequently I will dress like an ardent sports fan for much of the following years, once I am on my own and free of my mother's sartorial stipulations. At seven, I still love her implicitly, even though I have a sneaking suspicion that were she playing outfield for the Yankees and there was a choice between catching a fly ball or saving me from the path of a speeding train, before she chose saving me, she'd first check to see if there was a man on base. She hasn't lost her mind, divorced my father, tried to commit my beloved but damaged older sister to the state mental institution, or given my dog Bob (in whose honor I later rename myself) away to the local Vietnamese family because he barks too much for her liking, so everything is still fairly copacetic. I never see my furry best friend again after he mysteriously disappears, and I'm pretty sure his new owners barbecue him one Sunday while I am blissfully unaware and in church (of course) professing faith in the communion of saints, the forgiveness of sins, the resurrection of the body, and life everlasting. Amen. Really, no wonder we're all so fucked up.

To make matters worse, I am in love. Her name is Angela. She is a twelve-year-old goddess, forever maddeningly beyond my reach, and I begin my twisted hot-religious-girl complex right here, right now, at the tender age of seven, in this bastion of righteousness and morality. There is no mix of emotions more exhilarating, convoluted, and bewildering to my little mind than getting a stiffy as I stare at the stunning back of this angel with a ponytail while she kneels and prays, accompanied by the ancient melody of the wrinkly old vicar who drones on and on about God the Father and recites centuries-old, incomprehensible text without a hint of emotion to the faithful as I shove my hand in the pocket of my good pants to squeeze Woody Woodpecker because I inherently intuit that Angela and Woody are somehow connected. Simultaneously I am picturing in my mind, through a gauzy, sun-splashed filter, Angela turning around in her pew and seeing the love light in my eyes, stepping into the aisle of the boxy little church (which has now transformed itself into a majestic cathedral attended by kick-ass knights in gleaming battle armor), running to me while pushing past the astonished yet wildly applauding crowd of absolute-believers, picking me up (I am a smallish child), and spinning me round in slo-mo while professing her undying love as Woody and I rub ourselves against her crinoline dress and pledge allegiance to her forever. Whoohooo!! It is the upside of forced religion. The downside being that I am wracked with guilt at the same time. I instinctively know that what I am envisioning is very wrong. Horribly wrong. Completely against everything I am being taught that God wants and expects of me, frail and pathetic human being that I am. My mother would be horrified. How dare I defile God's house of worship with my stinky-boy carnal longings? It is an awesome amalgam! And mixed all together, the hot, intoxicating brew of these conflicting and uncompromisingly charged emotions is delicious and staggeringly mind-blowing. I am effing hooked.

The bar is surprisingly crowded at this hour. I wonder if any of these people think they've ever had a conversation with the Creator. Probably not. Everyone looks pretty content and oblivious to the worries of the wicked world. Fairly well adjusted, I'd say. But then they've probably all been drinking half the night. That's what I need. A little attitude adjustment. And a snack. At this hour pizza would indeed work.

I maneuver my way up to the crowded bar past some fairly stunning women and, sadly, equally stunning men who have their undivided attention. I try to catch the closest bartender's eye, but he's having none of it. Must be related to the stunning women. I glimpse my reflection in the mirror behind the bar and am shocked out of my self-pity by what I see. My dark hair is now long enough so the old ear issue isn't as noticeable. And my head has expanded a few sizes since childhood, too, thus tilting the proportions in my favor, cosmetically speaking. But as I look at my mirror image, I am more than puzzled. Is that an actual gray streak in my hair? As if a skunk has positioned himself like an ass-hat on the top of my head? A thick white stripe, an inch wide, weaves its way from the center of my hairline until I lose sight of it back beyond my crown. WTF? Despite all my stress, real and self-generated, I've never ever seen a single silver hair on my head. I don't think I'm overly vain regarding my appearance (obsession with the bat-ears aside), and I usually only look in the mirror to adjust the coif now and then or to check and see if I have a "bat in the cave" (visible nasal mucus), but I do *not* remember seeing a hint of this frigging gray hair coming. I am actually more than mortified to be discovering this drastic change while in a public place. It reminds me of the anxiety-ridden nightmares of my teenage years in which I'd dream I've shown up at my high school dressed only in my underpants or even worse, completely naked, displaying a very mortified Woody—small, limp, and not at his best—as all the cute girls from school walk by gawking and giggling.

Lost in thought, mesmerized, I am staring at my likeness when I hear a voice. "You want somethin', man?"

The Zen masters have been trying to drill it into our thick Western skulls for centuries—that which you seek will be irresistibly drawn to you once you cease the seeking of it. Case in point: the bartender I'd been trying to flag down is now parked in front of me asking what I want to drink. Okay, maybe not as much of a spiritual example as I would have liked but you get my drift.

"A beer, please. IPA if you have a good one."

"I get to choose for you? Lucky me," he tosses out and then disappears, along with his attitude, free to interpret my request as he pleases, charge me exorbitantly for it, and expect a healthy tip for being a putz. He is gone so fast that I don't even have time to get in the vital pizza order. I'm too distracted by my new Bride of Frankenstein dye job to chase after him.

I feel a sudden touch of vertigo. The room starts to spin and I am desperate to get to the restroom to check this gray striation thingee out. I decide to wait for the beer. At this point it couldn't hurt. The bartender returns and petulantly slams the drink down in front of me before vanishing faster than you can say, "I'd like a pizza with that, jerky-boy!" I take a large swig and check my reflection again. The white stripe glares back at me insolently and with attitude from the center of my head. What is going *on*? An image of Charlton Heston from *The Ten Commandments* flashes unbidden into my mind. He's coming down from the Mount (Olympus? St. Helens? Fuji? My theological knowledge is sadly lacking) with the stone tablets into which God has just blasted his ten rules for living and, yes, his hair has turned white, and his beard, and I am assuming his pubes as well. Is that what's happened to me? Do we instantly get a silvering of the follicles when we talk (or think we talk) to God? The beer's not having the desired calming effect so I chug the rest of it, push my way past the apparently carefree crowd, and head for the men's room. On the way I silently assure all the hot girls watching me that I am only going to the loo to check out this wacky new design in my hair. None of them notice or give a shit. They're all busy meeting and greeting guys their kids will eventually have to spend the weekend with.

Right now I'm thankful for the distraction they cause, as my mind races, trying to hold onto some sense of normalcy. The female of our species occupies my mind twenty-four hours a day, but my actual hands-on, in-the-field experience is sadly and embarrassingly minimal. And my choices, when those succubi have allowed me to choose, have not been stellar. I wish there was a litmus test for future possible mates. Way back in the Dark Ages of Jolly Olde England they used to toss women into the local river as a way of divining the good from the bad. If they were buoyant and floated, they were branded as witches, summarily hauled out and cooked to a crisp at the stake in the town square while everyone cheered. If they sank (and presumably drowned), they were deemed innocent and God-fearing folk—although, tragically, quite dead. Hell of a litmus test. But medieval England was so stunningly black-and-white in its ways and customs. You could even poop on the sidewalk, right in front of the local butcher's shop if the mood caught you. And there were rules of etiquette regarding the correct conduct one should employ upon meeting a friend as he's taking a very public crap in the local High Street. Whether one should acknowledge him or not, and possibly what to say. For the life of me I can't imagine what those appropriate greetings might have been—"Hail, Cedric, well met. All right, nice shape, good texture. See you at the next public hanging." Possibly uncomfortable, but refreshingly honest. Wait . . . where was I? Trying to grab onto some semblance of normalcy, obviously. And heading for the head past throngs of sublime but occupied women.

The bathrooms in these bars always smell like fat, hairy, naked men have been wrestling in them for a couple of hours without a break. I go to the mirror, where other male club patrons are washing their hands, faces, heads (the drunk ones always think water on their heads will sober them up—it doesn't), and I move in to get a closer look at my new 'do. Jeez. It's really there. I am staring at myself a little too long and hard, and it's making some of the guys around me uncomfortable. A couple of them back away with creeped-out sideways glances in my direction and head out to the bar before they're fully washed and styled, and I sense they think I have a look about me that says "Warning!!! I am about to go postal on this whole fucking place in about three seconds." I will, however, not. I feel lost, separate, marked, favored, cursed, but definitely un-postal. This can't be real.

I separate my hair with my fingers to get a better look at where this hoary stripe begins and ends. It grows from the very roots of my head, and there is a firm line between the definite white and the dark brown. I'm having serious trouble processing this when my groin buzzes. It does it again. And again. It takes me a couple of seconds to realize it's my cell phone on vibrate in the front pocket of my jeans. I glance down at my glowing crotch and move to a corner of the now fairly empty, slightly anxious and on-edge restroom to retrieve the intrusive thing. I look at the screen to check the caller ID. At this late hour it's probably Doug. It's not Doug. The caller ID reads: **"Big 'G,' little 'o,'** **'d'. "** That's when I lose it.

Ronan Young has been fishing the dark waters of Loch Ness for forty years. A native son of the craggy Scottish highlands, he has neither travelled nor been inclined to travel farther afield than his cozy home in Inverness. He lives for the stark beauty of this land, and he is fairly sure the land reciprocates. The pale-yellow winter sun hangs in a pewter sky ending its westward journey beyond the ragged peaks as though snuggling into the mountains for warmth. Ronan regards the day's catch with a schooled eye. Sea trout, char, a clutch of eels. A good haul for him and Evelyn. He turns his small fishing boat, the *Bonnie Bradana*, toward the Loch Ness inlet that feeds the much smaller Loch Dochfour before he will take the twenty-minute trip along the canal to the Caley Cruisers boat dock where he houses his girl between fishing trips. This morning a couple of visiting fishermen have cancelled their day trip on the great Loch, so Ronan has taken this opportunity to go solo. It doesn't happen very often, but when it does he is nurtured by the rhythm of the deep water, the mighty crags that surround the lake, the spirit of this land, and his soul soars. It's just Ronan and his *Bonnie Bradana* alone on Loch Ness. Once a fiercely defiant single entrepreneur, he has, through financial necessity and the changing face of the tourist industry, been absorbed into the larger Caley Cruisers with its twenty-odd fishing boats. And three or four days a week he takes a brace of fishermen out onto the Loch. He has a few *good* fishing spots to which he guides those travelers who are courteous and respectful, and a few not-so-good ones where he takes the paying passengers who treat him like a ghillie. He is no man's servant. The *great* spots he reserves for himself and his few local friends. It is from one of these, near the far end of the Loch, that Ronan has just come. On his mind the thought of a pint or two at the Steading Inn before heading home for Inverness to Evelyn and their two Cairn terriers, Toby and Jacoby. This time of year most of the tourists have returned to the ball-and-chain embrace of their workaday world and the cities that spawned them, leaving the great Loch relatively empty once more. As it was almost year round when Ronan was a small boy and he would visit these same fishing spots with his father, learning the angling craft that he now plies so well. A single osprey circles overhead, scanning the gunmetal-gray water for a meal. The flat calm that is the Loch's surface this late winter evening encourages the bird in her hunt as the *Bonnie Bradana* cuts smoothly across the Loch's surface. Ronan knows this lake and knows her moods, her sullen turns of personality. She is old and she has survived for eons. The weekend revelers who take to her with their rented boats and pleasure craft know nothing of the depths of her soul. But Ronan does. He feels her essence, knows her true self and loves her for it. And he somehow feels that love is returned. Or at least an abiding affection born of mutual respect. His *Bonnie* coasts along the smooth, cold surface. "It is indeed a flat calm, Mister Murdoch," dialog from a movie he'd seen years ago, surfaces in his consciousness. He wonders at that. It always held great portent for him, those words that were spoken on the bridge of the *Titanic* before she struck an iceberg and became legend. Were they inviting something in? Suddenly, the *Bonnie Bradana* rocks slightly, as though riding the wake of another boat. Ronan Young scans Loch Ness, but he is alone. Again the boat pitches. He is puzzled, but only fleetingly. Something in his fisherman's soul knows there is a natural rhythm to this movement and there is very probable cause for his frail craft to seesaw like this on the unruffled lake. He has heard the stories since he was a child, though he's believed none of them. He has been asked the question a thousand times by wide-eyed travelers and visiting fellow fishermen. He has shaken his head in incredulity as expedition after expedition has come up empty-handed, with nothing on their expensive sonar and video monitors but fish fins and sunken logs. He knows that what they are seeking is not down there. Until this moment he has believed that with all his heart. Then, alongside the *Bonnie Bradana*, while the dying sun is sending out her final fading rays of warmth and light, the skin of the dark water peels open and an arched and ancient wet, black back the size of a semi breaks the surface of the Loch as a creature of legend breaches.

I love monsters. I always have and always will. But at twelve years old, the whole boy/monster thing is at its zenith. It's huge. I believe everything I read and I read everything I can. Frankenstein's Monster was almost definitely, for sure real! Possibly the Mummy too—jury's still out. The Loch Ness Monster has in particular caught my attention mainly because there is actual photographic proof that this amazing creature exists . . . and confirmed sightings . . . by church guys . . . and official Government Monster Specialists from the USA . . . everything. It's been sanctioned. The very first sighting was by a saint, for crying out loud. In 565 AD, Saint Columba was recorded as having seen this staggeringly awe-inspiring beast. And I'm pretty sure that was before TV and newspapers and stuff, so it wasn't like he was looking for his fifteen minutes of fame. That firmly slams the lid on all the naysayers, I think. I have, scotch-taped to my bedroom wall, the classic "Nessie" photo—the long serpentine neck and snakelike head poking up out of the lake in silhouette like a defiant middle finger, flipping off all the doubting Thomases and nonbelievers. "Hah!! Fuck you!!" it seems to be saying. This grainy shot of the creature is the centerpiece of my whole monster collection. Proof that my mother can make fun of me all she wants but smarter people than she are certain that the Loch Ness Monster is as real as roosters' balls. Regrettably, years later the photo will be revealed as a complete and utter fake, apparently made from a toy submarine, some wire, and a bunch of moldable plastic wood. But for now it's all good! Incontrovertible proof!

I look up from my current project and put my musings on how I could manage to get my twelve-year-old ass over to Scotland to view this magical beast for myself on hold, in time to see two spiffily dressed young people walking up our driveway. A young man and a young woman, both wearing black and each carrying some sort of book that looks suspiciously like a Bible. They appear so clean and scrubbed that the ol' family homestead suddenly takes on the aspect of a white-trash, doublewide meth lab by comparison.

There is a knock at our front door and I hear Josephine, my older sister by six years, answer. Josephine is named, of course, after Josephine de Beauharnais, Napoleon Bonaparte's first wife, another trendy historical reference from our mother's canon. A muffled conversation ensues. Josephine enters my little monster-sanctuary of a bedroom minutes later with a tense, pinched expression on her face and fear in her green eyes. I know what she is about to ask me and still I have no answers although I have tried to find them these past three years. She is the one female in my life who is safe. She is all-giving, all-loving, all-tortured, and all mine. I would give my meager twelve years to free her from whatever it is that causes her to relentlessly interrogate me with the same crazy questions. Questions that I can never answer to her satisfaction. Even if I understood. Even if I had the answers. We are both helpless when this demon has her in its clutches.

Our parents are even more clueless and confused about her condition. Her obsessive fears have reached such a magnitude that she can barely exist in this world anymore and I am powerless to help my sweet, broken sister. She is also under the dominion of a debilitating depression that sends her into dark downward spirals where she cannot raise a smile even for her dork-stick of a brother. It is a one-two punch that literally cripples her. The young girl she once was, with the wicked wit, bright smile, and open-door policy for the world and all of its people is gone, apparently for good. For the life of me I cannot figure out, in my young mind, what changed in her life to cause this drastic change in her spirit. I have heard phrases bandied about—"brain-chemical issues," "Lithium," "long-term psychotherapy"—but I still really don't understand any of it and am completely and broken-heartedly baffled. The only passion she still has is for the music she loves. I think she finds some solace from her demons, earphones clamped tight to her head, eyes clenched shut, the guitars blasting, drums pounding. But the singer from her favorite band has just killed himself, so there is a tortured aspect even to this. And Nirvana is no more.

"Tio," she says to me as I sort through the pieces of a plastic "Creature from the Black Lagoon" model kit I'm struggling to glue together without getting them stuck to my fingers or the paper instruction sheet, "there's two people at the door." My sister is the only one I allow to reference my atrocious birth name. And in her beautiful compassion she picked "Tio" over the other possible syllabic choices—"Hor" (whore) and "rat" (rodent). My mother calls me "Horatio," of course, and I have no defense against it. My father calls me "boy." I answer my Josephine.

"Yeah, I saw them walking up the drive. What do they want?" I'm hoping the conversation will go in any other direction. But it doesn't.

"I think the boy has a sore on his lip," she says.

"It's okay. It's not herpes. And if it was, you couldn't get it just by looking at him."

"But I think he rubbed his mouth before I shook his hand."

"I really don't think you get it like that, Josie, honestly," I try, although I have no real idea what herpes is or how one gets the damned thing. I suspect it may have something to do with monsters I am not yet aware of, but I have no proof. I do know that my sweet sister is terrified, with her whole being, of contracting this herpes thing. I wish I knew how to help her. She who was always there for me when I was small. She who had comforting words that healed my little broken heart. She who cheered for me like I'd won when I came in seventh place in the 100-yard dash. She who protected me, even taking on a bully once on the way home from school. She who was my avenging angel against everything that frightened and intimidated me as a young boy. She who was more a mother to me than my own mother. But not now. And I am powerless to help her.

"So I couldn't get it, even if he touched his lips and then his hand brushed against me?" she probes.

"I don't think so, Jo. I'll go talk to them."

"Can you look at it? The thing on his lip," she plaintively begs my retreating back.

It's hard to believe sometimes that I am her younger sibling by so many years when she falls into one of these endless mental loops. She sounds like a little girl pleading for a favor from Daddy.

I walk down the hall to the front door. Two spectacularly clean young people stand as if to attention behind the bug screen. They are immaculate human beings.

"What do you want?" I ask a little defensively. The dude has already worried my sister, so that's a big strike against him.

The girl speaks. She is fresh, polished, and, to my young eyes, another of God's exquisite handiworks.

"We'd like to talk to you about Jesus," she states with a bright-eyed zeal that immediately attracts me. *It doesn't take much.*

The man has a small, dying zit in the corner of his mouth. I assume this is what has my sister in such a state. It doesn't take much.

Josie joins me at the door. "We already go to church," she says.

"That's great," replies the perky girl. "What church do you guys attend?"

"The Presbyterian on Edward Street. It's our mom's church," *my sister replies. She can seem like she's functioning fairly normally in public situations like this, but once she's alone, her demons will pounce upon her like frat boys on a drunken sorority sister.*

"We'd love to come in and talk to you about *our amazing church.*" *Again, it's the perky girl talking. She seems to pick up on me and my unyielding gaze, directed mainly at her sumptuous breasts, as the easiest mark and begins directing her carefully rehearsed spiel to yours enthralled.*

"We're Mormons," *she informs us, smiling at me. And I am suddenly interested in Mormons, whatever they are.*

"I'd like to sit down with you personally, young man, one-on-one, and tell you how our church changed my life, and how it can change yours, too."

Oh, she's good. She's very good.

I push open the screen door like a zombie Mina Harker inviting Dracula in. I hear my sister's stifled cry of opposition but I am powerless under the gaze of this bewitching . . . "Moron," *was it? Proof, I think, of what a truly crappy, selfish little brother I really was.*

"May we talk with you separately?" *Dracula asks me.*

Again, Josephine's stifled resistance. Again I ignore it.

"Okay. Are you going to talk with me?" I ask her. Really, what a dick I was.

"I'd love to. And Bradley here will discuss our Lord with your . . . sister, is it?" Dracula, the little stunner, continues.

"Cool. Her name is Josephine." My sister is giving me seriously angry, desperate looks now. I signal her, in the silent code that we've developed over the years, to stop worrying; that everything will be okay. But she is signaling back that everything will definitely not be okay.

"We can sit in the living room, and they can go to the kitchen," I say, taking charge and guiding the situation now, with visions of I don't know what but they vaguely involve Woody and this burning-hot arch-angel. It's a potent, intoxicating feeling. These two seem like they would do anything to have us become fellow Morons. I have no idea what price I would ask, but I'm willing to have some guidance. Miss Dracula looks like she knows a thing or two about this. We sit on the sofa, Drac and I. She is so close to me that I can see down her top at the tantalizing crest of her breasts as they rise and fall in remarkable rhythm with her breathing, and although most of the girls I know don't even have breasts yet, I am not immune to their charms.

"What's your name again?" Dracula begins.

"Tio—no, it's Bob," I reply, making an instant decision that might possibly have an impact on me for years.

"Okay, Bobby. I'd like to start by asking you a question," she says, instantly switching to the more familiar version of my brand-spanking-new name.

"Fire away," I reply, thinking that this sounds like a really mature and worldly thing for me to say and I'm quite proud of myself.

She smiles a flirtatious smile. Pretty sure.

"*Did you know that Jesus Christ came all the way to America to save your soul?*" *she asks, opening the book she's holding.*

"*Really? Did he come through New York?*" *I query. Obviously I haven't been paying much attention in church.*

She smiles again, and her teeth are so white that I begin to wonder if people suddenly become great-looking like this once they agree to be Morons. Kind of like vampires get a widow's peak, fangs, and a black cape when they turn into blood-sucking fiends from hell.

"*I'm pretty sure most people came to America through Ellis Island,*" *I continue. I believe I may be on a roll.* "*I'm pretty certain my great-grandfather did.*"

She laughs out loud at this and I don't understand why, but I'm happy to have made her laugh.

"*You're really sweet, you know that?*" *she purrs—or at least I imagine she purrs—at me.*

"*Jesus came here before there were* any *Americans. Long before any cities or highways or even McDonald's.*" *She seems to think this is funny, but I don't get the joke. McDonald's has always been here.*

"*There were only the Nephites and the Lamanites. The Lamanites were originally a white-skinned race that God burned because of their terrible sins, turning them into Negroes,*" *she offers up.*

I interrupt her. Breasts and all. I don't know much about my fellow Morons yet but I'm pretty sure black people aren't the color they are because they've been set on fire by God. Not that I'm listening, but I guess part of me must be, despite her staggering awesomeness.

"*I know a black kid named Evan and I don't think his skin is that burned,*" *I suggest.*

Dracula puts her hand on my thigh, dangerously close to Woody. She just won the argument by default. Sorry, Evan. Woody answers the call. But to be fair, this comely wench could sell binoculars to the blind, life insurance to the dead, and oil to the Arabs. Her hand's warmth seeps into my skinny upper leg, melting the frosty heart I suppose I have hardened all my life against these wonderful, wonderful people, the Morons.

"I wish you'd open your heart to Jesus," she whispers in my ear, but she's probably not really whispering, nor are her lips anywhere near my ear. But the ear hears what the ear wants to hear, especially when it's as acoustically superior an ear as mine, and I am sold on being a Moron immediately. We talk for an hour or more, which seems like a minute or less, and then she removes her hand from my fluttering thigh (yes, the little minx has left it there through the whole conversation; she is no dummy) and says they must go but she will see me at her church next Sunday. She leaves her book for me to read, with a personal note inscribed on the frontispiece that drips and reeks of sexual innuendo, I convince myself. Dracula and Bradley leave with one more convert to Moronism as my sweet sister Josie runs to the bathroom to see if she has signs of advanced herpes. She takes a thirty-minute shower, throws up three times, and changes her clothes twice. And I form another deep connection between sex and organized religious fruitcakes! My little thigh still burns from the Moron flirt's touch, and Woody will spill his beans later that evening with the memory of Dracula's soft, warm hand still smoldering in his loins. Or certainly close to them. Horatiodamnit!!!

I am in a corner of the men's room in the bar. I hit the "answer" button on my glowing cell phone . . .

"Hey. How'd you like the Chuck Heston thing? Pretty cool, huh?"

"What . . . ?"

"What? What? What?!"

"What . . . ?"

"Okay, you need to expand your vocabulary."

"God?"

"That's a neat trick, yes? Did you freak out when you saw it? The white streak? How long before you made *The Ten Commandments* connection? I love that. You accept this whole 'movie' element that if you speak to me, your hair, beard—and possibly pubics—turn white. Hahaha. That's a little wacky, but I get it. And the white stripe is a nice touch, I think, when you begin to doubt. Which you did. I was hoping you wouldn't want to start your own church or shave your head or God knows what else."

"This is so not what I thought talking to God would be like. You sound like me. Or 'me' if I was, I don't know, in charge and a bit drunk."

"But you are in charge."

"Well, no, I'm not."

"Well, yes, you are."

"This is surreal."

"Yes, it is."

"So you're not mad? You're not going to send a plague or something to kill me, right? Because I'm doing a little better now."

The bathroom is starting to empty at a much faster clip now that the occupants are catching on that I believe I'm actually talking to God about possibly killing me. I try to dial it down a little in intensity and volume. And I drop the surname . . . or Christian name . . . epithet . . . title . . . rank . . . whatever it is.

"Yes, you are."

"And this isn't some weird guy with a computer program or something that has information he shouldn't have plus a great relationship with my phone service provider?"

"What about the 'Moses' white-hair thingee?"

"Okay, okay. I can't even begin to process *that* yet."

"Have you had anything to drink?"

"Wouldn't you know that?"

"Of course. I wanted to see if you'd try to sneak that one by me. There's no point in talking to you people when you've had too much to drink."

" 'You people?' That sounds so . . . I don't know . . . callous. Like something I would say."

"You think?"

"Where's the burning bush? And how come you don't sound all Godlike and imperious and infallible so that when we hear you speak we all just want to drop to our knees and honor and adore you? Really. What the hell?"

"Adore me? Okay, how's this . . ."

The voice in my ear suddenly takes on a rich, sonorous quality. With a crapload of really cheesy echo. I think I detect an angelic choir humming angelically in the background. The whole thing sounds like some half-assed Oral Roberts program.

"My son!! I am the Lord thy God. Prostrate thyself before me and pay homage to my magnificence, for I am the maker of all things in Heaven and upon the Earth. I demand thy obedience, thy supplication, and thy occasional contributions of hard-earned cash via televangelists with too much hair spray. Fear me!"

One of the porcelain sinks in the now completely empty restroom explodes into flames, scaring the crap out of me. It burns with a ghostly purple/green fire like nothing I have ever seen before.

"Holy shit!!!"

"How's that? Better for ya? More Godlike?"

"You're out of your mind!"

"Hahahahahahahahahahaha!"

"I'm going back to the bar."

"I think you need a cup of coffee!"

The line goes dead. And this time it's not me ending the call. No wonder we're all insane. God is, too.

I pocket my cell phone and exit the bathroom and its blazing sink, at the approximate speed a gazelle leaves the Serengeti at the first whiff of a lioness. And I feel very much like that gazelle right now. I'm beginning to think it was a bad idea to call God in the first place. An exceptionally bad idea. God is apparently quite real, quite crazy, and clearly tracking me now, which prior to this encounter I would have thought either highly unlikely or extremely helpful. Not anymore. The only change to come out of these conversations is that I am, at the moment, no longer thinking about self-termination. It seems kind of lame to even consider it . . . considering.

I feel instantly better once I'm amongst mere fellow mortals again. Safety in numbers. Or at least a temporary diversion. I elbow my way to the bar a second time, keeping a wary eye on the ceiling as though I'll be able to spot a thunderbolt or something equally dubious before it hits me. I don't even know what I'm running from, or if I can run. It's time for another drink. God said there's no point talking to the alcoholically impaired, so maybe if I stay high from now until Christmas God will leave me alone. I probably should say "he" or even "she," but what's really strange is that there is no definite sex attached to the voice I've heard. That in itself is exceedingly bizarre and so politically correct it makes me want to hurl . . . but it's true. It's a kind of androgynous voice, neither wholly male nor wholly female.

Mr. 'Tude, the bartender from hell, ignores me again even though I have severe desperation and need written all over my face, or maybe he ignores me *because* of it. I should get out more so I can learn the societal signals. He is actually just watching a basketball game on one of the thousand TVs artfully positioned for mandatory viewing whether you're into the sports thing or not. While the other bartenders swirl and dart around him, pouring, mixing, and delivering their potent concoctions in a fairly impressive ballet, I am struck by the irony that although I just spoke with God for the second time, I can still resent the fact that this weasel is ignoring me on purpose and I'm not getting a beer when I want it. Evidence, I think, that if the Martians invaded, vaporized our president with a ray gun, and took over the world, we would all accept it in stride and continue to try to win this week's $25 million Powerball. We are shortsighted pea-brains, all.

"This guy is one of the reasons people shouldn't breed," I say to no one in particular.

"Spay and neuter them all," I hear to my left. I turn to face the voice, half expecting to see my sister Josephine. It's so much something she would say in one of her lighter moments, when her system was relatively free of the psychosis-numbing drugs.

It's actually Angela, the twelve-year-old beauty queen from the Church of my Holy Twisted Childhood, all grown-up and ready to have a crack at producing some healthy babies with yours dementedly. Okay, it's not really Angela, but this girl certainly has a similar look, although her dark hair is cut short and slightly spiked. Her eyes have that same almost violet color and they seem to be smiling without the rest of her face joining in. If we all have a "type" that we settle on early in life, I would say that this girl is hitting about 90 percent on my checklist. What the heck is she doing talking to me, let alone initiating the conversation?

"Can I buy you a drink?" I'm stunned that I can't come up with a better line. I've just spoken with God, for godsake, and I'm still working from the same sorry script.

She answers appropriately. "Well . . . I'm either looking for a dog or a boyfriend. I haven't decided if I want to ruin my carpet or ruin my life."

"Okay. Sorry. You just reminded me of someone. Two people, actually," I say as I sign off and turn back to trying to distract the lazy bastard bartender from his basketball game.

"I'd like another beer here, please!" I yell, but of course it falls on deaf ears.

"I think you need a cup of coffee," I hear her say.

The fact that I've just heard this exact phrase from another quarter (specifically, the bathroom—more specifically, my cell phone) a few moments ago sends a fleeting shiver down the back of my Cleveland Spiders (world's worst-ever baseball team) T-shirt. But things have been a little off-kilter lately, so why would it stop now? I get a sudden, paranoid, frantic thought and spin to face her.

"God?" I blurt out before I can stop myself. My hands literally reach out to try and grab the word back before it reaches her ears, as though it were an errant loogie I had accidentally hocked up at some passerby and was hoping to arrest in its flight before it embarrassed both of us by landing on her lapel. But land it does. With a mucusy plop.

"What did you say?" She is smiling with her lips now as well and even adds a small giggle at the end of her question.

"Sorry. That was . . . sorry." I'm embarrassed that she didn't just ignore it as you would some old lady who'd farted in church.

"Did you just call me God? With a question mark at the end of it?" she persists, seeming pretty amused by my discomfort. There is interest in her eyes, though I am lost as to the reason.

And of course jerky-boy picks this moment to leave the ball game and bug me.

"Somethin' else I can get ya?" he condescends.

I turn to him. "Hang on."

I turn to her. "Just a second. Don't go anywhere." I turn to him, "Can I order a . . ."

But he's gone, and with him all hope of that pizza.

"This guy must get paid really well, because he isn't surviving on his tips," she says, and I don't even know who *she* is.

"I'm Bobby," I say, extending my hand in the prescribed, time-honored, and incredibly asexual I-don't-need-to-get-laid manner.

"Alice," she replies. She doesn't take my hand but raises her drink in acknowledgment.

That was dumb of me, I think to myself, not to notice she already had a drink. In my head I am already blowing my end of the conversation. Never had the gift of the gab.

"So, were you asking me if I was God just now? Because it sure sounded like it." Obviously she's not going to let it drop.

"Ah . . . yeah, I think I may have," I answer. She's still hanging in there, and for some reason it seems to make more sense right now to go with a version of the truth rather than dance around and deny it. She is sharp. And she's waaaaaay too pretty to be talking to *me*. Again suspicion clouds my clouded mind.

"Are you going to tell me why?" asks Alice of the violet eyes.

"Your name's really Alice, right? This isn't God messing with me again?" I sound like a nut. No, I sound like a total loon bag.

She frowns, but with a slight smile, still. If the roles were reversed I'd probably be putting as much distance as I could between the two of us right now. But she's still here.

"Okay, that sounds really creepy and weird. Sorry. I'm a pretty normal guy. I mean, not *that* normal, but then I guess no one is really *normal* normal. And not 'boring' normal either. I'm kind of a 'fun' normal—with a little 'depressed' normal occasionally on the side, if we're being honest, which I assume we are, but I'm probably the most normal, in a 'harmless' way, guy in this whole room right now . . ." I stop. I'm babbling like a fool, again. And she is still sitting at the bar with me, looking quizzical. No real hint of fear that I can discern. No fight-or-flight urges battling inside her.

"I don't get out much," I offer as explanation.

She thinks for a second or two and then opens her mouth to

speak. "You seem really genuine. And the reason I'm not running from this bar at top speed is because there's something in your eyes that's kind of hard to deny. Not to mention the white lightning bolt in your hair is very Charlton Heston. You know, from *The—*"

"—*Ten Commandments*, yep," I finish her sentence.

"I'm not saying that you're *not* a wingnut, but I sense you're not a *dangerous* wingnut," she finishes.

I've been staring at her lips. They're curved up at the ends, which makes a really hot, dimple/crease thing happen in the corners of her mouth when she says certain words and . . . Whoa! Did she just say I might be a wingnut?

"No, no, I promise you I'm not a wingnut," I blurt out. I'm totally shooting from the hip here, fairly certain that I've blown this already by focusing on the wrong damn thing at the wrong damn time *again*. Screw you, ADD. "It's just that I'm pretty sure God called me on my cell phone just now and I'm still shaken up by it because it was so bizarre and he/she sounds like he/she's a bit of a freak, and if that's who's watching over us then we are all hosed." The words just hang there as charged as a racial slur yelled in Harlem at midnight. Or so I imagine. I have no idea how she will react.

Alice is now frowning without the smile. "God called you . . . on your cell phone."

"Sorry, I know it sounds completely freaky." I can't back out now, although they say you can, but you really can't most of the time, and this is definitely one of those times.

"Yes. God called me. On my cell phone. It sounds stupid, I know, but he did. Or I think he did." There. I said it.

I wait for minute or two, or what feels like a minute or two but in situations like this is probably more like six or seven seconds. She hasn't moved. I'm actually amazed. And then she speaks. "Okay, here's the deal. I'm kind of caught up in this, and I'm leaning more toward thinking there might be a truth in it rather than arguing that you're spinning me a line so you can abduct, kill, and eat me."

"What??"

"Maybe it's my line of work, or maybe God is trying to reach me, but I think I'm supposed to hook up with you in some way."

Her line of work? Hook up with me? What is she saying?

"Are you . . . you're not a hooker, are you??" I am clearly and seriously out of my depth now and have no idea what part of the outfield she's batting to.

Alice gives me a look.

"No, I'm not a hooker. I'm a sister."

Not what I expected, so I answer, "Well, I think most of us are brothers or sisters of someone. That's not so unusual. I myself . . ."

"I mean a *religious* Sister. A nun."

Woody and I are all ears.

He is an old man now. His wife is gone these past six years and Ronan Young, who jokes at the local pub that he is now Ronan Old, still takes the Bonnie Bradana out on the great Loch every now and again to wet her keel. He no longer plies his fishing trade and has been relegated to the ignominy of dependence on the local volunteer "Meals on Wheels" for his own personal sustenance: those helpers who are so effusive and well-meaning in their ministrations yet will never wish to comprehend the depth and breadth of his life. Nor, he understands, should they.

Each generation centers on itself. We learn very little from the generation before us and absolutely nothing from the generation before that. Ronan worries that there will be no one to care for his "girl" once he is gone. The *Bonnie Bradana* is a local legend, but people have their own lives and responsibilities. He has no children or extended family that would take on the care and upkeep of his beloved craft. The *Bonnie* has been a part of the community since Ronan's father built her and christened her into Loch Ness many a long year ago. Evelyn had called her Ronan's "second wife," so much a part of their lives was this vessel. And he has told no one of his encounter that lonely winter evening on the Loch, almost twenty years before. Not even his Evelyn. But the *Bonnie Bradana* knows. She was there and brushed against the dark, sleek skin and broad, powerful back of a myth as it passed by. A once-in-a-lifetime moment shared with the protectors of this powerful place. Ronan understands that he is one of them. Chosen. He would protect this land with his last breath and final splash of blood. The great creature knows this too and shows herself only to the faithful. An honor that is unspoken and buried with the few who are blessed enough to truly bear witness. When he is able, Ronan slowly walks the shores of this ancient lake and dreams of the encounter that has begun to define his remaining years. He sees her shadow in the dark, cold waters; he sees her spirit in the chipped and whittled mountains that ring this Loch. He feels her power brimming at the very surface of the tarn. It is palpable. How could he have missed it for so much of his life, and why did she wait so long to reveal herself? But he understands somewhere in his soul that perhaps he was not ready before this. Her pneuma, her vital spirit, the one thing that has enabled her to exist these many eons, has gathered wisdom and knows where and when to show and not to show herself. And to whom. She is beyond age and beyond reasoning. Ronan now understands that there is much he cannot fathom. So much he will never comprehend. The great cities of the earth and their people are even more removed than he from the truth of this spirit world. They exist so confident in their bright, clear knowledge and the crystal-cut understanding of how their universe works that many will not reach his level of comprehension in their lifetimes. They are in the grip of the tyranny of logic—the false diamond that seduces their beautiful and brilliant minds. They still believe that the more they read, the more knowledge they possess, the more information they amass: the closer they are to the truth. But they are not closer. Their astute minds accept only what is written, accepted, perceived, deduced. They miss entirely the path of the earth's soul. Ronan has always known this, though he never "understood" it. He understands it now. It has taken years. And a committed path. The ones who seek their way through knowledge and who chose spiritual doubt as a way of life are akin to those who use vacillation as a path to commitment. But such language drowns in deep lakes like this. It washes away like a child's chalk drawings on the sidewalk when the hard rains come. A sand painting that has taken weeks to create and seconds to blow away in the wind. The great creature has neither knowledge nor understanding nor time for such things. She is waiting. For one who was born here eons ago and has, through the cycle of birth and death, forgotten that they belong here, that they can communicate with spirits in this ancient place. She is waiting. For the one.

A*t fifteen years of age I am a card-carrying, moderately committed member of the MORMON Church. Thank Joseph Smith I finally got the name right!! Let me tell you, there were a few raised eyebrows when I first walked into their midst and announced I was here to become a Moron. I have been a Mormon now for eight long and peculiar months. Evan won't speak to me. And Dracula, the seductive coquette who first got me caught up in this odd religion, has neither shown her brilliantly brimming breasts at the services I've been obliged to attend nor visited me at home to rest an encouraging hand on my vacant, plaintive thigh. I've been through the whole Mormon gold plates thing (written originally in "reformed Egyptian," whatever the hell that is), the magic stone, and the hat, and I swear I did not laugh out loud even when they talked about their sacred skivvies (special underwear that's supposed to offer protection against evil and temptation), so committed were my little heart and wiener to the hot recruiter I was sure I would see at a gathering at some point. And if I'd been wearing this super-underwear in the first place, I might have been immune to Drac's religious-sexual come-ons and avoided this whole gonzo sect. But now, even at fifteen, when the seething hormones are pretty much resistant to anything that would knock them off their single-minded course, I am tiring of the chase. I have whacked the monkey almost nightly since I met this Mormon goddess, though I have seen neither angelic hide nor angelic hair of angelic her since. I have a severe rash on my wiener, from overuse of the old liquid soap in the communal bathroom, and a seriously deflated heart. Even at this tender age Woody has a direct line to my affections. I'm in the bathroom so much that my clueless mother is sure I have a terminal case of dysentery.*

And the guilt! I thought the Presbyterians were tough on us chronic masturbators, but the Mormons take it to a whole other level. They refer to it, mainly at church gatherings of boys my age and older, as "the problem," and drill it into our sexual-fantasy-filled noodles that the wiener is sacred and to be used only for procreation. I'm good with that—just let me begin procreating, then! But in lieu of the actual carnal act, I must resort to spanking frank or my head (and possibly my frank) will explode. Do these old guys who preach against self-stimulation-of-the-pork-sword even remember what it was like to be a teenager? It's a survival instinct to think of nothing but SEX at this age. From back when we all used to croak at the age of nineteen, eaten by some saber-toothed tiger or other predator with a hankering for the easily caught, upright monkey-thing. "Get a baby into the world before a dinosaur makes you its lunch" is hard-wired into us young males. My brain is screaming to me, "Get laid, motherfucker! You'll be toast soon." How does one fight that? Certainly not by thinking of football. Or kneeling piously in teen-prayer. Not that I've tried prayer, mind you. I'm usually elbow deep into my third wank of the day before the guilt gets so bad I start to run the alternatives through my mind. Let's see, "waxing the carrot" one more time or a little meditation and invocation. "Choke Kojak," yells my reptile brain. So I do.

And then there is the truly bleak side of my life: my sister, Josie. Never far from my thoughts, except when my thoughts go south to Sexytown.

At home, she continues her sad downward spiral and hardly ever leaves the house anymore. She showers or bathes three to four times a day and walks around her fortress of a bedroom with her red raw hands still dripping water and soap from the thousandth scalding scrubbing. She touches no one and handles every single thing as though it were riddled with contagion and vermin. The beautiful soul she once was is disintegrating day by day under the onslaught of her dark demons, and I am impotent to help her. I answer her repetitive questions when I am not at school, at Joe's church, or going door to door with a "recruiter" so I can learn the difficult craft of increasing the Mormon congregation myself. Our mother is beginning to hint that Josie would do better in a "facility." I'm not sure what type of "facility" she means, but her tone suggests to me that it wouldn't be something my sweet girl would be terribly happy about. The three-pronged relationship I have with the female of the species at this point in my life is neither fully understood by nor completely lost on my young mind. (1.) My mother: controlling, shaming, at times loving, lethal (when it comes to dogs), and increasingly less tolerant (when it comes to my father's infidelities.) (2.) Dracula, who because of her exasperating absence has caused my heart and Woody to grow fonder and has become the sole focus of my twisted pious/carnal longings. And (3.) Josie, my damaged angel of a sister whom I love with my whole soul, and who has been nothing but good and kind to everyone in this world but whose growing torment (that God has seen fit to allow) is the darkest cloud over my life.

Before I leave the Mormon-owned Church for the day I head to the Mormon-owned bathroom and crank the Mormon-owned casaba one more time (it's a wonder it doesn't drop off). I always have and always will get a special thrill from strangling the one-eyed milkman in an oppressed religious setting. Sorry. I know it's wrong.

I arrive back at the house after yet another class on how to be a stormin' Mormon. These people are taking increasingly more of my time and I have begun to give up on ever seeing the fantasy-inducing recruiter/bloodsucker again. In fact, I have an inkling she was just a hired actress from Hollywood who they brought in for the job, to tempt and draft. She may not actually have been a Mormon at all. The real Mormon girls I am meeting are staggeringly uninterested in yours hornily and I am truly tiring of the whole freaking freak show, such is my lack of any real commitment to the cause. I'm beginning to think I was badly duped by Dracula the babe, the breast-heaving siren-witch from Tinseltown.

It's not a short walk from the bus stop to our place, and I arrive at our humble home slightly out of breath; obviously I need to start doing some serious cardio. I enter the house to the sounds of an argument in full swing and stop just inside the door to try to get the drift of this quarrel before I have to join it. It's my mother and father in another of what have become progressively frequent altercations.

They're in the kitchen. She sounds hysterical. He sounds stoic.

She: *"Who is she? Why was she calling here? How did she get our number?"*

He: *"I've no idea."*

She: *"She said she was a 'friend' of yours."*

He: *"I can have friends."*

She: *"I told her I was your wife and demanded to know why she was calling . . .*

He: *"Oh, Jesus."*

She: *"Don't talk like that to me."*

He: *"Damnit, Julia."*

She: *"And she said she had no idea you were married."*

He: *"That doesn't mean anything."*

I move further into the entryway by a few steps. He sounds culpable even to my untrained ear.

She: *"I need to know what this woman means to you."*

He: *"She's no one."*

She: *"She didn't sound like she was no one. I know you're lying. You just said you didn't know who she was."*

The volume is going up. I move closer, unsure if I should let them know I'm here and get involved or stay hidden and stay out of it.

She: *"You said that other woman was the last one. I can't take this anymore. What must my people at church think?"*

He: *"I don't give a shit about 'your people' at the church. This is my—"*

She: *"Don't swear."*

There is the jarring sound of a dinner plate being thrown into the kitchen sink with great force. It smashes to pieces as silverware clatters around the tile floor and my mother cries out in anguish.

He: *". . . THIS IS MY LIFE! . . . and . . . you want to know who this woman is? DO YOU?"*

I sense this would be a good time to show myself or this is going to get even uglier. I appear at the kitchen entrance.

Me: *"Will you guys stop yelling and breaking stuff! You're upsetting Josie! She doesn't need to hear all this!"*

They both look like stunned rabbits on a railroad track as the train bears down.

"Horatio," is all my mother says, and she bursts into tears.

My father brushes past me without a word, knocking me into the wall, and exits the house. I run after him, unsure why I am doing it exactly. Somewhere in me I know he is only adding to my mother's pain by leaving. But he has driven away before I even make it outside.

At their bedroom door I can hear my mother inside, sobbing softly. I know there is a photo by her vanity mirror of them when they first married, and it flashes into view in my anxious mind. She looks happy. He looks sullen. I don't realize until years later that she is trying her best to conceal a slightly Rubenesque pooch to her belly that is my dear and distressed older sister in the very early stages of her life.

I lean against my mother's closed bedroom door for a minute or two, listening to her snuffle against a pillow. I have nothing to say. I'm a kid and I have no words. There is the clink of a bottle as wine is poured into a glass.

I think I hear Josephine crying as well, in the room across the hall. I'm sure she's heard the battle. I tap on my sister's bedroom door but there is no answer. I call her name so she'll know it's me but she still doesn't reply, so I crack the door. She is sitting, slumped over on the edge of her bed, her once beautiful auburn hair a dull, tangled mess covering her face, used tissues scattered around her small, delicate feet.

"Josie, are you okay?" I try tentatively.

Nothing.

"They're not going to argue anymore. Dad left the house."

Still nothing.

"Do you want dinner? Have you had any yet?"

"Don' wan' dinner," she answers. Her voice sounds thick and slurred. I know she doesn't drink, so this puzzles me.

I enter her room, sit next to her on the bed and put my arm around her slender shoulders. Usually when I do this she rests her head on me and we just sit until she feels a little better. But now her head only falls further forward.

She sniffs unhappily, takes a labored breath and begins to slowly talk.

"I know this'll never leave me . . . I'll have this crap for the res' of my life. I can't live on Luvox or Zolof' and I'm not going into any . . . fucking men'al hospital . . ."

"I know, babe," I reply, and I realize her unhappiness is not from the overheard argument. But there is really nothing I can say that will help when she is this low.

". . . and I'll never have a boyfrien' or get married. Never have kids . . . all I ever wanted since I was li'l was to be . . . mommy . . ." her voice is heavier-sounding. I pull back to look at her but her face is still covered by her disheveled hair.

Her neck and arms feel clammy to me.

"I'm going to make coffee, do you want some?" I say to her.

". . . coffee won' help . . . took too many . . ."

"Took too many what?" I feel like I've missed something.

". . . don't worry . . ." Her voice is barely audible now. She is slowly falling forward. I pull her back upright. Her breathing is shallow.

"Took too many what, Jo?" I'm starting to get concerned.

"Mom's osson . . ." she is slurring heavily.

"Mom's what??!"

"Os . . . ossonn . . . ossa . . . ossaconen . . ." she can't form words now. I look around and finally see the wineglass and beside it an empty prescription bottle. Alarmed now, I lay my sister down on her bed and grab the orange plastic container. OxyContin.

"Shit, Josie!!!!

I scream for our mother as I run to the phone, but I already know I'm too late.

My groin tickles. I feel a momentary surge of panic, thinking I could be peeing myself, such is the late hour. I look down to see if my crotch is dark with urine but it isn't. It's bright blue with modern technology. I meant to turn the damn cell phone off.

"Aren't you going to answer it?" asks Alice.

I hesitate, then retrieve the infernal machine and look at the caller ID. This ordinary cell phone has taken on extraordinary properties of late.

"It's Doug." I'm relieved to see it's not Yahweh. "I'll call him back. He's a friend of mine. He should know better, I'm usually asleep by now."

I look at the girl sitting next to me at the bar. It's just not physically phucking feasible that she's a nun. I begin trying to mentally picture her in a black-and-white habit, a small Bible, a crucifix, and prayer beads clutched tightly, reverently in her soft white hands. She's a nun, for Chrissakes. A nun! Can we please stop where this is going? I imagine her in her robe, cincture, and scapular—I know all the sacred and appropriate terms. She wears a wimple, as torrid beads of sweat begin to pop out and encircle her flushed and almost flawless face. She's on her knees groaning in ecstasy, her dark tunic hiked up over firm, round, pale buttocks. I am also on my knees, taking her from behind as Woody and I penetrate her untouched, unspoiled, extremely holy places and make her glad she's a woman. Oh, my God, that's terrible!

I turn off the fantasy in my mind as though it were a brilliant, award winning, super-cool, highly watchable, 3D TV show. Click!

"I think we should go somewhere a little less crowded and noisy where we can talk, do you agree?" I suggest, trying not to sound like a mass-murdering wingnut cannibal.

"Okay. I'm open to that," answers Alice, grabbing her purse off the bar and standing. She is long-limbed and slender but with curves and a pleasant fullness. She is actually wearing a dress that displays her attributes. I am even more perplexed, intrigued and yes, seriously turned on, Bobdamnit!!!

We leave the bar/club/pickup joint where I didn't get the pizza I so seriously craved and head off into the well-lit metropolis.

Out in the relative sanity of the city streets I see she is wearing fairly sensible flat shoes. If she'd been strapped up in high heels I would have had to rethink the whole "nun" thing. She carries herself with a calm confidence and appears completely unaware of her beauty. So that's a point in favor of her whole story—and then I realize: Who am I to doubt *her*? *I* told *her* I've been chatting with the Almighty . . . the Almighty Whack Job, I'm beginning to suspect.

"That's quite a pick-up joint, that bar. You must have been hit on fairly regularly tonight," I begin, still trying to drag my reeling imagination out of the cesspool of lust and longing in which it seems happiest to abase itself: it's always been a difficult task.

"The 'nun' word usually quashes any interest," she smiles. "Although it seemed to have had the opposite effect on you."

I color with the rush of blood to my cheeks.

"Not really," I lie. "I felt like I had to talk to someone, and you seemed open to the insane possibility that God had my cell number." This part is very true, I realize as I say it. "I don't even know where to begin," I offer. "Me having a most bizarre conversation with Jehovah, or you, Sister-Inmate-Escaping-Over-the-Barbed-Wire-Encrusted-Convent-Wall as the Mother Superior releases the hounds and busts open the shotgun rack."

She smiles at this but says nothing.

A couple of young guys walk by and toss out a few lewd comments from the safety of the group at this holy, burning-hot bride of Christ, and I think we are all going to hell, we men. Alice hears them but says nothing.

"Well, let's start with me, since there's probably a little less to my story than there is to yours," she says.

"Not necessarily," I suggest. "Now that I'm away from it I'm starting to think I could have just imagined the whole thing."

"Okay then, let's start with you." She seems fairly affable without any real hint of a hidden agenda, and I'm now pretty much buying into the whole escaping-nun thing. As odd as it seems. But I am hardly the one to talk about odd.

We pass one of the three thousand coffee bars that crowd each side of the street and I guide her inside, where the warmth and the smell of ground coffee seem to say, "Come on in and have a cozy chat. All your crazy shit will seem much more plausible after a large, skinny, triple-shot, cinnamon dolce latte, served extra hot with whip."

We order something simpler and sit in a corner, as far away from the students with their glowing banks of laptops as possible.

"There were no dogs released or guns drawn when I left the church. In fact it was my Mother Superior who suggested it," she begins. "She's a remarkable woman and did something that she could be easily chastised for, letting a neophyte free on her own recognizance for two weeks so she can find herself. It's not something that's encouraged within the order. They'd rather have the ones who are struggling or having a crisis of faith hunker down with books and religious instruction from counselors and other sisters. Grace, my Mother Superior, said she didn't think that I was cut out for the life of a nun and that I might be better suited to doing God's work living in the outside world. So she suggested I take a short sabbatical and, with God's help, try to locate my rudder and find my course."

"That's like a scene from *The Sound of Music*." I think I'm trying to be funny but I regret it as soon as I've spoken. A fairly regular occurrence in my world.

She smiles anyway and agrees, "Yeah, it does a bit. 'Locate my rudder?' I don't even know where the *boat* is."

"I'm sure the boat is out there somewhere. You just have to find it," I reply, having no idea at all what I mean by this! After the obligatory uncomfortable silence, I continue.

"So what were you doing in a bar at one in the morning?"

"Seeing if the high life was something that still had a hold on me," is her answer.

I'm trying to grasp where this is going. "Isn't that like saying 'I used to have a heroin addiction so I'm going to do a little heroin now to see if I'm still hooked?'"

"Maybe," she answers, "but I was thinking I had a grander view of it than that. Maybe not."

"You said 'still' had a hold on you. What does that mean?" I am possibly probing beyond my capacity to actually help here and maybe doing it for more prurient reasons. I hope not. Stand down, Woody, damn you!!!

"I was very young and got caught up in something I wasn't ready for. A group of guys who were supposed to be friends took me away from a pretty messed-up home life. My father was an angry man. He beat my mother—and me occasionally—any time he felt bad. These boys gave me somewhere to feel like I had a place, y'know, where I could belong. They introduced me to alcohol and drugs and the party life. And then one night they gang-raped me. I was sixteen."

Silence from me. Mr. Clueless has no idea what to say. Prurient interest is out the fucking window. The longer the silence, the more embarrassed I am at not having said something after my probing. All the possibilities sound lame—"That's terrible"? "I'm sorry"? "Wow"? "Must have been awful"? Sometimes it's better just to shut up. In a very short space of time I have learned a stranger's dark secret because she has entrusted it to me.

I stumble. "I didn't mean to . . ."

"It's okay," she says, and I feel she is being truthful. "I think it's part of my path to see where I fit into this world I've been cloistered away from since I was twenty-two. And of all the pick-up lines I heard to-night, you asking me if I was possibly 'God' got my attention, considering where I had come from and what I am looking for," she finishes.

Oooooowwweeeeee!!!!! Although I'm pretty sure it wouldn't work on most women, I actually came up with a winning opening line and this burnin' babe wanted to talk to me over all those other handsome dickheads in that place! In your face! YEAH! . . . Wait, what am I saying? Damnit, Woody, shut the fuck up!!!

My mind pole-vaults out of the gutter.

"I'm sure there's a whole lot more to your story," I say to her honestly, though I am still uncomfortably aroused, given the proximity. But Alice is apparently done spending time on it for now. Or she senses that my libido has taken a sudden turn to the left.

She sips her coffee.

I look around the atmospheric room. There are a few other couples (if I may be so bold as to call us a "couple") as well as the previously mentioned overcaffeinated students prepping for exams, sucking down Adderall and studying last-minute CliffsNotes on their computers. I focus on a guy in the corner. Big. Slightly menacing. Kind of out of place. He glances up and we catch each other's eye for a second. He breaks the connection and looks down into his coffee mug as Alice speaks.

"So, Bobby . . . tell me about your phone call."

The massive weight of the great Loch pushes against the peeled and faded blue husk of the old wooden boat. His recent stroke has left Ronan Young with a heavy limp and only one working arm, making life considerably more challenging. It is with this good arm that he now steers the *Bonnie Bradana*. They are heading out into deep water, he and his faithful girl, neither of them really sure of the destination nor the exact reason tonight. Something in Ronan has driven him to make this journey, no doubt inadvisable in his current physical condition and at this late hour, but he has lived by his own rules so far and sees no reason to abandon that path at this point in his life. The Loch is calling. He knows that at some point in their lives, every human being dreams of a great and meaningful end when the time comes. But most of us will spend our last hours in small, antiseptic, windowless rooms, hooked up to beeping machines, attended by a scrubbed impersonal staff, when a good death is all that is really and truly desired. The moon crests above the snow-dusted crags that have watched over the great Loch since she first filled and formed. They have borne witness to the creature that found its way into the then salted sea, before the world changed and shifted and closed. Ronan has learned that there are things on this earth and under the sky that we will never fully understand and he realizes that he now, at this late stage in life, accepts the unacceptable, trusts the impossible, and sees logic in the illogical. He has been schooled by the great creature. She who seems to be a spirit of this lake as much as she is real flesh and blood. The lapping of waves against the hull and the sleepy purring of his craft's small motor are the only sounds Ronan hears as the surrounding mountains reflect their faint echoes back into the darkness. It is chilly out here on the lake but Ronan is at peace. His life has been both arduous and enviable. Small successes have been hard won and he has felt at times as though the weight of the great Highlands were strapped across his shoulders. Then again, in the quiet company of his precious Evelyn or travelling the great Loch at the helm of the *Bonnie Bradana* he has believed he was as blessed as any man on this earth. Now everyone he loved is gone. And he is no longer the man he once was. Life has become painful and exhausting. His mind swims in and around old memories. Meaningful now in their precious distance and the irretrievable moments lost. He thinks of his childhood family. His mother and father who loved and were loved . . . and his brother.

His elder brother Devin had moved to Glasgow in his early twenties to make his fortune, or so he vowed, and seldom contacted the family nor made his whereabouts known. Devin always loathed this brutal and beautiful land. Was sure he was made for the comforts of the "civilized" world. He had been a brawling, brutal bully of an older brother who seemed to care little for his immediate family and even less for his friends and workmates. His anger would boil over often and cause mayhem for whoever was standing nearby. Ronan frequently took the brunt of Devin's irrational rage and could never understand where all the fury came from. "I'm just fuckin' angry is all," spat out in a hoarse brogue, was the only explanation given to Ronan for the beatings. Devin longed for what he referred to as "the comforts of progress and culture" and swore an oath that he would never come back to the Highlands once he'd made his way and even if he were on his deathbed would not cry out for home or family. And he never did. Such is the power of a vow uttered in passion. Ronan and his kin heard little from Devin after he left. A short, curt letter stating matter-of-factly that he was heading to America to pursue his dream of a better life, believing, he said, that Scotland was no place for a man of ambition and vision like himself. Ronan's not-overly-maudlin mind still hovers on the outskirts of a memory of his older sibling. At this late stage in his life he wonders about a life missed with a brother he should have known and loved but really barely knew. Visions of the two of them as small children playing at the lakeside a half-century ago that are now reduced to nothing more than a scratchy black-and-white movie stored in his memory. Age-old visions of life as it was meant to be before his brother's ego, desires, and lunatic imaginings took hold of his soul and drove him away. So much gone so fast. All of it in an eyeblink. Ronan listens to the gentle thrum of the engine and the restful lapping of the waves against *Bonnie*'s hull. Light is leaving the slate sky. The birds disappear from the air. There is a presence on this great inland sea.

Soon the motor's repetitious thrumming and the rhythmic splashing of the swell are joined by a third sound. In the dark distance a giant breaks the surface of the Loch and a rush of warm, moist air is expelled from massive, primordial lungs. Ronan hears the wash of a wake as a large body begins to move through the ancient expanse of water.

Unsure exactly why he is doing this, he turns the small craft in the direction of this new sound. And it turns to him.

W*e are in the empty hospital waiting room. My mother is perched long-sufferingly upon one of the chairs, my father is slumped into another on the opposite side. I understand there's been an argument, but I think to myself, "This is about Josie now, isn't it?" And I'm* *wondering why we aren't all in a tight, affirming circle in the center of the room, offering spiritual and emotional support to my sister. Despite all our feckless crap, we are family first and foremost, are we not? My mother dabs softly at her eyes with a white handkerchief that has colorful flowers embroidered at the corners. It was a gift from her mother, the embroiderer, and to me it has always linked her to something earnest. Something deeply and simply human, despite what we have all morphed into as a fairly flawed family of late. I know that at some point in her young life she was an innocent, open girl who only wanted the best for herself and the ones she loved. When does the ruin set in?*

She smelled of alcohol on the ride over. My father is staring at a wall. He is hard-eyed and stone-faced. I fear him too much to even try to get close. I'm leaning against the vending machine, struggling to distract my racing thoughts of blame and "if only" with a plot to free a bag of peanut M&M's. I think I can stick my skinny arm up through the dispenser window high enough to knock the candy off its rack with a ruler or something equally viable. I'm also trying to use Jedi mind-power to will the yellow package free of its little metal corkscrew holder. But dark images of my sister keep pushing through my meager defenses.

Josie was deathly pale, damp-skinned and barely breathing by the time the paramedics got to her. I told them my mother didn't know how to drive and asked if we could ride with them in the ambulance, so they let us. I didn't want to say I thought she'd been drinking. My father met us at the emergency waiting room, in stony silence like my mother, both with their own thoughts to which I was not privy. We'd seen my sister briefly after they'd pumped her stomach and shot her full of something called Naloxene or Naloxone. She didn't look like she was alive, so pale and fragile, with cables and wires running from her small body to vital life-sign machines bedside. I couldn't tell if she was breathing or not. She didn't appear to be. Her eyes were closed and with her head lolling to one side she gave me the impression that this is what a dead person must look like. And that I had been too late. Guilt comes naturally to me. A nurse has hustled us out into the waiting room saying the doctor is on his way to assess her condition. It sounds ominous to me and I hate the tone of it but at least she isn't telling us they'll send the body home after they've harvested her organs and given her clothes to Goodwill. Now contrition and despair are winding their way like boreal, binary serpents up my spine and into my brain no matter how many ways I come up with to free the damn peanut M&M's.

If I hadn't been at that stupid church trying in vain to get Woody some female attention or ingratiating my little ass to some Mormon mucky-muck and if my pea-brained parents hadn't picked tonight to try and settle some scores, I would have seen what was going on with Josie sooner. Or I might have been able to talk her down off her desolate ledge. I could usually make her smile, even if I couldn't chase the demons away completely. And now all my selfishness, all my abhorrent degenerate pursuits, and my fucked-up, eternally combative parents have caused the death of my beautiful sister. The only one I really cared about anyway. Hot tears sting my eyes and burn my cheeks at the realization that I will probably never see her alive again. I am so goddamn angry. I decide right then and there that I am done with the Mormons. I am done with the Presbyterians. I am done with my loony parents. And I am DONE with girls and their wanton disregard and toying with my and Woody's heart. Forever!! In my Josie's memory and in honor of her sweet, tormented and much too short life. Done!!! Finito! Terminado! Expletum! Finished!! My new life will begin here and now!! A grand and staggeringly significant celibacy! A brand-spanking-new and meaningful destiny that will heal the cosmos in honor of my precious and never-to-be-forgotten sister!

So who should walk past the waiting room window pushing a small trolley and dressed in a fairly tight-fitting, non-regulation nurse's outfit, awesome hoo-ha's mocking my freshly uttered declaration that I have just sworn on the memory of my precious sibling in four languages (and obviously God is in on this and having a really good laugh as well) but none other than Dracula herself!!! The intoxicating Mormon hot-hand-on-my-hot-thigh recruiting goddess. Woody springs to attention before she even clears the window and I go straight to hell. I move with such speed through the waiting-room door that no radar system on earth would be able to track me, so mom and dad don't even look up. I almost bump into her, or more accurately, because I am still a kid and relatively short, her awesome hoo-ha's.

"Hi . . . (she never told me her name), it's ME!" I say, beaming, stifling my present broken heart for this until now very absent succubus.

She looks kind of bothered that I'm in her way and holding up the delivery of her much-needed plastic pee collectors, and says, "Do you need something?"

"Yes I need us to go forth and multiply for the Mormons" I want to say but don't. My whole damn tortuous libido-driven devotion circuit is reconnected and firing away, despite my newly sworn oath. She is even more astonishing than I remember. And clearly she has no idea who I am.

Instead, I reply with a slight whine, "I'm Bobby Cotton. I'm the guy you introduced to the awesomeness of the Mormon Church, remember?"

She brightens momentarily, smiles and says "Super!" then appears to be ready to move on. It's not quite going how I always thought it would.

"I have friends who want to join," I lie like a bastard, trying to keep her attention at any cost.

"I don't really do recruiting anymore," is her disconnected reply.

"You're fucking kidding me???" is what I, again, want to say, but I settle for "Oh."

"But I'm happy you let Jesus and the LDS into your heart."

"What's an LDS?" I ask, still pitching to her catcher's mitt, but she doesn't return the ball.

"Excuse me, I have patients to see," she says, and brushes by me with her cart and a curt, tight smile.

Like a man wronged, steely-eyed and determined to set his woman straight on his affections, I march after her, although I'm sure I look more like a whipped puppy running for a corner to hide from a well-aimed hose.

"But I've been going to that church for months now. You told me you'd see me there," I whimper pathetically.

She stops and turns to face me. "Look, I must have recruited fifty boys your age, and I wouldn't recognize any of them if they came up and bit me. Sorry. God bless you." (God bless me?) And with that she turns and continues pushing her wheelie-tray full of tinkle collectors down the bright, antiseptic hallway—and out of my life. Camera pulls back, music rises. Fade to black. Cut and PRINT!!!

Woodydamnit!!!

I limp back into the waiting room, where the stone statues that are my parents still have not moved. I want to say something about the ignominy of life, woman's inhumanity to man, the delicate balance of emotions that is "love," and how life couldn't possibly get any friggin' worse if I stood up on my principal's desk and told the whole damn faculty to go fuck themselves. But instead I cross to the vending machine I had been trying to rob earlier and give it a swift, hard ass-kick. Only my mother looks up briefly and then she goes back to staring at her folded, blue-veined hands. Is God really this careless with our hearts, I wonder, though probably not in those exact words, and as if in answer there is a muted, papery "plop." I look at the vending machine dispenser drawer *where the sound came from and see that my hostile punt has dislodged a yellow packet of peanut M&M's. Obviously God is still mocking me. So I grab it, tear it open, and stuff the M&M's into my mouth in a sort of "substituting food for the absence of love, resulting in severe depression" thing. I am aggressively chomping away when the waiting-room door opens and a thin, balding man in pale-blue scrubs and an off-white coat steps into the room.*

"Mr. and Mrs. Cotton?" he asks my parents.

"Yes," answers my mother.

"I'm Doctor Ellis."

We all freeze and time stands still. I am thinking now only of Josie.

"Uh-huh," says my little, crushed, heartsick mom.

"We have managed to save your daughter's life . . ." he says, with no flicker of emotion and no hint of what may come.

"There've been two calls, actually." I don't really know how to explain this as we convene over coffee at this late hour, the blistering-hot postulant and I. In my reeling mind the phone conversations all sound like scenes that might have been cut from *Agnes of God,* or maybe even *The Exorcist V.* And with good reason.

This is really freaky. I know it. And I suspect she knows it.

"Two? Lucky you," she says lightly.

"Yeah, you'd think so, right? But it turns out he, God, may be a bit crazy, or a lot crazy. Or something totally different than we all thought he'd be."

"Well now you're not saying 'he/she.' You're just saying 'he.'"

"Yeah, I know. When you talk to this voice, it really doesn't have a defined sex to it. Like there's no real gender distinction. It's so strange. I don't know how to explain it, and it's not something you really notice, though it caused me to almost involuntarily say the 'he/she' thing, but it's a bit of a pain to keep repeating and repeating it. It makes me sound like more of a freak than I already do."

"As well as painfully politically correct," she adds.

"I know. How hard does that su . . . how funny is that?" I avoid saying "suck" because she's a nun and it seems like the appropriate thing to do, although she looks like no nun I've ever encountered. I did encounter more than a few at school—vicious, punishing, remorseless, sexless beasts who did everything they could to brutalize and devastate their young charges. Except for Sister Mary, who was awesome.

I smile at Alice. I'm still trying to find some common ground that isn't inhabited by things I know would seem insane in the cold light of day, if not under the coffeehouse lighting, which is at this late hour warm, cozy, and as yellow as chicken fat.

Trying my best not to scare her off but really needing to tell this to someone, for maybe the first time in my life I opt for absolute honesty as an opening gambit. I don't recommend it.

"I've been thinking about death and dying a lot in the past few months."

A beat. Nothing from Alice. She seems to be waiting.

"I've heard that's when you start looking within, around your early thirties, isn't it? I read that somewhere." I inhale deeply . . . and GO! "I've been really depressed lately and worried that maybe I've already shot my wad as far as life goes, excuse the expression, but it seems like my existence on this earth is completely laid out before me now with no more surprises, no more wonder or discovery, just a long, monotonous, dull gray grind until I finally flop over like a dead fish from a heart attack or a stroke in my late forties, so I've been thinking about suicide as well, trying to figure out which would be the best way to go, either drinking myself to death, which in all likelihood I'm sure I'd enjoy, versus jumping out of my apartment window, but it's only on the second floor so I'd probably just break an ankle or a hip or something and that would then make me even more depressed having to hobble round in a leg cast for six weeks and pee through a catheter, plus I've already just gone through a hellacious divorce, though I'm sure what I'm feeling is pretty normal considering, but I don't know if maybe I just conjured all this God stuff up in my imagination as an alternative to my brain actually exploding in a bloody nerve-cell-and-myelinated-fiber spattered mess on the kitchen wall from all the friggin' pressure, and who knows, maybe I even dyed this dopey stripe in my hair myself in the bathroom sink and then blocked it out of my memory and I *could* actually be insane, come to think of it . . . I mean . . . that's a possibility, right?" It's a staggeringly convoluted and ambitious sentence delivered without a break and without a breath. As I accept the award I thank the *Guinness Book of World Records* for naming it "longest and lamest speech in the history of humankind!" And *muchas gracias* to all those who voted.

A look has slowly crept onto Alice's face that tells me there may be good reasons why absolute honesty is not always the best policy for a balanced and positive first impression.

I glance around the hazy room to see if anyone is listening in to my mad-as-a-March-hare monologue. No one is, but Alice still says nothing so I counter argue *for* her. "Okay, that's dumb. Obviously I'm not crazy. I'm just stretched a little thin right now and I've been through a very strange couple of phone calls that I . . ."

She's watching me with, I imagine, the same look a mouse might wear when confronted by a hungry but slightly deranged pit viper.

"Sorry, that was . . . ridiculous," I try, "Let me have another shot at explaining this. Okay, I'm just going to tell you the story without my interpretations or side comments and then if you still want to run for the hills I'll open the door for you, give you a push on your way, and pay for both of our coffees." She relaxes slightly. Just *slightly*.

I launch into the whole, extremely anomalous tale and for some reason start at the point where we met at the bar and tell the story backwards. I figure it wouldn't seem any more plausible going in the right direction, so what the hell—and that last disturbing phone conversation is still fresh in my memory. I don't mention my divorce again, or my desire to get myself iced by the Holy Spirit, and I end with the beginning of the first cell call I made from my bachelor digs. She has relaxed her guard a little more, enough to ask a question.

"How do you know it isn't just someone you're familiar with or who's familiar with your life messing with you?"

"Because this . . . voice knows stuff about me that no one else knows. I mean, someone could, if they dug deep enough I guess, but who would bother, for a joke or whatever," I answer, then continue the thought. "And I swear to God, okay, bad use of a phrase considering, but the men's room sink really *did* catch fire. It was the most bizarre thing. It burst into flames and he laughed like a maniac in my ear. It scared me."

I still don't know how far from believing me she is when she asks, "So where did you find this phone number?"

"In some book I bought at a bookstore a couple of days ago." And no, I am not going to tell her I stole it. "It was written in pencil on the inside cover. That in itself is pretty eerie. I haven't read the book yet; I only got as far as the phone number. I think it's called *Magnificent Vibration*. It's a book on personal growth. I was in the store and the book just seemed to kind of jump out . . ." I stop talking. Alice is reaching for her purse slung over the back of the chair. She's leaving.

"Wait," I say.

But she doesn't halt her movement, and her movement, I realize, is not to leave but to retrieve something from her purse, which she does and then drops it in front of me on the dark, fissured wooden table. Comprehension takes me a second but I do recognize the object. It's the same book I've just finished telling her about. *Magnificent Vibration* is the title. "*Discover Your True Purpose,*" says the caption underneath.

"Motherfucker," says I.

"I bought it at a bookstore a couple of days ago," says Alice.

I look at her in complete confusion. She's wearing a similar expression, which doesn't help.

After a few beats she adds, "Unlike yours, mine came without a phone number."

The blood-drained winter sun is an impotent, diffused ball hanging low and idle in the haze of a dawn sky. A light drizzle further filters out her anemic warmth and color. Silence hangs inside the low, settling lake mist. High above the bleakness, morning birds call and wheel as they prepare for yet another uncompromising day of gathering nourishment for themselves and their nurslings. The damp Loch Ness fog offers small counsel and limited guidance for the shadow that is slowly finding its way through the aurorean blur. The dark shape looms. Its movement is steady, like a living thing, and it leaves a gentle wake as it cleaves the fascia of the water. Concentric circles form on the still lake as fish break the surface to breathe in the oxygen-rich air-water layer, sending ripples ever outward until they resemble diminutive black sand dunes stretching to infinity. Lakeside trees drip dew back into the great starless Loch.

A half a world away, as two people sit over a table in a late-night coffeehouse and struggle to comprehend the incomprehensible, people here are waking, rising and greeting the coming assault of a new day with hope, fear, apathy, and all the colors in between.

Rubbing eyes, stretching limbs, and heaving sighs, some heavy, some joyous as the day breaks in through their bedroom windows. Life awakens, coffee boils, eggs fry, engines rev, and the repetitive path of the school/workaday week begins anew. But some will not see this day. Nor any days beyond. On the Loch the shadowy silhouette moves out of the gloom and into sight where it begins to take form.

While most of the world is either rising or retiring, stepping into or out of their daily routines, the world ticks on. Few understand that the ticking will not go on forever and the clock is running down. There are fabled guardians: spirit creatures who intuit this and understand that their brethren are being hunted, murdered, and crowded out of existence. Poisoned, polluted, and lost as is the world herself, by the very ones who have been her self-elected caretakers, stewards, shepherds. Such a spirit lives in this lake, unmolested and hidden from all but a few. And there are other spirits, in lakes, on mountains, throughout forests and plains and in the deep, deep oceans, who know that the world is on her knees and fighting for her life. They understand that alone they are impotent to stop the onslaught. And how can they seek the allegiance of humans when humans are the cause of their downfall? From where shall their salvation arise? A savior to heal what has been almost irreparably damaged. To fix what has been broken. Their collective eyes are open, searching for the one who will come to them, in whatever unlikely form. They search, in their own way. Even as time runs out.

The mist is rising as the meager warmth of the day heats the surrounding air. The shape moves beyond the damp morning fog and no one is witness as it bumps against the gravel edge of the lake, comes to ground, ends its journey. The vessel is old and in need of repair but there is no one on board, no passenger, no oarsman, no captain, and she has drifted half the night. As her keel scrapes against the glacial shoreline stones, a painted and once loved name is her only identifying mark: *The Bonnie Bradana.*

The three of us sigh in collective relief, yet I sense there is a rather sizable and conflicting "but" coming. *The doctor stands in the* waiting room . . . waiting. "Can we visit Josie?" It's little me who pops the question. Suddenly all I want is to see my sister breathing with the light of life in her eyes again. I want to hug her till she yells "Get off me, retard!" like she used to—before she could no longer bear to be touched at all, even by me.

The doctor (did he study drama in high school? Because that's about the level of his acting expertise) finally lets the cat out of the bag.

"We've managed to save her life but she has had a cardiac episode."

Another pause, like we're all supposed to know what the hell "cardiac episode" means, with all its thousand-and-one possibilities.

"Can you just spit it out?" I want to scream, but don't. I just hang there and take it, letting him have his little movie-of-the-week moment. The room is starting to swim and my scalp is cold and tingling with possible imagined scenarios. Mother lets out a pathetic whimper.

"So what does that mean?" I ask, since no one else is talking.

Another theatrical pause.

I'm going to kick him in the balls, I swear to God.

"Her heart stopped, and it took us some time to resuscitate. It was fifteen minutes before we could get her vitals going again," the bad soap opera actor masquerading as Josie's doctor finally offers.

We are all leaning forward like dogs trying to will the cookie off the kitchen counter.

"What does that mean?" This time it's mother reading from my script, same intention.

I can stand it no longer and say with some force "For Chrissake sake will you just tell us what's wrong with my sister?!!"

"HORATIO!" mother yells in embarrassment, though my father says nothing. The doctor looks extremely put out. I've veered away from his script.

"I agree with the boy," says my father in one of the few times he will ever stand with me. "What are we talking about here?"

The doctor, sensing he has lost his audience, lets us have it with both barrels. "She is alive, but there is significant brain damage. How much we won't know until she comes out of the coma, if she comes out of the coma. Her brain has suffered severe oxygen deprivation during the time her heart was still, and we have good reason to believe there is gross cell destruction as a result. She is on a respirator at the moment, which I suspect we will be able to remove eventually. But she will, in all probability, need twenty-four-hour-care for the remainder of her life."

He stands there, the despot. Is he waiting for applause?

"When may we see her?" asks my poor, lost mother. She sounds exhausted.

He turns and exits, tossing back his reply like a sore loser. "I'll send a nurse in."

We all wait meekly for some unfamiliar nurse to come in and tell us what to do next. I could really use some more M&M's.

My mother and I bring my sweet, broken girl home one autumn evening after the doctors, nurses, consultants, a PR dude (wanting to know if our stay was satisfactory—"Yes, we had a fabulous time, thanks for asking") and the jerk demanding payment in full of the hospital bill before we bail, have all had their way with us. The only light in my Josie's eyes is a dull fire that seems to recognize nothing and see no one. I've spent the three weeks of her hospital stay by her side talking to her, trying to get a reaction to all the stupid shit I've been saying, bad jokes, worse impressions, and even, so help me, a thorough explanation of the grand mysteries of the Mormon church, with which I assure her I am no longer affiliated. She does not respond. She allows me to brush her hair, hug her, kiss her slack face, with no objections or questions about my cleanliness, where I have been, or who I might have touched beforehand.

We move her back into her old bedroom and begin the feeding, cleaning, turning her over, talking to her incessantly. And that is all we do and all we are told we can do by the powers-that-be who seem to know so much yet still offer so little.

"There are no easy answers," is their generic response. "Do the best you can." Another good one. Love that. "There are facilities that house people like your daughter." That's one I particularly despise, although mother perks up at the suggestion. So insistent am I at not having Josie sleep anywhere but in her own bed here at home that I voluntarily include myself in the cleanup detail, which to a young teenager is highly gag-inducing as well as extremely disgusting and unpleasant. But I do it. And it actually gets easier. The stink, the washing, the medicated cream on her bedsores, the caretaking of the soiled laundry actually begins to feel like love to me. Now that I am free of the Mormons' persistent and invasive grasp I have more time to spend with my tragic and beautiful sister. "Beautiful" is no longer a word that an outsider might apply to

my girl—she drools, her skin is sallow, and she lives in a perpetual bad hair day. There is dried food clinging to her nightdress and matted in her tresses, but she is my Josie and as my mother slowly backs off and leaves her more and more to my care, she becomes the real reason I run home after school every night, forsaking friends and even possible potential (though in reality, imaginary) girlfriends.

The big moment arrives when I catch her eye one evening. She points at me with a shaky finger and smiles a big goofy grin.

She has "seen" me, I am sure of it. I call out to our mother.

"Mom, Josie just recognized me!"

No response from the matriarch. So I point to myself, and like a parent teaching a baby new words I say slowly—"Tio. TIO."

"Sho," says Josie.

"Motherfucker," says I. "Yes, Tio, Tio. I'm Tio." Honestly it's like she just memorized the whole frigging Encyclopedia Britannica *and recited it verbatim back to me in Swahili.*

Now let the healing begin!!!

One of the doctors had candidly admitted there was so little they actually knew about the human brain that it was possible some healing might occur. Rewiring, rerouting of electrical impulses, that sort of thing. I asked if we were talking about my sister or my laptop? Mother swatted me. But here it is, and she would soon be back to her normal self, laughing, going out on dates, and living the life she was meant to live. She would, however, not. She smiles when I enter her room, but "Sho" is about as far as we will ever get. I am happy for that at least. So I now become "Sho."

One day I hear voices in the living room and head out to investigate. There isn't a lot of conversation in this house these days, apart from the occasional screaming match between the parents, but I don't really count that as actual dialog exchange, so the chatty tone drifting in from the living room perplexes me. It is an uncommon sound in this house, the easy, relaxed notes of a one-on-one conversation. It's weird how something so commonplace can be missing for so long that its sudden intrusion makes it seem almost exotic, alien. My parents are standing talking to an older man who reeks of organized religion and clutches a small book. "Oh no, not the Mormons again," I think to myself.

My father breaks the casual color of this anomalous exchange and switches to parent mode.

"Boy, this is Reverend Whiting from the church. You know him, I'm sure?"

"Yes, of course," I lie, finally putting a face to that droning, somnolent accompaniment of my constant erotic fantasies while struggling to get through another Sunday morning at the old Presbyterian.

Mother jumps in before I say something stupid.

"Reverend has come to offer us some Christian help with Josephine," she says.

Christian help? No idea what that means. Will I now hear him pontificating from Josie's room, poor girl? Is there an exorcism in the works? "The power of Christ compels you to stop crapping in your bed!!!" Or will he be absolving my sweet, childlike girl of her many, many heinous sins?

"The Father is offering us some aid in the feeding and maintenance of your sister, for a while. To give us a little breathing room so we can decide what's to be done on a more permanent basis." This from mother. I don't like the sound of that at all! Plus, "feeding and maintenance" sounds like something you do to a houseplant.

"I can handle taking care of Josie. I don't need anyone's help," I covetously object.

"I would like to be of service to your family, Horatio."

What the hell? Who else besides my mother calls me Horatio? The small voice has come from behind me. I turn.

I didn't even notice her when I entered the living room, so invisible does she make herself. She is thin and very pale, with fragile blue eyes.

Quite a few years younger than the older dude, but not young enough to be a daughter. Her severe ankle-length dress runs all the way up to her throat, covering her completely from head to toe, making her seem exceedingly prim and dour. Like a visitor from another century. There is a fatal meekness to her that is somewhat off-putting to me. Suddenly it lands on me. She's his wife!! *And as if in concert with my realization, my mother says,* "This is Virginia. Reverend Whiting's wife and a wonderful, wonderful woman. She will be coming to help with Josephine four days a week for the next few months so we can have some time to ourselves."

I can't stop myself. "You've got all the time to yourselves you need. I take care of Josie!"

"Excuse my son, Father. He still hasn't come to terms with the full scope of his sister's disability." *Again mom, misreading.*

"I don't need anybody's help," *I repeat, a little loudly and possibly petulantly.*

"Mrs. Whiting starts tomorrow, Horatio, and that is the finish of it!" *Mother slams the lid down hard on my small-scale rebellion.*

I storm out, too much like a little kid for my own liking, and head to Josie's bedroom for consolation, validation, and just to be near her.

I sit on her bed holding her soft hand as she stares into space and sees I know not what. The conversational tone from the living room soon drifts toward the front door and disappears out into the night. Silence reigns in our home once again. I know what's coming next, and sure-as-death-and-taxes, it does.

The bedroom door flies open, frightening Josie and causing me to leap to my feet. I am her knight in shining armor rising to defend her. Actually I'm just a needy little weasel in dire fear of being usurped and removed by degrees from the most meaningful ritual in my life: caring for my sister.

"How dare you embarrass me in front of the Reverend like that!" Whoa! Mom's on fire.

I push past her into the hall to get the brunt of this away from Josie just in case her mind is able to register the sudden elevated emotions. She does get agitated from time to time and I don't want to be the cause. The harpy follows me, continuing her rant.

"Don't turn away from me!! Virginia, Mrs. Whiting, is starting here tomorrow and you will be courteous and help this good Christian woman administer to your sister or you can leave this house right now, you ungracious little bastard!!!"

Okay, she never swears so this is a rather large red flag to me.

I have no retreat. I would run from the house at full speed if I could take Josie with me, but even in my agitated state I recognize this is a solution somewhat full of major holes. For one thing, I don't even have a job. At seventeen I have spent most of my free time either sucking up to the Mormons or taking care of my sister so the job thing is fairly nonexistent and when I say "fairly" I mean "totally." And if I did leave, mother would stick Josie in a home faster than you could say, "Life isn't fair so stop your whining."

I slump onto my bed while mother stands in the doorway, claws barely retracted, wings tucked in behind her, tail lashing angrily.

"Fine," is all I say. Having recently considered writing as a possible career path, I'm furious with myself that some answer a four-year-old might be satisfied with is all I can manage. "Fine"? That's all I've got?

My mother leaves with her righteousness defended and intact and I head to the family bathroom for a quick, stress-relieving wank in order to deal with my raging emotions. Nothing calms the spirit of the beast like soothing music, meditation, the counsel of a wise sage, or a good monkey-spank. I choose this last option fairly regularly, and when I say "fairly regularly," I mean exclusively.

God (or the entity's preferred moniker, "Omnipotent Supreme Being") creates a phone, creates a dial tone, then hesitates, momentarily distracted by something happening over in Galaxy 5,325,708A. The line disconnects. The life forms that identify themselves as the Vee-Nung on the planet they've named Ete Mee-Qwa have just fully grasped the concept of quantum entanglement and, utilizing the uncertainty principle, are, predictably, about to turn this really beautiful reality into a really ass-ugly weapon. This is not good, considering the global war—like state that is currently their evolutionary high point. The Vee-Nung are a technologically and organically advanced race of intelligent mucilaginous amphibians, and even though they dwell both in the water and on the land, they are having difficulty grasping that their planet is a living organism, and that constantly polluting, pillaging, and pummeling it and its inhabitants has its consequences and definite term limits. The people of Earth are even less connected to their caretaking responsibilities. It's enough to make an Omnipotent Supreme Being weep, for crying out loud. WTF! No wonder there are so many goddamn atheists in the Universe. After two conversations with the human named Horatio Cotton, the OSB (Omnipotent Supreme Being) is having even more serious doubts about the orbiting celestial body that the inhabitants have unimaginatively called "Earth." Earth? Seriously? That's the best they could come up with? It's like naming it "Bunch of rocks" or "Dirt, water 'n' stuff." Unbelievable. The OSB's original name for the planet translates, roughly, though incompletely and inadequately into "Beautiful Blue/Green/White Majestic Starlight." And they picked "Earth."

The OSB feels pain on this planet. And when the OSB "feels" something, it includes the whole of the Cosmos and time before and time to come as well as the extra fifteen dimensions that most of the "intelligent" Universe failed to grasp and have hence self-generated all kinds of whack-job theological explanations for something that to the OSB seems very natural and as obvious as swinging dog's balls. It makes you wonder. The OSB is aware of it all. The devastation, the brutalizing, the destruction and torment of those who are meant to be nurtured and cared for. The poachers who recently rode into a herd of elephants (one of Earth's more spectacular inhabitants) armed with rocket-propelled grenades, AK-47's, and chainsaws to destroy whole families, even generations of these magnificently aware and frighteningly imperiled beasts just to savagely hack off their long, pointed teeth as they lay dead and dying in the blood of their brethren and children. And don't even start the OSB on these humans' proclivity for hyper-breeding. You'd think they'd invented sex. Not to mention their industrialized powers, who still pour unfiltered and untreated waste, filth, and poisons directly into their own waters, killing and contaminating the once-abundant ocean life, as well as themselves and their descendants as an indirect result. Friggin' idiots! And living on a planet where a few degrees of orbital shift would result in complete and utter annihilation of all inhabitants, they continue to send garbage into the sky, destroy life-giving vegetation, obliterate whole species of flora and fauna that hold curative secrets, and then kill one another as fast as they can over their thousand-and-one names for God. Truly. Self-serving, short-sighted disappointments, the lot of 'em. Thank the Omnipotent Supreme Being that the life that walks, swims, crawls, or flies around this big blue marble aren't the only sentient beings that exist there. There is another. It has always been that way. The OSB made it so. And this one has a mother's survival instincts and a hunger to protect her helpless and decimated children at all costs.

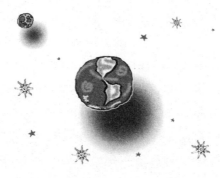

I wrap my Houston Texans (America's worst-ever football team) hoodie around me as the biting wind picks up. Obviously I have some odd penchant for wearing sports-team merchandise that advertises the ultimate losers in their fields. Pretty sure there's a deep subconscious point I'm advertising about myself by doing this, but I haven't really had the time or the inclination to sit down and fully analyze it yet. It does concern me, though not enough to stop Googling "worst sports teams" and consequently buying their wares. Although it's chilly at this late hour, we *are* in Hollywood after all, so we're in no danger of getting lost in a blizzard or contracting frostbite. But it's definitely a bit nippy for the West Coast. Alice loops her arm around mine and huddles close to me for warmth against the cold breeze. "All *right*!" thinks Woody. "Shut up!" thinks I.

The extremely odd situation in which Alice and I have found ourselves has brought us closer than might be normal under, well, normal circumstances. We are both, after much conversation, and the occasional furtive glance from me at the outstanding shape of the tops of her breasts (sorry, but the rounded cleavage, the part that women *show*, is, to me, the most awesome part—and believe me I *am* trying to keep these stupid non-sequitur comments to a minimum, so bear with me), at a loss to come up with any real explanation for what we are both now pretty sure went down tonight vis-à-vis Alice, God, and me.

I have offered to drive her back to her temporary digs since the cab she caught to the club has long since vanished beyond time and space, where all Los Angeles cabs seem to go when you really need one.

She feels warm against me and I'm thinking this must be what they call a power connection. How long ago did we meet? Three hours ago. It feels like three minutes—underwater! Hahahaha. Of course I don't really mean that, but it's an age-old joke that I'll probably tell our kids. Hang on; I may be getting ahead of myself here.

My thoughts are racing. I haven't been this close to anyone so beautiful, sexy, and religiously inclined since my mother rented the videotape of *The Sound of Music* when I was a little kid and I sat glued to the TV screen for the next week playing it over and over and over again.

It's getting very late and we turn up a side street heading to where I'm pretty sure I left the car. We almost walk right into my whoreson of a boss. At least that's my first impression of the shape looming ahead of us. My immediate thought is, "Damnit, did he follow me tonight so he could bust me for some imagined screw-up at work just to make me look like a goofus in front of this smokin' wife of Jesus, who I am feeling seriously more and more attracted to by the minute?" It's an anomalous thought but it might be something he'd do just for the sadistic pleasure of it. But I quickly realize I am about as far off the mark as I could possibly be. And Alice's sharp intake of breath signals that this may not be someone either of us actually knows. The large figure is just standing there, in the center of the sidewalk, blocking our way. It certainly has the girth, heft, and approximate poundage of the bastard I slave under from nine to five, but as I look closer and my eyes become more accustomed to the darker side-street lighting, I see that the figure's open mouth is mercifully free of secretions of any kind. This is not The Right Whale after all. So the next jarring thought I leap to is "Uh, oh. Are we going to be statistics on the morning news?" *The bodies of some loser and his totally stunning companion were found on a side street in Hollywood in the early hours of the morning. Though what such a sizzling-hot honey was doing with this clown is beyond all of us here in the Channel 13 newsroom.* Jesus, I can't even get a break when I'm *dead.*

Alice pulls me out of my reverie and to the left to pass around this now threatening figure. The man mountain moves as well and blocks our way. Always ready to defend a lady's honor and prevent my own ass from being beaten, I whip out my wallet. "Here take it. I've got (I actually start counting) twenty, thirty, thirty-two bucks. It's yours."

No movement from Goliath.

"You can take the credit card but its already in receivership and has about a 17,000 dollar deficit attached to it so you'd actually be *losing* money on that one."

Still no sign we have reached an agreement.

I begin to review the single karate class I took as a teenager when my father suggested I stand up to Steve the Jock and stop being such a goddamn pussy. Let's see, there was the stance—both feet together, fists at attention. Nope. That won't help. There was the step-forward-and-punch-the-air-while-yelling-"Kiai," or some such verbiage. Pretty sure that wouldn't be a terribly intimidating move at this juncture considering our differences in size and mass. Skip that one. And then there was the respectful bow at the end and I think the word "Osu" was uttered with an accent on the sibilant "ssss." This move is a distinct possibility, in that Goliath would understand that I am bowing to his superior brawn, might, and mastery, he will feel sympathy, and pity me for having to degrade myself in front of my woman and be obliged to let us pass unmolested.

I settle for, "We're just walking to our car."

He moves a step closer. We move two steps back.

"What's going on?" says the behemoth.

I'm confused. Is he making idle chitchat at two o'clock in the morning on this deserted avenue? So I answer as casually as I can.

"Not much, my man. What's goin' on with you?"

This immediately feels like the wrong response.

His breathing is labored and heavy.

"What does it mean?" That's what he says to us. "What does it mean?"

Silence from me. Finally I squeak out a response.

"What does *what* mean?" I answer, even though we all know my mother said you should never answer a question with a question.

Is he going to eat us? My mind is in flight-or-flight mode ("fight" is pretty much off the table at this point), trying to figure out how best to extricate us from this bad and possibly cannibalistic situation.

"I was at the coffee bar. I saw you. I overheard the two of you talking," he blurts out, and it suddenly hits me that he's the big guy I momentarily locked eyes with over coffee. Okay, so this is now a stalker thing. Who's he stalking? Obviously my bewitching companion.

"Dude, we just want to get home, okay?" I try. I feel I may not be winning chivalry points with Alice.

The behemoth reaches his right hand inside his long coat. Shit!! He's got a gun! He's going to shoot us! I push Alice away and dive onto this big freak, driving us both to the pavement. Even as I do it my whole being is screaming,

"Have you lost your fucking mind?! Good-bye, Charlie!" I can almost hear the muffled "pop, pop, pop" and smell the burned cordite, feel the warm, wet, sticky ooze as my life leaks out of me through the hot bullet holes while the city lights go dim and Alice weeps. "Just another true-life story from the City of Angels! Coming soon to a theater near you!" This is Hollywood, after all.

Goliath fights back . . . but not with the energy or conviction I would have expected from an insane, carnivorous serial killer bent on adding two more innocent notches to his long list of beautiful and tasty victims.

"Get off me!" he actually shouts.

"Give me the gun!!!" I scream, because I heard it once in a movie and it sounded really good.

"I don't have a gun, dipshit," is the very unexpected reply. We continue to wrestle on the ground.

Mindful of "my girl," I yell back, "I am light years from being a dipshit, my friend!!!" Not really apropos, but I am in a highly stressed condition. The giant finally pushes me off him so easily that I feel like a two-year-old wrestling with his dad.

I jump to my feet. Goliath struggles to his. Probably due to the handicap of the extra poundage. Should I kick him in the balls, grab Alice and run? It's such a violent move, and I guess I'm not one of those tough guys who kicks first and asks questions later. I'm more the "I think we need to talk" type of person. Maybe it comes from idolizing an older sister.

By the time all this has run through my brain, he's back on his feet and in his former advantageous position as the threatening stranger. Fuckit!!! I grab Alice's hand, dodge, weave, and dodge again then take off to the other side of the street, figuring if he doesn't have a gun, we can at least outrun the fat beast.

"Stop!!! Please!!!! Pleeease!!!!" he moans almost pathetically.

And we actually stop . . . and look on in wonder.

"What's he want?" I ask under my breath. This has been a most unusual night, so why should it stop now?

"What do you want?" It's Alice this time, voicing my sotto voce mutterings aloud.

Again Goliath reaches inside his coat with his right hand.

Gallantly (since he's already claimed he doesn't have a weapon) I jump in front of Alice. She pushes me to the side so I don't block her view of this dangerous giant.

"He already said he doesn't have a gun," she remarks somewhat disingenuously.

We look on as the colossal anthropoid speaks and his sonorous voice echoes off the brick buildings around us.

"Help me to understand," is all he says as he produces something from the folds of his long coat. He holds it up at arm's length so the streetlight hits it. It's quite dramatic. And, again, it could only happen in Hollywood.

"Holy shit," I say under my breath as light reflects off the raised object.

We both recognize it instantly. *Magnificent Vibration.* The third one I've seen today. This must be the best-selling book of all time, because everyone I run into seems to have a friggin' copy.

"Mine has a phone number written on the inside, too," says Goliath.

It's late Friday morning. Both of my parents are at work and I've blown off school, after a shouting match with my mother, of course, who has stormed out of the house yelling back at me (and to the whole neighborhood) that, at seventeen, I am already a LOSER. Which I most certainly am not, having just bought myself my first electric guitar! My head is currently filled with visions of famous billionaire musicians who dropped out of school because the pull of the music was so strong. And how they struggled and fought, persevered and climbed until they finally reached the top of the mountain, where they plugged in and played their songs for all the world to hear, adore, and throw money as a result. At this moment I can play a C chord. Not well. And it hurts my fingers.

I can hear Mrs. Whiting reading to Josie. She is actually doing a pretty good job of caring for my girl. My sister's hair is no longer matted, her nightdresses are clean, and she seems pretty oblivious as the Reverend's wife sits with her and reads her page after page after page from the Bible. Although I still consider myself Josie's main caregiver, Mrs. Whiting has lightened the load a little and I have begrudgingly accepted her. She is a wispy, almost ethereal woman with ivory skin, flaxen hair, and modest clothes that all have a hand-scrubbed, ultra-sanitary look about them. She seldom talks and almost never to me but when she does, although she may be looking toward me, her pale blue eyes have a downcast aspect.

It's now early afternoon and I have frittered half the day away as we adolescents who have forever to burn tend to do. I am still lying in bed, daydreaming of the possible rock-star future that could very well become real once I get beyond this single, extremely difficult and pain-inducing

C chord. The voice of the Reverend's wife drifts in and out of my periphery as she delivers God's word to what could only charitably be described as a captive audience. I am about to get up and give my sister a break from the holy bombardment when the words drifting in from her bedroom suddenly take shape. Mrs. Whiting is reading:

"Yet she increased her whorings, remembering the days of her youth, when she played the whore in the land of Egypt and lusted after her paramours there, whose members were like those of donkeys and whose emissions were like those of stallions . . ."

What the hell? What is this? How come her husband never reads that stuff in church?

This gets my and Woody's attention—I'm lying half-naked in my bed as this ecclesial wife talks dirty just down the hall. I don't even begin to wonder why it turns me on, but it does. I rise and head to the communal bathroom to start my day with a little healthy self-stimulation accompanied by confused and disjointed mental images of naked Egyptian priestesses mounting donkey-dicked men.

None of us has any idea why the things that turn us on do turn us on, and in our teen years we are mere puppets of the powerful sexual forces that will drive us into adulthood and consequently ruin our marriages and our lives but provide hours and hours of crazy, freaky shit to masturbate to.

So I am standing there, perched up on my toes over the bathroom sink, jammies around my ankles, vertical Woody in hand, when the bathroom door (which I am sure I have locked) bursts open. Jesus save me, it's the Reverend's wife!

We both stand there frozen for a second in what I assume is abject shock for her as much as for me. Neither of us moves. Though there are no train tracks anywhere near our house, I believe I hear a train whistle honk mournfully in the distance . . . a cold coyote calls . . . a cricket chirps . . .

"Who's watching my sister?" I ask feebly. It's all I can come up with, dick in hand.

Her colorless face is suddenly flushed and her eyes are pinpricks of blue fire. She moves aggressively toward me and I flinch and hunker down, ready for the righteous blow I am sure is coming, already conjuring up explanations for the rather compromising position in which she has stumbled upon me. But the wallop does not come. Instead, my eyes still squeezed shut against impending doom and/or severe embarrassment, I feel, for the first time in my life, a hand other than my own wrap itself around poor, shunned Woody and start stroking the little guy for all he is worth. Her hot and labored breath is on my neck as she works her unexpected magic, and although he hardly produces the emission of stallions, Woody makes me proud by shooting his meager load into the sink and I shiver with pleasure, confusion and, yes horror. I look down just to make sure I'm not imagining things, and it is indeed the Reverend's wife's hand swaddling my quickly deflating member. Without a word from either of us, she turns and bolts from the bathroom, slamming the door shut, and I am left there with a mixture of nakedness, shock, guilt, wonderment, fear, euphoria, shame, distress, joy, chagrin, confusion, excitement, insecurity, virility, daring, defeat, triumph, awkwardness, self-consciousness . . . did I mention joy? I feel usurped, stunned, in peril, and completely at a frigging loss to explain what has just happened. I actually say under my breath, "'the fuck was that?" I stand there for a few minutes trying to decide the next best course of action, pajama pants still around my feet, shrunken wanger hanging limply against the cold sink. That was nuts! Did that really just happen? I can't pull all the disparate pieces together to make any kind of sense *of this unlikely equation. ME: a kid/jerk that no girl seems interested in and whose only sexual release has been self-stimulation of the old beanpole + SHE: Adult woman, churchgoing, pious, a mature member of the real world = HER HAND on my little Woodland Hills whitesnake, stroking it into ecstasy.*

In a fog, I pull up my pants and bolt from the bathroom to my bedroom to get back into bed so I can think about this and try to process it. Does this mean I am no longer a virgin? I'm pretty sure it means something along those lines, and I punch the air in a salute to my newfound manhood. Then comes the guilt. I begin, mentally, to go through the screaming matches as the Reverend and I face off over the attentions of this suddenly desirable and comely woman. I hear my mother crying and berating me for the destruction of her church. I fear the inevitable condemnation by God. She is, after all, the wife of one of His servants. Could I actually go to hell for this? I see newspaper headlines spinning at me with that cheesy effect the old TV cop shows used to use—

HORATIO "BOBBY" COTTON: PUBLIC DEGENERATE NUMBER ONE!

GEEKY KID MAKES CHURCH LADY WHACK HIS MOLE!

HE SAW, HE CONQUERED, HE CAME.
THE DEBAUCHED LIFE OF BOB COTTON!!

Oh Jesus!! I try to breathe through it to calm myself and then begin conjuring up possible explanations to everyone peripherally involved as to how this could have happened in the first place. Could I possibly explain it as an accident? She rushed in, seriously in need of the restroom, stumbled, tripped, mistakenly grabbing my wiener on her way to the floor; I tried to pull away, which only applied more friction to the afore-mentioned wiener, thus resulting in a "finishing move" and subsequent loss of manly bodily fluids. We were both shocked and embarrassed and apologized to each other profusely, she backing out in tears, me damning my manhood to a lifetime of abstinence and myself to a commitment of service to the Church for the rest of my existence, Hallelujah, we are all saved, and no harm, no foul.

And then there is Josie. I have used and abused her caregiver. Appropriated an angelic and innocent woman who was committed to my sister, just so I could have my wanton way with her while she struggled and fought to save her honor and get back to her duties. I'm sure Mrs. Whiting is in Josie's bedroom right now weeping for her maiden-hood and her innocence lost, thanks to my uncontrollable and lustful desires. Damn mankind and his erect penis! We are monsters all! I need to go to Mrs. Whiting, fall to my knees and beg her forgiveness for my wicked, almost-copulating ways. I am clearly the sinner here and she shouldn't feel that she's in any way responsible for the shameful act that just went down.

There is a noise at the bedroom door and I look up from my insanely lame mental meanderings. It's the Reverend's wife. She is still flushed and has maintained that slightly hyper-intense look in her eyes. She's swaying ever so slightly as though she's high or something.

"Are you okay?" she asks, and her voice has lost its timidity. She sounds like another person entirely—her voice is almost husky and somewhat out of control. I fake a casual attitude, but inside, my soul is whipping like a flag in a gale.

"Yeah, I'm good," I lie.

"I'm glad," she says, but the words have more attached to them than

if she were merely pleased about my current state of mind. She moves into the room and closes my door. Oh yeah, there is waaaaaay more going on here.

"How's Jo—" I begin.

"She's sleeping," she interrupts and moves farther inside the room.

Okay, I'm seriously in over my head.

There is that pregnant pause again as we face off where the train honks and the cold coyote calls, etc., etc.

Then she reaches up behind her back and I hear a long zipper-unzipping sound. It's almost comical, it's so loud and so blatant. But I am not laughing. Not at all. I go cold . . . hot . . . I don't even know anymore.

Her scrubbed, Reverend's-wife dress falls to the floor and she is completely naked underneath. She's not even wearing some mildly modest underwear, a petticoat or some unnamed and secret church garment à la the Mormons. Nothing. She is BUTT NAKED!!! Although I am confused, nervous, and scared, Woody is paying serious attention and she seems to sense this. A slight smile—one could actually say a "devilish smile"—curves one corner of her now quite moist mouth.

I have never seen a live, completely naked, full-grown woman before and most certainly not in my own bedroom. I am in awe. She's frigging naked!!! In my room!!! With me!!! Even as freaked-out as I am I take note of her attributes. She has very white, almost translucent skin. Her frame is thin and her breasts are only slightly larger than mine, but they are larger, so I note this as a major plus, now that I'm a man of the world! There is a thick, dark patch of pubic hair between her pale thighs that kind of scares me, but I finally learn what the phrase "the carpet doesn't always match the drapes" means. Blond hair, dark pubes. Noted.

As she comes closer and sits on my bed, I realize I have been holding my breath since she entered the room.

This is no longer the demure, numinous acolyte I thought was tending to my sister. She is now a supreme, fire-breathing, chest-heaving succubus intent on, apparently, seducing me. Instead of her usual awkward sideways glances, she is staring right into my eyes. Through my eyes. It's pretty intense. And freaky.

Her hand goes under the covers and finds that Woody has been paying very, very rapt attention to the proceedings. She leans in and kisses my neck, then slides the covers down, climbs up onto the bed, and straddles my hips, handing Woody a skilled shiatsu at the same time. I'm thinking this woman has some serious talents that her ecclesial community may not be aware of. I feel her naked skin against MY naked skin. I have NO idea what to do or what is going on, but she does. "Am I about to actually get laid??" is the only thought I can register as my head swirls and I feel the pressure and weight of her body on mine. I watch, absolutely flabbergasted as she reaches between her legs, takes authoritative hold of the Woodman and, saints be praised, guides him up into the saddle like a champ. She moans and begins to ride me up and down, eyes closed, head swaying back and forth, and I hear her muttering softly, breathlessly. And what I hear is, unbelievably, ". . . She played the whore in the land of Egypt and lusted after her paramours there, whose members were like those of donkeys and whose emissions were like that of stallions . . ." and other crazy shit I never even knew was in the Bible. She is reciting it all from memory between gasps, sighs and whimpers as she rocks her hips back and forth. It is a heady cocktail for yours virginally.

I don't yet realize what it means but she is as wet as a Vietnamese monsoon down there and Woody throws his nut after a dozen or so strokes, such is the inexperience of youth. It is a magical moment. Yes those words actually form in my brain as I orgasm for the second time under someone else's power. "Whoa!" is pretty much all I can squeak out verbally. *The Reverend's wife—should I call her Virginia now?—seems to sense I can do no more (at least not right away) and disconnects us. She leans in and with that weird husky voice I don't recognize whispers in my ear, "This is just between us, okay? No one else needs to know."*

"Uh-huh!" Again, all I can manage.

She rises silently, dresses quickly, and is gone out of my room before I even land back on planet earth. Un-spanking-believable. There is a moment of rustling, a chair squeaks, a sigh, a beat, and then in her original voice (the one the Reverend's wife usually uses when she isn't naked) I hear her once again begin strafing my sweet sister's brain with the "non-rude" verses of the Bible.

I lie there listening, trying to piece together how this could all possibly have happened. And it is, for me, another good, hard, and permanent tie to sex and religious freakdom. A further melding of the crash, heat, and intoxicating power of the forbidden. An intense fettering of aberrant sexual ties to organized faith.

Amen, Sister.

At one, as the OSB is, with the universe, he/she can simultaneously experience the methane hydrate ice volcanos on the high plains of Kwoffle 5 and the atmospherically condensed and precipitated moisture falling on a side street in Hollywood, Earth. "All right!" thinks the OSB to his/herself. "Everything's moving along nicely."

We are all squished into my super-lame rent-a-car because it has now started to rain. Alice with her hyperactive, forbidden-fruit hotness alongside me in the front seat while the behemoth takes up most of the back. It's a small, low-end-model Kia, and Goliath's knees almost touch the roof. I think momentarily of my ex, driving around in my/our/her C class Mercedes (possibly with a staggeringly hot guy resting his brawny and restlessly roving hand on her upper thigh) and I get momentarily deeply depressed. So I look over at Alice, the alluring human Prozac.

"I just realized I don't know your last name," I say apropos of nothing.

"It's Young. Alice Young." She turns to our titanic new friend and extends a hand. He takes it in his giant paw. "I am Lexington Vargas. It's very nice to meet you, Miss Young." He seems less like a homicidal maniac cannibal and more like a fat Hispanic house cat right now.

"I'm Bobby Cotton," I conclude the introductions. "Can we see your book?" Lexington Vargas hands his copy to me. Same cover, same title. I open it to the first page and there, in a familiar hand, is indeed a phone number. "Did you call it?" I ask. Really, where do you start with this?

"Yeah," he answers and briefly regards the skunk stripe down the center of my head.

"Did you reach anyone?"

"I did," answers Lexington Vargas as he tugs on a long, snow-white, Shirley Temple–like curl that has been tucked behind his ear till now, to let it hang free in all its *Ten Commandments* glory, no longer lost amidst his quite prodigious perm.

"And . . . ?" I ask. Dude, it's like pulling teeth.

"A voice said, *Lexington, go get yourself a cup of java,*" is his reply.

"That's it?" I feel instantly way more significant than I truly should, given that I had a fairly lengthy though extremely weird conversation with the entity we think we have identified as God. But then I realize that God didn't mess with this Vargas guy like he/she did with me. And actually, now I come to think of it, he/she seems to have taken great pleasure in wigging me out. But Lexington Vargas is fairly okay with the fact that he might have talked to possibly God.

"The voice also told me a couple of things that happened when I was a kid back in Mexico that I'd forgotten about. Stuff no one else really knows. It scared me a little," he continues. "But it made me think it was legit."

Alice and I are waiting for more.

"So, I went out into the night and started looking for a coffee joint," he says, slightly wonkily.

Alice gives me a furtive sideways look that if you weren't paying attention you might have missed.

"I didn't really know where I was going so I got on a bus, walked, got on another bus, walked some more, got a ride, walked again, and ended up in the same place you both did. I was sitting there wondering what the hell—excuse my language, ma'am—I was doing there and then I seemed to tune in to the two of you talking. And when you, Miss Young, pulled out the same book I have, it all made sense. Well, not really, but kind of." He finishes with a loud sigh and in the close confines of the small Korean auto his breath is quite stinky and almost asphyxiating.

"Can you drive me home?" Lexington Vargas asks.

"Where do you live?" I answer distractedly as I whip out my cell phone and light it up. I have a new number in front of me and I intend to see who is on the other end of the line now that the number I have is not available from my calling area and if I feel I have reached this recording in error I should check the number and try my call again.

"La Crescenta."

"Where's that?"

"Just past Glendale."

"Seriously? That's like an hour and a half away! It's—" I look at the illuminated clock on the dashboard of the death trap known as the Kia—"almost two in the morning."

Alice finally speaks. "I think you guys are focusing on the wrong fucking things."

I sense a stiffening of Lexington Vargas's body that intimates he is not used to a woman with a potty mouth. I, on the other hand, knowing that she's still connected to the Nunnery or whatever it's called, am exceedingly aroused by it. She is oblivious to both our reactions.

"Obviously we were meant to meet. Maybe we should try to figure out why," she says with some vexation.

I see her point. I think so does Lexington Vargas. He sighs again. We hold our breath and I crack a window.

Reading off the inside cover of our brand-new acquaintance's copy of the book, I begin furiously dialing with loud beep, beep, bippity, beeps echoing around the inside of the plastic car while the face of my phone flashes like a crack-crazy munchkin's discotheque. I am calling God. Yes sir, I am. Possibly. Alice reaches over and smacks the front of my phone closed to disconnect the call. (Yep, I ended up with this cheesy cell phone because my ex, who is probably delta-deep in the throes of passion at this moment with Mr. Studly Roving Hands, took my new iPhone, too.)

"Wait a minute," says Alice, the burning Prioress. Okay she may not actually be a Prioress, but I am in love with all those intensely religious and sanctified words, names, and phrases. "Let's discuss this before you place any more calls, okay?"

It's a fair request, and I concede, although I'm thinking she must be on fire to talk to God, I mean considering her vocation, even as up in the air as it may be at this point.

Just then, as if in answer, the heavens open up with a muffled, rolling detonation and a very rare burst of Los Angeles–based thunder echoes over the Hollywood Hills as the rain truly starts to come down in earnest. Regrettably, to keep dry, I roll up the car window, hoping Lexington Vargas has no more sighing or serious exhaling to do. I can at least introduce him to humanity's finest invention for the single man, the breath mint. I begin searching the cheesy polymer center console in the Kia for the Listerine tab dispenser I know I have. It's amazing how at great and meaningful moments I can only focus on trivialities and insignificant shit. An avoidance mechanism, possibly, or could it be that I just don't like funky breath? Nope, it's probably avoidance—and/or my ADD. I do have *that* in spades.

"Has anyone actually *read* this book?" asks Alice, holding up Lexington Vargas's copy, and I stop my rummaging for the mints, such is the obvious yet totally overlooked import of her question.

"No," says I.

"No," says Lexington Vargas.

"Yeah, me neither, but don't you think we should at least check it out?" It's a legitimate query from Alice.

Lexington Vargas opens his mouth and we instinctively flinch. Thankfully he does this to speak and not to sigh. "I don't read English so well. I speak it but I never learned to read it," he says. "I live in LA. There's no real need."

I have to ask. "Why would you buy a book written in a language you can't understand?"

Our large new friend wears an expression that seems to suggest he hasn't thought to ask himself this question. There is a perplexed beat, then:

"I don't know. I liked the cover," is his honest reply.

And I realize that's the same reason I bought (sorry, stole) my copy. It seems like a staggeringly inconsequential rationale—because the cover isn't really *that* great.

I look at Lexington Vargas's book, which Alice is still holding aloft to make her previous point.

"Motherfucker," I exclaim for the third time tonight. I really need to watch my language or at least curb it a bit. Then again, Alice did drop the very charged—and from her mouth, stunningly sexy—F-bomb a minute ago. "Damn it, focus, Cotton, focus!!! And damn you, too, accursed ADD. To hell with you and your petty distractions," I think to myself.

But I am back on track, and I point to the copy of *Magnificent*

Vibration she still holds. The title now reads *Magnifica Vibración,* with the subtitle *"Descubre tu verdadero propósito."*

The ample dude in the backseat emits a slight gasp, grabs his book from Alice's hand, and begins flipping through the pages.

"It's all in Spanish now," he says with childlike wonder.

I am suddenly amped, "It's a miracle. It's a friggin' miracle, right? Doesn't that qualify as a *miracle?*" I turn to Alice. She is the resident expert after all. "Well, doesn't it?"

Alice is stunned. "Wow. What's going on here?"

"Read some of it. What's it say?" I urge Lexington Vargas, having unfortunately left my own copy at home. He begins to scan it in silence, lips moving slowly. Apparently he's not so good at reading Spanish either.

"Where did you get your copy?" asks a slightly dazed Alice while the big guy painfully peruses his text.

"Some bookstore on Melrose."

"By the high school?" Alice again.

"Yeah, just across and up toward Fairfax. You know which store I mean?"

"That's where I bought my copy," is the not unexpected reply from the babe-nun. I don't tell her I *stole* mine in a fit of pique at losing most of my financial power in the divorce, though why I would take that out on some poor guy trying to make a living selling books is beyond me. Kick the dog I guess. Terrible human trait.

"I too got mine at that store," says Lexington V.

I jump the gun a bit and show what appears to be a little back-end racism. "What the heck were *you* doing on Melrose Avenue?" The question is out of my mouth before I can slap a hand over the offending orifice.

Lexington Vargas seems to take no offense.

"I work at the school there. Fairfax High. I'm a groundskeeper, janitor, handyman, anything they need."

I babble to cover my faux pas, "I just meant since you live, like, what, forty miles away, wouldn't you go to a bookstore a little closer to home—but I see your point . . . I didn't mean anything about, y'know, you being ah, foreign or . . ."

"Don't worry about it," says Lexington Vargas. It truly seems not to have fazed him at all, and I'm beginning to like this guy who recently scared the piss out of me and whom I thought was bringing my doom by way of me being his late night snack.

"I'd really like to go home soon," moans Lexington Vargas, but his lips move silently as he scans his copy of the book.

I've started up the gerbils or whatever they are in the Kia's engine compartment that under-power this thing and am already heading in the direction of Glendale and its environ known as La Crescenta to drop off Big Boy.

It's actually not as far as I'd first lamented. The traffic is pretty skinny this time of night, given the weather. I think Angelenos worry about melting in the rain.

"We should check out that bookstore tomorrow," I opine, but Alice is lost in her own thoughts while we wait for Lexington Vargas to deliver his book report. I am already speeding (well, "speeding" is a bit of a misnomer considering what I'm driving) to the 101 freeway.

"What's the gist of the book?" I ask as we barrel through the fairly deserted city, sending the odd, meager rooster-tail of water into the opposing lanes.

"What's the *what*?" asks the Leviathan.

"What are you reading about? What's it say?"

"It's about me," is his reply.

Wait . . . WHAT?!! I bark incredulously.

"The first few pages are about me growing up in Morelos. My home town in Mexico."

"*Magnificent Vibration* is a book about YOU?!" I am flummoxed.

"I guess," is Lexington Vargas nonchalant reply.

I slow the car. I can't drive *and* process this kind of information. Multi-tasking has never been a strong suit.

Alice perks up and dives into her bag to retrieve her copy of the book as I pull over onto a side street near the Hollywood Boulevard on-ramp. The rain beats down like the ghost of Keith Moon is drumming away on the roof of the vulnerable Kia. Alice opens her pages. Silence. I am hoping she reads faster than Lexington V.

"Oh my God," she says to no one in particular.

"So it's a book about *this* guy?" I toss a dispirited and slightly disappointed thumb in the direction of the man mountain in the backseat.

She looks up at me, eyes like saucers. "*My* book is about *me*," she says breathlessly.

My face betrays disbelief or some neighboring emotion. I don't actually feel disbelief, but I am feeling something. Definitely feeling something.

She turns back down to her copy and there is a moment of restless quiet as she continues to peruse the pages. She raises her head and looks out into the rain, lost in a memory.

"I just read about," she takes a sharp and shuddering breath, "when I was eight years old and I was in the kitchen of our old house in Ohio, and my father was angry and cursing and beating my mother. I jumped in between them screaming for him to stop and he hit me against a wall and knocked me out cold." There are tears in her eyes now. "I'd forgotten he did that. My father. Punched his eight-year-old daughter unconscious," she sniffles. "My mom hid her bruises, black eye, and other damage from the neighbors but I had a concussion for three weeks. I'd completely erased that part from my memory. I didn't . . . I . . ." she stumbles to a stop and hangs her head. Tears drip onto the open book, staining the pages. She looks again like she must have felt at that long-ago moment. Sad, frightened, pathetic, broken, lost. I put a hand on her shoulder. Lexington Vargas lays a meaty palm on her back and rubs gently. Her pain is palpable. We sit in tableau for a few moments, three strangers strangely connected. Then without a word, but my mind whirling like the growing storm outside, I kick-start the Kia's gerbil and we head onto the freeway in the direction of La Crescenta, wherever the hell that is.

Ronan Bon Young.
Beloved Husband of Evelyn Beryl.
Friend of this land. Now in God's hands.
April 24, 1941–January 14, 2013

is how the small, incarnadine headstone reads as a group of white-haired and bent figures shuffle away from the freshly filled grave. It is a marker only, his body having never been found. The handful of mourners and the priest who officiated agree it is unusual, but it's how Ronan would have wanted it, such was his love of this place and in particular the Loch and her deep, dark, and restless spirit. His stone lies in tandem with his bride Evelyn's own marker, which Ronan set in place himself not four years earlier.

At the "local" later that evening, all who knew Ronan Young toast his memory and agree to a man that the *Bonnie Bradana* should be mothballed in a museum, so much a part of the local culture and legend has she become. But no one has the means, the real inclination, or the time, and the shared desire is more of a nod to Ronan and his beloved vessel than anything that will be acted upon. Instead the *Bonnie Bradana* will be left to gather cobwebs in a boat shed until the money for the berth Ronan had always paid in advance runs out and she is broken up for her cured wood or torn apart and cannibalized for whatever is still salvageable within her. But there is a petite, well-loved home and a modest bank account that needs to find an heir. Devin, Ronan's older brother, has been dead these many years, but there is talk of a child that Devin conceived, who may still live somewhere in America and who, if living, should be located and informed of the humble windfall, being the only surviving family member. Both a local lawyer and a family friend are sending out smoke signals to the west trying to locate this child. Good people doing good deeds.

But the yin and the yang of the universe must always be in

balance. There is no other way. Everything is a whole. A circle. Complete. With every gift comes something dark and with every misfortune comes the seed of an equal benefit. All seemingly opposite or contrary forces are interconnected and interrelated. There can be no front without a back. No up without a down. No zig without a zag. No black without white. No life without death.

And ten minutes' journey from the hill on which Ronan Young's memorial has just been placed, there is a gloomy and anonymous apartment in Inverness where a young man is piecing together, from homemade parts, a handgun that will be sold for one purpose. To take a life.

If I think that's all I'm going to get from the horny, but possibly slightly nuts, Reverend's nympho, I am very much mistaken. She keeps on keeping on. She extends her hours of service to my sister, and I make sure first that Josie is treated well, bathed, taken care of and read to: the Bible from the Rev's wife; Dracula, The Picture of Dorian Gray, and True Tales of the Loch Ness Monster from me. Then we get down to business, Mrs. Whiting and I—and that feels just plain creepy calling her Mrs. Whiting. She has already suggested, mid-romp, that I call her "Virginia." That's disturbing, too, because she's older than me by more than a decade and a half and it's generally uncomfortable all round to even call her anything, so I don't. She teaches me things about the female body that I never would have even considered were possibilities, let alone my task and duty to attend to as the male sex partner. I get better at it, too, and although I'm still racked with guilt and a feeling of absolute phantasmagoria pervades every encounter, Woody is having the time of his young life. And he doesn't jump the gun quite as much anymore, either. We (Woody and I) both learn about new and interesting coital positions as this wild sexual fruit-loop gives us both the instruction of a lifetime.

I feel a certain confidence as well, in social situations that previously intimidated me—at school and around the communal circles in general—now that I am actually having full-on, penis-to-vagina sex. And not just with some dopey girl from school, either, but with the genuine article: an adult, married woman! It just reeks of "grown-upness" to me. I do try, in my guilt, to talk myself out of the position I'm in, but Woody outsmarts me every time. He's obviously better at debating than I am. At the end of every—dare I even call it "lovemaking"—session, she continually admonishes me to "keep it to ourselves," and that "it's our little secret." Not sure why she keeps saying this, because I'm sure as hell not going to print up posters saying I'M OFFICIALLY PORKING THE REVEREND'S WIFE, SO SUCK IT! *and hang them all around my school. I am a randy young boy/man and have since come to understand that most boys my age are open to screwing pretty much anything remotely female that shows them even the slightest affection of any kind whatsoever, but at this point I'm regrettably aware of the cuckolding nature of our trysts, and, sadly, I am also slightly in love. My mom would kill me. Then there's the public shame to consider (though it would probably be mixed with a certain amount of bonhomie and back-slapping from my schoolmates).*

So we, Virginia and I, continue to screw our brains out like teenagers on prom night. I even send her hackneyed "love" notes and pathetic little gifts through the mail. This is very dangerous behavior considering the situation, people involved, and ease with which the missives could fall into the wrong hands. She is quick to put a stop to it, hinting at possible embarrassing scenarios should we ever be "discovered." My mind kicks into overdrive concocting these "embarrassing scenarios" that ultimately culminate in me being publicly hoisted on a long pointy stick with the sharp business end shoved up my ass and protruding through my open mouth while neighbors and friends scream, cry, curse, and throw old, rotten fruit at my corpse as my poor mother beats her breast in shame and ruin and flicks boogers at me. Then mom comes home early.

We are banging away on my little bed, she breathing heavily and leaking her lust all over my bottom sheet, when I hear the front door open with its characteristic squeak/honk.

We both tense, unable to actually make a move to hide the fact that we are seriously in flagrante delicto when I hear my mother yell, "Horatio, where are you? Mrs. Whiting?" Funny she should call out to both of us. I am shaft-deep in the aforementioned Mrs. Whiting and we are both butt naked. I leap off Virginia and pull on my pajama bottoms, already coming up with ailments that are possibly fatal and that have kept me in bed all day. The bitch is on her own. Well, not really, Mrs. Whi . . . Virgi . . . the reverend's wi . . . damn it—nympho-woman jumps up, runs headlong into my closet that houses my cheap mismatched Abercrombie and Fitch outfits, and slides the door shut. (???!) As mother walks into my bedroom I see the Rev's wife's one-piece saintly garment lying on the floor where she disrobed in her wanton abandon. I give it a swift kick and send it sailing under my bed.

"What's going on? You look flushed," says mother with frightening intuition.

She should work for the CIA, I swear to God. I grab my stomach, mainly to hide the fact that Woody is "tent-poling" my pajama bottoms, and feign severe ill health.

"I've been throwing up all day," I answer as convincingly as possible, given the circumstances.

"Where's Mrs. Whiting?" She is relentless and seems determined to decipher the mixed messages she is apparently receiving.

Flying by the seat of my jammies, I stammer, "She had some kind of emergency at home. Left about an hour ago. I've been watching Josie," I lie like a bastard.

"Humph," she says, then, "What's that awful smell?"

"What smell? I don't smell anything."

She sniffs the air, unknowingly breathing in randiness, lust, and the effluvium of human sexual secretions.

"I'm going to check on Josie," I say, feeling bad for using my angel girl as an alibi, but I would hope she'd understand given the lay of the land.

"Just a minute, Horatio!" My mother's voice freezes my blood.

"Something's going on. What are you hiding?"

"God, nothing, Mom."

"Don't blaspheme," she says, apparently taking a page out of my book on severe ADD. "I can hear breathing."

I start to puff and pant like a fool in a vain attempt to distract her and make her think it was me.

"I told you I don't feel good," is my unrelated answer.

This woman has the ears of coyote, the mistrust of a jilted lover, and the instincts of a TV psychic! I am so screwed. She is eyeing my closet.

I turn and reach out a useless hand as she moves to the closet door.

"Mom! Stop!" is my best shot.

She slides it open and, God help us, there is the Reverend's wife, naked as the day she was born but with a lot more pubic hair. She has the look, I would imagine, that a tuna might wear as a ton-and-a-half white shark roars in for the kill, and she is vainly trying to cover said *pubic hair along with her rather small breasts as if my mother, not see-ing the actual body parts, will say something other than what is about to come out of her mouth.*

"Jesus CHRIST!!!!" screams Mom.

"Don't blaspheme," I try as a distraction.

She backs away from the closet, white-faced, stuttering, mumbling . . . she is obviously and understandably having real trouble computing this.

"What? . . . How . . . YOU HUSSY!!" this from Mom; I believe the term is from the 1800s. She's starting to turn red now, which indicates to me that possibly a little anger is creeping into the equation. I am speech-less. So is the Reverend's wife, although I hear some serious rustling coming from my closet indicating that maybe she's grabbing some of my teenage wardrobe to cover her nakedness.

"This is unconscionable!!!" says mother. I don't know what that means but I'm pretty sure it doesn't mean "It's all good in the 'hood."

The Rev's wife takes a few tentative steps out of the closet (so to speak) and I see she is now wearing one of my T-shirts.

"It's not what it looks like, Mrs. Cotton, honestly," she fibs.

Sadly, Virginia has chosen a rather unfortunate article of clothing from my stash of wrinkled, faded T's. It's one I bought on a whim to boost my public image, wore once, was soundly laughed at by my peers, and was retired to my closet shortly thereafter. On the lower part of the shirt is a large, red arrow that, on me, points in the general downward direction of my crotch, but because of her smaller size is positioned precisely over Ground Zero. Written boldly across the front of the chest is the awkward phrase, "Sex Machine!!" It is an unlucky choice of cover-up, considering. The meaning is not lost on my, by now, apoplectic mother, either.

"Get out of my house!!! NOW!!" is the fair response from Mom.

"Mother, look . . ." I begin.

"You SHUT UP!!!!" is all I get.

Back to Mrs. Whiting. "Grab your whore clothes and leave my house this instant!" Where is she coming up with this shit?

The Rev's now totally freaked-out wife is vainly searching for her "whore clothes," scanning my bedroom floor, panic-stricken.

I dive under the bed and retrieve her dress from where I had kicked it in hopes of avoiding this unbelievably surrealistic scene.

Mrs. Whiting grabs it from me and runs to the bathroom, where this whole thing started in the first place. Mother turns to me.

"You disgusting, loathsome boy. THAT is the wife of my PASTOR!!! She was married to him before God and all his angels!! Wait until your father gets home!!!" I guess we resort to these clichés when real words fail us.

"Dad comes home? When?" is my insolent retort. I really have no explanation or excuse or defense, but I do resent the "loathsome boy" comment. She takes a swing at me. I duck.

Mrs. Whiting leaves the bathroom, dressed, and at a fair clip as she heads for the front door.

"I will be calling your husband!!!" my mother yells to her and the door slams shut with a ringing finality.

Mom storms out, probably heading to the liquor cabinet and only then, after mild fortification, the telephone. In an absolute fog I make my way to Josie's room, sit on her bed, and tell her what has just happened. My girl does not judge, does not criticize, does not hear. But I feel safer with her. I always have. I always will. I decide to try to prevent the nuclear war that my mother's phone call will instigate and wait until I think she's had enough to drink for me to reason with her. She is pretty well buzzed by the time I approach her in the living room, and the conversation does not go at all well.

"Please don't do this," I try one final time as she reaches for the Phone of Doom. "I'll never see her again. It's over. I'm sorry I hurt everyone. I'm a terrible person, I understand that now." I'm trying everything short of knocking her unconscious but she is hell-bent on ridding the world of the Devil and his minions and I leave the room as I hear her say "Reverend, it's Julia Cotton. I'm afraid I have some very, very, very, upsetting news for you. I've just come from my son's . . ." She halts as though being interrupted by the voice on the other end of the line. I stop to hear more. It's too awful not to. But what I hear is definitely not what I am expecting to hear.

"The POLICE?!" my mother says with shock and disbelief. "They're at your house now?!!"

My whole body goes numb and I feel like I'm floating.

The police?!! I didn't know it was illegal to have sex with a reverend's wife! Or maybe it's just anyone's wife. Mother has banged me over the head with the Ten Commandments since I was small enough to focus and I know "adultery" is definitely in there, along with murder and stealing, I just didn't realize it was an actual punishable crime here on earth! I thought it was more like the "taking the Lord's name in vain" or the "carved image" thing. And how did they find out already? Did they bug my room? Have they been spying on us with one those surveillance vans that have all the recording and video equipment inside, antenna on the roof, disguised as a plumber's truck? Have they been filming, listening to (and possibly laughing at) all my pathetic thrustings and soft proclamations of love, in fact our entire illicit goings-on??? Will I be sent to prison?! I've heard all the stories of what they do to young men like me in prison. I think I'm going to faint. This whole deal just took a major step to the left and I am cold with terror. I hear mother hang up the phone with nothing more said. Then the words drift out of her like a bad dream neither of us can wake from. "The police are on their way over here."

Woodydamnit!!! This is all your fault!

"Oh, crap," utters the Omnipotent Supreme Being. But not because of my sad little situation. The Vee-Nung have just turned their beautiful and fragile planet into a permanent black hole. All those millennia to create the perfect orbital star and "Poof." Gone like Mrs. Whiting's whore clothes in a randy moment. The OSB looks at "Earth," which could quite possibly be the next in line for de-beautification by its destructive, ignorant, negligent masses. It's enough to make an Omnipotent Supreme Being weep. The OSB has watched as "Earth" has struggled to rid herself of the lethal virus that is causing the infection and gradual destruction of her body. But the more intelligent elements of that same lethal virus have thwarted her plans again and again. Well-meaning scientists, doctors, and geneticists have all nipped AIDS, Ebola, and SARS in the bud. Where's the frigging Black Plague when you need it? The OSB does not, as a rule, interfere in the workings of the Universe, but on "Earth" it may be time to move another chess piece.

We are beetling down the freeway to deliver Lexington Vargas to La Crescenta as the inadequate windshield wipers make a mockery of their name. Visibility is low. Keith Moon's ghost still wallops the fragile roof, and I begin to wonder if this rain could actually punch holes in the flimsy ceiling and douse us all as we chug along at an astonishing forty-three MPH.

Both Lexington Vargas and Alice are deep into their own copies of *Magnificent Vibration* with the help of some hack, low-wattage interior lighting, which is making piloting the Kia in the rain even more difficult, but honestly, if I had my own copy of that book I'd be balancing it on my knees and reading it right now even as we careen toward La Crescenta. Not a word from either of them except for the occasional, sigh, moan, or *"Dios mio."*

What the heck is going on? I wish I hadn't left mine back at the divorcee's apartment complex I sadly refer to as "home." I begin to hope that my sexual indiscretion with the whore of Babylon isn't detailed too heavily in my version. But my head is also spinning at the greater potential meaning of the three of us coming together like this. Not to mention possible conversations with possibly God. I can come up with no reason or significance for any of it. And Alice has temporarily nixed the phone call that I am burning to make to the number in Lexington Vargas's book. I think she's scared. That's a pretty reasonable reaction I guess, considering he's the CEO of her company.

"STOP THE CAR!!!" suddenly screams the colossus in the backseat at the top of his quite prodigious lungs, and I react as though a SWAT team has just lobbed a stun grenade into the vehicle.

As I slam on the brakes, the lightweight Kia instantly and predictably launches into hydroplane mode, spinning in impotent circles across the mercifully fairly vacant lanes of the 101 and causing several cars to dodge and weave around us. It all happens so fast. A giant, thirty-foot green-and-white freeway off-ramp sign crashes down onto the asphalt right next to us, scaring the crap out of me, sending sparks flying, and tearing itself to pieces on impact, none of which, thankfully, hits us, as I would guess the sign is made of much sturdier stuff than the auto that's currently still spinning like a kid's top. This is all accompanied by a deafening, end-of-the-world-type howling roar that is getting more thunderous by the second. I'm suddenly aware of something gigantic looming overhead. I finally get the damn Kia under control as an object the size of a football field comes into view through the upper edge of the windshield and very, very close.

"OH, SHIT!!!" we all seem to scream in unison as a colossal Airbus A380, the largest passenger jetliner in the world, thunders through the downpour, all lights blazing, and attempts to make a landing directly in front of us on the freeway. It looks monstrous and out of control as it descends. Large pieces begin shearing off the wings as they come in contact with walls, signs, pillars and posts at the edges of the roadway, sending sparks and debris in every direction and causing the giant airplane to lose what remaining control it is under.

I frantically pump the brakes as this incredible event unfolds right before our eyes. Even straddling all the north- and southbound lanes, the airplane is still too big for the freeway to give it a clear landing path. Cars are weaving, pirouetting, crashing into one another, the divider, and the off-ramp walls and generally adding to the shitstorm that is coming as the giant tires finally punch down onto the wet and shining blacktop. They hit so hard that most of the rubber shreds like gray string cheese on impact, the front wheel-strut collapsing altogether, causing the immense nose of the aircraft to drop, hit, and light up like the fourth of July. We're all still screaming and the jet engine noise is deafening as the giant metal flying machine roars down the highway—inexorably screeching, pitching, yawing, and sparking—destroying everything it happens upon until it finally lurches to a halt mere yards from a concrete overpass.

We're all holding our breath as our little toy car bounces to a stop as well. Great gouts of black smoke are pouring from the stricken craft and chaos is everywhere. A yellow evacuation slide suddenly pops open from a lower rear door on the whale-like fuselage of the destroyed airliner and we watch transfixed as a single person jumps into it and glides to relative safety—then starts running in our direction.

"I think we maybe ought to back up some," says Lexington Vargas with characteristic understatement.

But the escaping figure is passing stationary cars between our vulnerable little vehicle and the giant plane and looks to be heading directly toward us. My first thought is that it's a woman with long black hair but the running motion and general outline are masculine. He stops at our car, yanks open the rear door, and squeezes in beside Lexington Vargas amid grunts and groans from the latter.

"We would be wise to leave the area," suggests the hitchhiker with Lexington Vargas–like restraint, and I momentarily catch sight of his extremely beautiful and completely undamaged, coffee-colored face. I'm thinking this is one lucky dude. I'm also wondering why more passengers aren't exiting the wreckage, but I get my answer as a violent fireball explodes out of the open rear door of the Airbus, windows pop from the heat, and flames begin to lick the outside of the plane's now-boiling skin. Anticipating what may come next, I slam the car into reverse and bang right into the front end of a stationary Mercedes. This is no time to exchange numbers and insurance information, so I spin the wheel and we begin racing the wrong way back along the freeway we've just travelled. Other cars are turning to follow suit when it happens. I see the blinding flash of light reflected off every wet surface before me—followed by the thump/whump of the detonation as thousands of gallons of ridiculously flammable jet fuel ignite and turn the three-hundred-million-dollar aircraft and the five-hundred or so travelers into gore and cinders. Then comes the heat. I look in the rearview mirror at the inferno that was once an airplane. Cars between us are bursting into flames from the high radiant temperature as the mighty Kia makes good its escape with not much more to show for it than a slightly crumpled ass-end.

I whip out my phone and juggle it open to call 911, watching for oncoming traffic as I pilot the life-saving automobile up an open on-ramp to the comparative refuge of the side streets.

"There's no need to do that," says a calm voice from the back. "Everyone is calling. Believe me."

Alice and I exchange a look. The stranger's relaxed demeanor is disconcerting, to say the least. Like it's no big deal that he seems to be the only survivor of what could conceivably be the single worst airplane disaster in the history of aviation. Is he a terrorist? Did *he* bring the giant plane down?

"I am Merikh," he says, extending a smooth, dark hand to Lexington Vargas. He has a very subtle, impossible-to-place accent. And a stunningly beautiful face. My first thought is that he's black. But he has the long hair of an American Indian, lustrous and iron straight, and his eyes tilt to a slightly oriental aspect but are the pale blue/green of a shallow tropical sea. His full lips and skin are African but his strong nose is almost Middle Eastern. He looks like an amalgam of every fine feature of every known race. I almost can't take my eyes off him, he is so physically fucking attractive, but I must steer this awe-inspiring, life-saving Korean auto and avoid any possible head-ons.

"What happened?" asks L.V., his voice slightly tremulous and clenched-sounding. He does not offer his hand in return.

"The plane crashed," is this guy Merikh's monumentally vapid answer.

"Did you do that?" L.V. quizzes, jabbing a fat thumb back at the fast-retreating firestorm. Obviously Lexington Vargas has had the same thought that I did.

"That is not my doing, no," is the understated reply.

"There's been a lot of terrorist crap going on lately," L.V. continues, more to us than the new guy.

"Why did you run to our car?" Alice interrogates. Her voice sounds strained, too. We're all in shock trying to deal with this horrifically unreal situation.

"It seemed like the correct course of action," Merikh replies.

"You are one lucky mofo," I respond, my voice too loud.

"I am, as you say, one lucky mofo, yes."

"We should probably drop you at a police station or hospital somewhere."

"I am uninjured and will contact the authorities tomorrow, thank you." This guy is sounding weirder by the minute.

"I don't know, dude, this is pretty strange you surviving that crash and not seeming wigged-out or in shock or anything. You don't even have a mark on you. How is that possible? Why did that plane go down?" For some reason I tend to ramble in stressful situations.

"I had a feeling when we left Narita that the plane would crash," Merikh answers, again oddly.

"Never heard of any country called Narita before. Sounds Middle Eastern." Lexington Vargas either still thinks this guy's a terrorist or, like me, he just never paid attention in geography.

"Narita is the Tokyo airport . . . in Japan," Merikh explains.

"Okay, we know where Tokyo is," I say, somewhat peeved, although in all fairness to the guy there was no condescension in his tone.

"What were you in Japan for?" Alice again takes over with a fine non sequitur.

"I was there for the tsunami event."

"Doing what?" I can't keep the slightly suspicious note out of my voice. We all sound like we don't trust this very pretty man. And we don't.

"Helping," is all he says.

There is a moment of silence that I would like to suggest is for all the poor souls who have just lost their lives in the recent air-travel-related conflagration on the 101 freeway, but in truth we are all trying to piece together a logical line of questioning for this very strange person. Merikh seems willing enough to provide answers, but somehow he's not really telling us much.

He is handsome, though. It's almost ridiculous how good-looking this dude is. I covetously check Alice, my sizzling-hot Christ-bride, for any signs of attraction. I blame Woody for this sudden switch of focus, but at least it's proof that the trauma is starting to wear off.

"Honestly, I think we should hand him over to the cops, man. There's gotta be a lot of questions people are gonna be asking that he can maybe answer." This really sensible idea is voiced by none other than our once-perceived-as-a homicidal-maniac, Lexington Vargas.

"I agree, I think that's the right bet," I add. "It's best for everyone if you just tell the police your story. And I don't think we should be driving aimlessly around Hollywood with the only survivor of the world's worst air disaster in our backseat."

"That sounds like a plan," Alice chimes in, and I believe that means she is not sexually attracted to this gorgeous but weird fellow. Damnit, Woody, shut up!!!

"LAPD's on Wilcox," says L.V.

"You sure?" I ask.

"Yeah . . . I'm sure," and his tone suggests that Lexington Vargas has some possible skeletons in his very large closet. I make a left and head the great and powerful Kia toward Wilcox Avenue.

"That's not a good idea," suggests Merikh. No one responds.

There is more silence. This time it's quite unnerving. Honestly, none of us know this guy from Adam. He could be capable of anything. The sooner we drop his ass off at a cop shop, the better we'll all feel.

"You two seem to be reading the same book," Merikh finally adds.

Both Alice and Lexington Vargas still have their copies of *Magnificent Vibration* on their laps.

"This has been a really weird night," is what I answer. "And that book started it all."

"Perhaps this will change your minds," says Mr. Hot Stuff.

In the rearview mirror I see he is now reaching into his brown leather jacket. I know what's coming.

"No way! You've got to be kidding me. Not *another* copy of that freaking book?" I exclaim.

But it is not. What it *is*, is a gun! And it's big, too. And really, really old. This odd hitchhiker is threatening us with an eighteenth-century flintlock pistol that has a bore so big I think I could squeeze my head into the barrel's opening. An ornate piece of antiquity with scrolling designs adorning its body and an elegant silver cap at the end of the handle. The gun looks like Jack Sparrow's piece from *Pirates of the Caribbean*, the last movie I filled the void of a lonely night watching. In fact, it looks *astonishingly* like that screen weapon! Almost identical. WTF! But who's looking at the details (other than a guy with ADD) when the business end is pointed in the general direction of your head. How could we have missed that he had this frigging cannon under his jacket? And how did he ever get the thing on a plane??

"Oh, Shit!!!" we all exclaim once again in unison.

He directs the large-bore opening at Lexington Vargas's temple. If the thing went off, I would suspect a major part of L.V.'s cranium would be decorating the interior of the silver Kia.

"Wait, wait, what are you doing?" screams Alice, wigging.

This guy has now proven himself to be *completely* unpredictable.

"Take it easy, just . . . slow down a minute here," I chime in, pretty much as wigged as she is. Only Lexington Vargas seems unruffled. Has he had a gun pulled on him before? Perhaps.

"My suggestion is that you do not drive me to the police. Instead, we stick together," says Weirdo.

"Why would we want to do that when you're threatening us with a gun?" Me trying on my best hostage-negotiator voice.

"Because I am here to help," he says.

"Help who?" Alice almost pleads.

"You," he returns.

"Help *us*? To do what?" she asks.

There is a beat or two. Then the very pretty nutball finally answers: "I don't know."

I'm still sitting on the floor by Josie's bed when the dreaded but anticipated knock at the front door finally comes. I've had the most horrific visions while I've been waiting for this visit. Awful prison scenes have flashed though my masochistic mind. One where I am badly man-

handled, punched, kicked, poked, and coerced into becoming a fully tattooed, white-supremacist skinhead in order to survive in "the joint." Another, I am a "bitch" married to the big, hairy fat guy with the most cigarettes. And yet more where I'm beaten and raped daily by inmates as the guards stand around, laugh, and shoot video. Supervised phone calls with my mother where I listen helplessly as she collapses into inconsolable tears. Even, God help me, conjugal visits from the Reverend's now-ex-strumpet. It has been a terrifying hour and a half. I hear footsteps down the hall and I look up. My mother is standing there with two sheriffs; both of them appear to be armed to the teeth and ostensibly trigger-happy, ready to shoot first and plant a gun on me later. No point in making a break for it now, anyway.

"These gentlemen would like a word with you, Horatio." She barely gets it out.

"Yes," I answer. "Is it okay if we talk in the living room? I don't want Josie to hear this."

The serious men in brown seriously nod their serious assent. I rise, bend down, and kiss my girl good-bye. Then, like the condemned man I am, I walk out into the hallway. The sheriffs follow. I am so screwed.

We all take seats in the modest living room as a blond, blue-eyed, Caucasian Jesus looks on from a frame above the mantel with a mixture of sympathy and barely suppressed horror.

"May we speak with your son in private, Ma'am?" asks the older sheriff. "It's completely up to you, of course, but there are some delicate matters to discuss and we feel he may be more forthcoming if it's just us men." He smiles conspiratorially at me. Uh-oh. Is he the "good" cop? I make a mental note that the younger one has now been identified, by a process of elimination, as the "bad" cop. They get ready to work me over, rolls of quarters in their meaty fists, phone books at the ready to wrap around my ribs so the bruises won't show. I almost want my mother here with me but the humiliation would be too much, so I say nothing as she sighs tragically, rises, and walks into the kitchen like the martyred saint she is.

The sheriffs wait until she's gone.

"Now, son," begins the "good" cop, with some condescension. "We understand this is difficult for you, but we need you to tell us the truth. Do you understand? This is off the record for now—we're just gathering facts, okay? Nothing you say will be held or used against you."

I nod, white-faced. They're probably recording it.

"This conversation is about Virginia Whiting, Reverend Whiting's wife," he continues. "We've heard from quite a few boys now that Mrs. . . ."

"Boys?" I squeak. He just lost me.

The "bad" cop chimes in and I flinch. "They've come forward about Virginia Whiting's alleged sexual advances," is the shocking answer. I am already reeling. She's been telling people about us???!!! And telling young BOYS??? What the hell!!!

"Good" cop continues. "Young men, around your age. Seventeen, eighteen, nineteen."

I am having serious trouble following all this. Why would she tell other people when she was always admonishing me about the necessary secrecy of our trysts? My shaky little-boy voice asks the big, mean men, "What did she say about me?"

The "good" cop looks puzzled. They both seem to be getting impatient with how thick I apparently am, so they decide to spell it out for yours half-wittedly. "Virginia Whiting has allegedly been having sex with a number of young men," is the unbelievable response from the "good" cop. "Men both attached to her husband's church and outside it.

As young men will do, some of them have been bragging to their friends about their sexual encounters with Mrs. Whiting. A concerned mother overheard something that was said and came to us. Our investigations have turned up quite a few boys, both under and over the age of consent, that Mrs. Whiting has allegedly been sexually involved with."

I am fucking stunned!!! My Virgi . . . Mrs. Whi . . . the Reverend's wi . . . SHE has been having sex with other guys??!!

It finally lands in my lap. The cuckolder (me) has been cuckolded. A lot.

I am devastated.

I have to ask. "Is it illegal to have sex with a Reverend's wife in this state?"

They seem amused by this. "Good" cop says, "We're investigating Virginia Whiting for having unlawful sex with young men not of consenting age and also abusing her office."

So I'm off the hook?

I am deeply relieved that they are investigating her and not me. But still devastated. Yes, quite devastated.

And although extremely grateful, I categorically deny any sexual involvement with the Reverend's apparently very horny and oversexed wife. The sheriffs both look doubtful.

"Son, we're aware that Mrs. Whiting has spent a lot of time in your home . . ."

"I never touched her," I lie like a bastard.

"HORATIO!" my mother reprimands from the kitchen. Damnit, she's been listening the whole time.

They both look at me expectantly. I look back. "Nothing happened between Vir . . . Mrs. Whiting and me."

I'm no stoolie. And I'm sure as hell not going to testify in some court of law, in front of a jury of my peers, that I have been snaking the Reverend's missus. The sheriffs give each other a look and both rise. They call to my mother, who enters so quickly she must have been standing right by the friggin' door.

"Bad" cop hands her his card. "If your son changes his mind, please give us a call. Thank you."

Apparently I am dismissed.

The men in brown exit the premises without me in handcuffs being shoved unkindly ahead of them. I am momentarily relieved.

Then my mother enters the living room after seeing them out and stands before me with her righteous hands on her righteous hips.

"You're as bad as your father," she begins as I hightail it out of there and head for the border like every bad guy does. But my south of the border happens to be my sister's bedroom.

"Sho," she cries as I enter her room. She is wearing a sweet and goofy smile for me and I sit with her while she stares at I know not what.

"Don't you walk away from me while I'm talking to you!" yells mother after me. "We have more to say about this, you and I, Horatio! You can lie to the police but you cannot lie to me. I was there. I saw that harlot in your bedroom and I can just imagine what was going on before I got home. Under your sister's very nose and in MY HOUSE!!" She drones on and on but I tune her out now that I am in Josie's room, secure in the fact that at least it was not under my sweet girl's nose that these heinous acts were committed. I am back in the safety of her world and reading to her from an old "Tales from the Crypt" comic book. This room has become the only place I really feel safe. It's time to come back to some sense of normalcy. Start getting my life back on whatever track it was on before this whole "Thou shalt not commit adultery nor prong the Reverend's freaky wife" thing began. Set about doing stuff for just Josie and me. But it doesn't happen.

Three days later, my mother walks into the kitchen, where I am heating up a frozen pizza in the lethal microwave, and announces that she is finished with us men. All our lying and cheating. All the secrets and the sex. All our irreligious behavior and denial of the Holy Scriptures. (???) She has had it and will brook no more wanton conduct. She is divorcing my father, and as soon as my school year is up I must move out and get a darn job. She is done with all of us. I ask her why she is lumping all the bad behavior of us male Cottons into this one act of divorce. Well, two, counting the moving-out-and-getting-the-darn-job thing. But she won't talk about it anymore. Her mind is made up. My father has heard from her and has agreed to the divorce. Now all that's left is for me to do the school/job dealy. She has HAD it!!! She storms from the kitchen and out of the house. The front door slams shut as a kind of exclamation point on her monologue and I hear the car engine cough and turn over. She takes off with a small but angry squeal of burning rubber. I traipse out after her as the frozen pizza turns into radioactive goo in the nuke. But she is gone.

Their divorce is not a surprise to me, but the reality of it hurts like hell. I feel responsible. Like the whole Reverend's-wife fiasco was the straw that broke the large, long-necked, arid-climate-dwelling ungulate's back. I never see my father again. He moves his stuff out while I'm at school and doesn't bother to contact me. "Boy" is off his radar. So is his more-loved daughter, I guess, now that she can no longer reciprocate what I think I always saw as his preening love for her. We're on our own, kids!

I go through weeks of depression that thankfully Josie is spared. Our parents' divorce at this late stage of the game would be exceptionally hard on her, were she aware. My girl is not. I thank heaven for small fucking favors.

Not much changes in the physical appearance of the house. The furniture—all selected by my mother—stays. The only thing that's missing is the photo of them on the mantel by our Lord and the one in their bedroom. They are permanently retired from public view. His clothes are gone, too. The only shot that exists of my father and me remains on my desk. It was taken on our one and only trip to Disneyland when I was six years old. I'm smiling into the camera, as happy as a squirrel with an acorn hat while my dad stares distractedly off to the left of the frame as though he has no interest in being in a photo with his son. A few weeks later that photo magically disappears as well. Zap!

I don't quite understand why I am so down about this dissolution of our parents' laughingstock set of matrimonial vows. I knew their marriage wasn't good, clearly headed for if not already on the rocks, but the *finality of it is almost as devastating as discovering that I wasn't the only monkey who was getting his banana peeled by sweet Virginia, the Reverend's horn-dog.*

At school I begin to flirt with the mixed bag of pleasure that is marijuana. It makes me feel a lot less depressed and a little less lame, even though I know I'm deliberately lowering my I.Q. and flatlining my drive to succeed. The silly nonsense word-jumbles Josie has begun to babble now and then sound even funnier when I'm high. "Door up, down." "Sho read curtain cabbage." "Bathroom face." "Daddy touch no-no." Phrases that make absolutely . . . Wait!! Back up! . . . What was that last one??? Probably just her brain misfiring. Okay, we have enough shit to deal with, and at this point everything else is just more shit.

Unbeknownst to my mother, who has upped her intake of her drug of choice (red wine) I drop out of school so I can take better care of Josie. My grades were sucking anyway and I'm pretty sure the whole Nobel Prize–winning scientist career is off the table for good. I have mastered the G chord now on my guitar, so possible rock-star fame is still quite alive, although it could be coughing up blood. Not sure. Fingers really hurt too.

We all hunker down for the long winter that seems to be upon us Cottons. And life just keeps getting increasingly surreal.

One morning I notice that the left side of Josie's face is looking a little slacker than the right side. Over the course of a week or so I'm alarmed to notice that instead of self-correcting, it begins to droop even farther. One morning, concerned that she may have had a stroke or something, I bundle her up, guide her into the car, and take her to see her doctor, hoping we'll be back before mother realizes I am driving the car without her permission and without a license.

Her doctor is a nice enough guy, but whatever his specialty is, it doesn't include asymmetrically drooping faces. So he refers us to a neu-

rologist, who then refers us to a radiologist, who then orders a series of MRIs of Josie's head. By the time we get home it's dark and our mother is well aware that I've taken the car without asking her or bothering to apply for a valid driver's license. She's convinced that I just took her sick daughter for a self-centered joyride.

I try to explain, but she has already hit the wine rack and will hear none of it. I'm just doing what I want, when I want, with no regard for anyone but myself, "You selfish little bastard!!"

I take Josie to the bathroom and then tuck her into her bed. I head to the kitchen to try again with Mom. She is still on her rant until I override her with a childishly shouted, "Josie's face is lopsided. The doctor thought it could be bad!!!"

She falls silent. Her pinched, furious expression softens to a more dumbfounded look.

"What?" It's as if the words I just yelled are taking their time to land.

"One side of her face is kind of sagging, so I took her to the doctor to check it out," I say. But she's off again.

"Without asking me if you could? You just take my car?! And with no driver's license? Is there any illegal thing you will not do, Horatio?"

I stuff it down, doing my utmost not to go south with her. I try again. Equably.

"Mom. Just shut up and listen, okay? The MRI guy told me he saw something in her head."

She stops one more time.

"In your sister's head?"

We are finally on the same page.

"Yes."

"Like what? What did he see?"

"Some kind of lump."

"On an MRI he saw this?"

"Yes. He said he was only a technician and wasn't supposed to say anything but I told him she was my sister and I really needed to know, now. He's been doing this for fifteen years and seen a lot of MRIs and he said that we should get the results from the neurologist as soon as we can."

It takes a few seconds for this to register but register it finally does. She slaps a hand to her mouth as if to shut herself up and stop any further discourse, then turns and bolts for Josie's bedroom to be with her daughter, all anger and blaming gone. That is the part of her that is still our mom. It's unexpected, but I start to tear up, seeing her run to her baby's side like that. With the amount of stress and the blitzkrieg of crap we have all gone through, I lose it. I drop to a kitchen chair and burst into tears like I am six years old again.

A few days later we three journey in to see the neurologist on a cold and rainy November afternoon, as united as we'll ever be at this stage of the game. Mom drives, of course, and I'm in the back with my bundled-up sister, who drools and doesn't seem to see the bare trees as they fly past her window in a blur. What's left of our family arrives at the doctor's and we sit silently in the waiting room while the girl behind the front desk sexts her boyfriend on her cell. We are both, my mother and I, fearing some pretty bad news. But when we're escorted into his office and the doctor finally enters, it's not bad at all!! It's fucking terrible. Beyond terrible.

"It's called a glioblastoma multiforme. It is, unfortunately, the most aggressive form of brain cancer, and it occurs predominantly in young people," is what we hear from him.

He points to a series of cranial MRI's on the desktop of a computer sitting to the side of his hard oak desk. We'd all missed these when we came in, such is our collective state of mind. The soft-tissue outline is so obviously my sister's face that I audibly gasp. There is a diffused white mass at the base of her skull.

"What we are seeing here is a stage-four tumor on her brain stem. Our options are pretty limited at this point, I'm afraid."

"What are the options?" I manage. I assume my mother's in shock.

He looks to her to see if this is her question also. She nods silently, sadly. He seems to be a regular guy who is just doing his best to deliver this awful news, but we've already been set up to expect some "options." Like there will be a couple of reasonable choices.

He takes a breath. "Honestly? I would suggest that you take Josephine home and make her as comfortable as possible," is the first "option" he offers.

"That's it?!!" I respond, maybe with a little too much energy for the small room. He shifts in his seat ever so slightly and I sense that I've made him more uneasy.

"Well, we could try chemotherapy and that might add a few weeks, perhaps even a few months to her life, but it would certainly make her quite sick and with a relatively insignificant result," he says. "Truthfully, I don't think it's worth it."

We sit there in silence, trying to grasp the death sentence he has just delivered.

"How long does she have?" My voice sounds far away to me, and I think I'm just parroting a line I heard in some movie, but it's the only thing I can think to say. And it feels like a movie we are all in. Where the worst that could possibly happen, does.

"At best, I'd say three to six months." He has a gentle and understanding expression on his face and his eyes are kind, but the words hit us like a hammer blow.

So we will go from four Cottons to two Cottons in a matter of half a year.

"Sho mom love smile," our girl blurts out into the quiet room. And I begin to think she understands more than I suspected.

I wrap my arm around her. She rests her sweet head on my shoulder. I try really hard not to cry.

In the small, ancestral law offices of McGivney, McGivney, and Mc-Givney in the city of Inverness, where the shelves are overstuffed with the myriad of paperwork and legal volumes that are the necessary evils of the profession, the shrill ring of a phone pierces the quiet. Weak afternoon sunlight filters in through four-hundred-year-old windows that looked upon this same room when Shakespeare was a contemporary playwright. They distort the light, creating diffused shadows and imbuing the furnishings with muted edges. Clive Mc-Givney rises and answers the phone, his voice colored with a warm Scottish burr. He listens and grunts a short, satisfied reply, then sets the phone back in its cradle. Turning to his father, who is sitting across the room, he shouts for the benefit of the old man's rapidly declining auditory faculties. "Dad, they think they've found Devin Young's kid in the United States. Apparently it's a lass named Alice."

"Then get the gun out of my face," says Lexington Vargas, reasonably enough.

"Dude, there's no need to threaten us. Really," I add, shooting furtive looks in the rearview mirror at gonzo Gorgeous George, who still has the large weapon pointed at the large man's large head.

"I am here to help," Merikh repeats as if it were a mantra.

I slow the muscular Kia, the Rolls-Royce of the Korean auto industry, down to a stop at an intersection as the light changes from green to yellow to red. The rain has subsided a little but it's still a downpour.

"If you really mean us no harm, then put the gun down. Please. I'm not going to the cops, I promise." Again I am trying the role of negotiator on for size. I must be getting better at it because Merikh slowly lowers the angst-inducing firearm until the business end is no longer aimed at its former and sizable target. He looks skittishly at Lexington Vargas, as though trying to judge if this is the right move or not. Then he puts the gun back inside the brown leather jacket from which it first appeared.

It's the right move for us but possibly the wrong one for him, because L.V. is suddenly all over him like a cheap suit, wrestling Merikh for the now-concealed weapon, accompanied by grunts and much seat-kicking. Alice, bless her heart, starts whacking the handsome intruder with a small, balled-up fist, inflicting limited damage I'm sure.

The door nearest Merikh abruptly flies open and he is unceremoniously shoved out of the car and onto the roadway by way of Lexington Vargas's substantial foot. The fact that he got it all the way up to Merikh's chest in the first place, restricted by the confines of this tiny car, impresses the hell out of me. He reaches over and yanks the door shut, wrenching the whole interior side panel off in the process. Okay, it's a puny car, but it still saved our lives—and it seems to be doing it again as L.V. yells, "Go man, GO! Let's get the fuck away from this guy, excuse my language, Miss."

He is a gentleman to the end.

I gun the Kia's hamster and we roar through the red light at a hair-raising twenty-one MPH. Mercifully, because of the late hour, there is no intersecting eighteen-wheeler there barreling through to smash us to smithereens. Merikh is already up on his feet and running after the car just like the damn T-1000 robot in *Terminator 2*. He's shouting something, but it's inaudible to us over the hamster's heavy breathing.

Inch by anxious, nail-biting inch, the Kia pulls away, and once again this impressive Asian automobile delivers us from possible annihilation.

I watch in the side mirror to see if Merikh whips out the gun to take a pot-shot at our retreating, slightly rumpled butt, but he does not. I turn my eyes back to the road as our brawny Kia gobbles up the highway.

"That's so weird," says Lexington Vargas, looking back at the fast-disappearing figure on the street.

"Yeah, totally," I agree. "What a nutjob."

"No, I mean . . . I couldn't find the gun. It was nowhere on him."

"Is it on the backseat . . . or the floor?" asks Alice.

"No," says our giant friend and bodyguard.

"Where did he put it?" I'm having a hard time with this now, too.

"He didn't 'put' it anywhere. I think it disappeared."

I give Alice that "WTF" look you see on kid-actors' faces in bad teen TV sitcoms and then suggest to our small group that, since it would now be a logistical nightmare to get Lexington Vargas to La Crescenta due to the exploding plane, and if Alice is good with it (please God, please oh please!) maybe we should all crash at my place so we can discuss what, if anything, we should do now about our curious coming-together, it being the weekend and all.

L.V. is only too happy to finally find a bed now that his own has been rendered fairly inaccessible, but Alice hesitates, understandably.

"It's cool if you want to go back to your own place," I offer unconvincingly as I ease on the brakes in anticipation of changing course yet again.

"I don't think I want to be alone right now," says Alice. "And since we've all been through this weird night together, it's probably a good idea to circle the wagons at your place." (Insert "smiley face" re: Alice.)

I turn the proud Kia toward the part of town that harbors my divorcee's home-away-from-home and put the pedal to the rodent. The Kia fairly hums in agreement.

Alice is dialing a number on her cell phone (nuns have cell phones?!) and I hear a thin, faint, scratchy voice say, "What is the nature of your emergency?" I realize she's dialed 911.

"We picked up a guy in our car and he pulled a gun on us," Alice says breathlessly.

Scratchy voice in the earpiece.

Alice answers, "No, we pushed him out and drove off."

Scratchy voice again.

"I don't know. I wasn't really paying attention to the street names." Alice turns to me. "Where were we when we kicked him out?" she asks.

"Yeah, I was kind of focused more on the gun, too, and the fact that he might possibly blow my brains out the side of my head," I answer.

"Somewhere on Barham. Before the studios. I was a little busy, too," answers the ever-cool Lexington Vargas.

Alice relates what little information we have. Then she adds, "Wait a minute! What am I thinking? He's one of the people from the airplane that crashed on the freeway tonight. He came down an evacuation slide and got into our car. That should help you locate him. It didn't look like there were very many people who got out before the plane exploded," she continues.

"Funny what small details escape you when someone points a gun in your face," I say with no slight irony. Self-preservation comes first, right? But Alice isn't listening to *me*.

"What?" she says into the phone. There is an odd note to her voice.

Scratchy, barely audible voice.

"But we saw him jump out of the plane. It happened right in front of us."

Scratchy voice again.

"Are you sure?" asks Alice.

Scratchy voice one final time.

"No, no never mind. I'll go in and file a report tomorrow," she finishes and disconnects the call, looking a bit lost.

"What'd they say?" I ask.

"She said all the news channels are reporting that there *were* no survivors," is what Alice answers.

We drive on through the wee hours, all our minds working overtime, trying to make sense of all of this or glean some understanding, or at the very least wake up from this *non compos mentis* freak of a dream.

I run a second red light just to be sure we further distance ourselves from the whacko, Merikh. Or ghost of Merikh; whatever he is. Alice lets out a shriek. "STOP!"

"Shit!!" I answer because she scares the hell out of me. But I have obediently slammed on the brakes again, thinking, "Jesus, not another airplane." But there are no more crash-landing jets in our future, at least not tonight.

"Go back and turn right down Fairfax," commands Alice.

"Why? My apartment's *this* way, on Sunset."

Alice holds up her copy of *Magnificent Vibration*.

"The bookshop where we all got these is just down the street."

"Pretty sure it's not going to be open at three o'clock in the morning," I reply. I'm tired, so the heat I'm feeling for Alice is tempered somewhat by the late hour. A look from her, however, convinces me to come to my senses.

"But hey, let's check it out," I add, literally and figuratively turning on a dime.

"Maybe we'll learn something." I spin the wheel and head the Kia in the general direction of Fairfax High School.

We are already in the neighborhood, and we arrive at our destination a few minutes later. I think this is time well spent as I eye the outlines of the sizzling nun's thighs through her skirt. Woody, not now. Please! Jesus!

I park in one of the metered spaces that—at this late hour—isn't occupied by a car full of rapists, drug dealers, or couples innocently making out and waiting to be the next victims of the Westside Slasher. The scarce-as-hen's-teeth Los Angeles rain has started to fall a little heavier again, but we all exit the Kia and head to the bookstore where we all bought (or stole) *Magnificent Vibration* "Discover your true purpose."

Not surprisingly, considering the way the night has generally gone, we can't find it. The building that we all concur housed the missing bookstore sports a sign announcing that it is now a travel agency!

FAIRFAX GLOBETROTTERS
Your partner in travel for 35 years.

The "35" looks pasted in, as though it's been added at some point to update the claim.

The shabby marquee and general design of the store add credence to the boast that this business has indeed operated here for the advertised three decades plus. We all stand there staring in slightly jaded awe as if the bookstore will suddenly materialize before us like some genie from a bottle if we just psychically rub the fucker hard enough.

It doesn't.

And we are getting soaked to the skin. Alice wears it well. Lexington Vargas and I, not so well.

The shop is very bare-bones. I peer through the be-dusted window. In the relative interior gloom I can make out two desks, some chairs, and a set of shelves housing a selection of books—but none of them look like *our* book.

"Figures," says Lexington Vargas.

"This is freaky," breathes Alice.

"You mean compared to the *rest* of the night?" I reply, and yes, my tone is somewhat sardonic.

If Alice hears me, she doesn't respond.

As we head, wet and weary, back to the car, I turn to look one last time just to make sure we didn't miss anything in our present, highly tweaked state. I notice a single travel poster taped to the agency window that I guess I'd missed before.

"COME TO SCOTLAND," is all it says, and I'll be damned if the photo isn't of Urquhart Castle, perched on a low hill overlooking Loch

Ness. Somewhere inside me I am still the twelve-year-old boy who loves monsters. Especially *that* monster.

"Fuck me," I exclaim softly. I am, of course, referring to the whole night, as well as to the serendipity of seeing this awesome poster in the window, but I may also be projecting and referencing something a little more intimate and unholy, considering I just accidentally touched Alice's fairly soaked-through butt as she got into the Kia via the door I am holding open for her.

Thankfully, Lexington Vargas is already in the car and out of earshot because he'd probably beat me to a bloody pulp for swearing in spitting distance of a nun, now that he knows she is indeed a cross-carrying member of the sisterhood. Alice has already shown a proclivity for the occasional cuss-word herself and doesn't seem to mind my lapses. It being the extraordinary evening it has been, I think she'd agree—although she may not be quite so on board with my secondary, more intimate meaning. I don't know. I *have* caught her looking at me. Sideways glances when there hasn't been a giant anthropoid blocking our path, a plane crashing, or a gun being held to our collective heads by an extraordinarily lovely madman. Maybe she's wondering why I wear my hair so long. Unless she's already caught sight of the twin sidecars I jestingly refer to as my ears, and put it together.

After a comparatively uneventful drive, Alice, Lexington Vargas, and I hole up in my BP (Bachelor Pad) and agree unanimously that it has been a fairly unusual night, to say the least. We've changed out of our wet clothes and showered. Alice is wearing my robe and I suspect not much else. L.V. has somehow managed to squeeze himself into one of my T-shirts and a pair of board shorts. I am in my jammies, once again.

"Alice, you can sleep in the master bedroom," I offer magnanimously. "Lexington and I will take the single bed in the second room and the couch here. Is that cool with everyone?" I say, pointing to the couch as if they've never seen a couch before and need immediate illumination.

"I've got dibs on the couch," says Lexington Vargas graciously. I admit I have a vague and unrealistic hope that somehow Alice and I will end up in the same bed tonight. Sheesh, what morons Woody and I are sometimes. We are a dangerously impractical pair, I think.

Alice and L.V. nod their agreement—on the sleeping arrangements, that is; not my private, mental note about my quixotic relationship with the Woodman. "I have spare toothbrushes," I offer to both but leaning heavily and hopefully toward L.V.

"We should turn on the news," says Alice, so I do.

The plane crash is on every station. There is also shaky videophone footage that some quick-thinking citizen has captured and probably sold to the networks for billions. The amateur video plainly shows the moment the evac slide is activated. Then the horrific explosion that follows. Of course the channels play this footage over and over and over but for the life of us all sitting watching in my living room, we don't see a single soul come down that slide.

The newscasters announce it again and again: No survivors. They show the video. Then say there were no survivors. Then replay the video . . . and say again, in case we missed it the first fifteen times, that there were no survivors. It's an endless loop and what news channels do when actual fact-gathering is slow.

We are too tired, too bewildered, and too numb to make any sense of the last few hours and what it all might mean. But we are united in the belief that it means *something* and that we are now involved in an anomalous event, possibly preternatural. Either that or someone spiked our coffee at Jafar's Java Joint.

"When we wake up tomorrow, I'm dialing that number in Lexington's book," I announce adamantly. The truth is I'm nervous about calling in case he/she harasses me again. Anyway, it's really late and I figure even God has to close up shop at *some* point and go home to the wife and kids. I still haven't looked at my copy of the book yet beyond checking out the 800 number. There's only so much information I can cram into my tiny brain in one cataclysmically eventful and astonishing night. I already feel like my head is about to detonate like the guy in that awesome scene in *Scanners*. BOOM!

Lexington Vargas nods his agreement at my suggestion of getting God on the horn in the a.m. I think he's too bone-weary to chat now, anyway. Alice continues to stare at the TV. She's hard to read. I don't understand her reaction, or rather her non-reaction, to the fact that we have some new, possible holy digits. If you were a sophomoric stockbroker and someone handed you Warren Buffet's home number, you'd want to give him a buzz, right?

Why doesn't she want to place the call? It's her BOSS!!! I let it go for now. Instead I suggest we all get some sleep. Lexington Vargas finally switches off the TV and its frightening replay of images we witnessed just hours ago and will never forget. I can only hope I'm too tired to dream.

Under cover in the darkened street below, a figure watches as the last light goes out in the apartment.

The rain has stopped but the wind still blows, whipping his long jet-black hair across his beautiful face. He brushes the errant locks aside with elegant fingers and continues to observe.

---

*J*osie's health heads south rapidly. She no longer babbles her sweet, childlike phrases to me in any language I can decipher. What little speech she has is taken from her completely in a matter of months as the tumor grows and presses on new and crucial areas of her brain. Our mother does her best, but she is struggling with the emotional and financial impact of the divorce as Dad, three weeks into post-marriage freedom, reneges on the monetary aid he'd promised her. The church is her only salvation, and I've even sullied that with my wanton sexual meanderings. She is waiting for the new pastor with bated breath. Me, too.

My "darn job" has failed to materialize, but I have now progressed to the slightly easier D-chord on the guitar and am hoping all my hard work will soon pay off and the much-anticipated rock stardom is just around the corner. That said, I'm pretty sure I could be kidding myself, so on weekends, when mother is home all day, I go door to door to see if anyone wants to employ a depressed, directionless, deviant high school dropout. So far no one has jumped at the offer.

The doctors (yes, "doctors" plural, because once you get cancer, everyone wants to climb aboard the gravy train) have been giving my sister high doses of steroids in the hope that this might shrink the tumor and relieve some of the pressure on her brain. Although it's a stopgap measure at best, the dexamethasone/prednisone concoctions have caused her once narrow frame to swell dramatically, as though someone has attached an air hose to her. Everything about her appearance is bloated and distended, and she no longer looks anything like Josie. Her skin has thinned drastically thanks to the self-same steroidal abuse, causing the weakened epidermis to tear randomly and painfully all over her body under the added pressure of the weight gain. I can tell she's suffering, though she makes no sound or movement, and I am unable to do anything to help her.

I read to her in the beginning, hoping Melville will get through. If Moby-Dick can't reach her, nothing can. I even clamp headphones over her ears and crank up Nirvana. She doesn't react to either. So I just sit with my sister and watch her die. I really wish we still had a dog.

I've even given up my fruitless hunt for the perfect girl, which at this point actually means "any girl who finds me even remotely attractive and has half a mind to climb into the sack with me and Woody." I begin to believe that maybe the Reverend's freak of a wife was the high point of my sexual career. Heaven forbid.

My girlfriend prospects are limited anyway, now that I'm caring for Josie most of the time, unless I start opening up the qualifications a tad to include 55-year-old, morbidly obese nurses and the occasional snobby, balding doctor. It's a thought.

I come home one evening from another fruitless day of who-wants-to-hire-an-incompetent-loser and hear my mother talking to my sister as though she were aware and coherent and might actually respond. It's silly and heartbreaking at the same time.

Mom says, "We have a new pastor coming into the church soon, Josephine. It's very exciting. We're all very excited."

Crickets!

More from Mom: "I might paint the bathroom. It looks so drab, that awful green color. I think it's time for a change, don't you?"

Again, crickets.

"Doris—you know Doris, Mark Brewer's new wife?—well, appar-

ently she's got a bit of a history and may actually have a criminal record. At least that's the talk."

As before, crickets. I walk into Josie's room to free her from this inane jabber, but she actually seems to be taking an interest in it. She's looking at Mom with big, wide eyes and appears to comprehend it all, ready to gossip herself, chat, shoot the shit, throw the bull. I sense that a change has occurred in our girl. This could be good. Is this the rewiring of the brain the doctor had mentioned? The miracle of miracles?

So if this was real life—and it most certainly is—what would be the guess? And you are correct, Sir or Madam!! Go to the head of the class. Pass "GO" and collect 200 dollars. Pick any stuffed animal from the third shelf. It is NOT the miracle we have all been praying for.

I sit on Josie's bed. My mother gives me a look that says she is making some serious progress and not to interfere. I have a sneaking suspicion it is not progress. At least not the kind she is imagining. I touch my girl's face. She is ice cold. I black out for a second. I put my hand on her ribs. There is no rise and fall or breathing of any kind. Josie is dead. She has silently passed, and our mother, with all her disconnected craziness, has missed this beautiful/awful moment. Our girl is gone forever. I fall into her lifeless arms and hug her for the last time. Mother is reduced to silence.

"I love you, my girl," I whisper into Josie's cold shell of an ear. I know she knows this but I must tell her once again. I am an inarticulate nineteen-year-old and I have no words to express either my pain or the staggering profundity of this moment. All I've got at my command is this simple, timeworn phrase. It is the purest and most simply meaningful final sentiment I can offer my avenging angel/harpy who was my rock, even with all her afflictions. And I offer it to her as she leaves me, on a journey to I-know-not-where.

So I say, one final time to her: "I love you." And mean it as much as I ever will in my life.

The hospice nurse comes in to confirm that Josie is actually dead, and a couple of men from the mortuary arrive to collect her body. We are in a daze and assume they know what they're doing, though who has the wherewithal at a time like this to judge that? A day later they deliver to our home a small wooden box of ashes that is all that remains of my sister. I set them on the dining room table, where we used to fight over who got the most Jell-O for dessert when we were kids. Her beautiful hair, the tortured eyes that could still show love, the pale skin she used to scrub until it was red and raw, the good heart that beat, the brain that turned on her, the musical voice that could soothe my young soul, the face and form of my sweet sister—all reduced to a pale gray, granulated powder. Her ashes. The container sits there for weeks. I don't want to move it because it's Josie. My mother won't go near it. Mother wanted her buried, whole and in the ground with all the attendant church rituals and hallowed recitations but Josie had (maybe presciently) expressed to me her desire to be turned into ash and given back to the earth should she go before me. And so I have made certain that this wish, at least, has been fulfilled. It is the least I can do for all she was to me. Sorry, all she is to me.

I walk into my monster-shrine of a bedroom a few days after she has passed and see my sad, pointless guitar sitting against a wall. The last time I wrestled it to the ground in search of the perfect "D" chord, Josie was still living and breathing in the next room. It seems to be mocking me. Now that she's gone, the guitar looks like an alien artifact. From a place I can't get to anymore. And music is basically math, isn't it? I sucked at math. Super-sucked! And the electric guitar is probably the algebra of the guitar world.

I think about selling the damn thing as it sits there and scornfully *plays back my ineptitude to me. But trading the torturous thing for cold cash seems crass. That very afternoon I walk my guitar outside and lean it against a tree in front of the house by the street. I write up a cardboard sign, place it between the strings, and then head back inside. The sign has the magic word written on it:* FREE. *Underneath, for my own benefit, I have added:* TO A GOOD HOME.

I look out an hour later. The guitar is gone. And so are my rock-star dreams and my big sister.

"Oh my god, what's that horrible sound?" is the first thought that comes to me as I surface from my deep and stuporous sleep, like a diver with narcosis. Did I doze off next to the rhinoceros pen at the zoo as they bellow and shriek their way through hot rhino-love? No, I'm in a bedroom, but it isn't mine. Maybe I got drunk and passed out somewhere? And then in a giant, mind-melting rush and crash, the whole previous night comes flooding back into my still severely overtaxed brain. I'm in my own guest bedroom because the provocative proselyte, Alice, is in *my* bed and that hideous, guttural pig-squealing noise must be Lexington Vargas snoring away on the couch in the living room! It's light outside so I rise, knowing I haven't slept nearly enough, but I'm determined to get back on the case, maybe even dialing up the Big Dude, although in the cold light of day I'm feeling a lot less confident about actually making the call. And I think I had some weird dream about a plane I was on crash-landing in Loch Ness as the passengers were trying to photograph the amazing monster of the Loch that turned out, instead, to be the spire of a sunken church. (??) I read somewhere that in dreams, flying and water are both symbolic of sexual desire. Guess who the sunken church is? Yep. And she's wearing my robe, right now.

I shake it off, grab my slippers, and walk out into the living room and confirm that the farm-critter noises are indeed being cranked out via L.V.'s ample nasal passages. Wow, he's *loud!* Any minute I expect to hear neighbors banging on the ceiling, floor, and walls. Maybe these walls are thicker than I thought, although I *always* hear the guy next door's bed bumping rhythmically against my living room wall and the *Oh my gawd*s every time he scores, and he scores a lot, the lucky bastard.

I stop in the doorway at the vision before me. Alice is already awake and on my computer, the blue-white glow of the screen lighting her fetchingly as she sits there, legs tucked under her. And, yes, she is still in *my robe.*

It's the very same computer I sometimes watch free Internet porn on as I spank Woody Woodsman into mild ecstasy to ease the pain of my loneliness and also get a good night's sleep, such is the pathetic cliché I have become, post-divorce. Until now. There is nothing clichéd about this *Three's Company*-with-a-twist I find myself in.

"Good morning," I whisper to Alice, though why I'm whispering I have no idea. If Livestock Boy on the couch isn't waking *himself* up with his own high-decibel log-sawing, I sure as shit am not going to rouse him by whispering a soft greeting. But wake him I do. As Alice looks up, Lexington Vargas snorts, snuffles, sneezes, and gracelessly hauls himself up onto one elbow, blinking at me with sleep-suffused eyes.

"Why are you yelling, man?" asks L.V in what I presume is his "morning voice." It's rough, congested, and extremely woolly-sounding.

"Well, good morning to you, too, Sunshine," I reply. I actually feel better than I've felt in years. Something seems to have come alive in me that has been comatose for a long, long time. A feeling I haven't felt since I was a boy. I think it's hope. And as weird as it seems, even as the words form in my head, I believe I am connected to these two strangers in a way that feels like family (and, so far, without all the flawed, dysfunctional crap that came with my own). L.V. grunts and rolls over, presumably to try to snore his way back into dreamland.

There's something unsettling about the way Alice is looking at me. I go cold. Did I leave some cheesy porn site up on deck for her to stumble on when she lit the computer up this morning? "Ham-Slam-a-Thon"? "Let's Play Stain the Couch"? "ShavedGoat.com"? I open my mouth, poised to apologize profusely if this is indeed the case.

"I've been scanning the passenger list for anything like 'Mereek,'" she says. I breathe a relieved sigh that she didn't ask me, "What the heck's a dirt-pipe milkshake?" "I've tried spelling it all the ways I can think of," Alice continues, "but there's nothing even close to it there."

"On the passenger list?" I ask. I'm trying to catch up.

"Right, there is no Mereek no matter how you spell it on the list

146

of passengers that boarded the plane in Tokyo," she answers. "Not as a first name or last. But I played around with the spelling and got a hit on Google—for M-E-R-I-K-H. It means 'death.' "

"Death?" I echo.

"Death," she reaffirms.

"What are you saying . . . ?"

"I'm not saying anything, I'm just telling you what I found."

"But you're implying that he's, what? Like the Angel of Death or something?"

"I don't know, Bobby. It all seems so crazy. But a lot of people did lose their lives last night. And there were some very peculiar moments with this guy that can't be explained in any conventional way. Abnormal stuff to say the least."

I have to agree, although I *had* been thinking Merikh might be a cyborg from the future, not the Angel of Death, but maybe that's just the twelve-year-old in me doing some wishful thinking. I parenthetically really like that Alice, the blazing apostle, called me "Bobby" just then. It sounded intimate, especially considering that we're both in our jammies and in very close quarters. I begin to imagine us having risen early after a night of ardent and animated lovemaking: I'm brewing coffee while she reads me the morning news and says things like, "Oh, Bobby, let's go out and get a dog today," or "Why don't we have breakfast on the pier?" And then I realize it's just the old ADD kicking in once again, aided and abetted by the Woodman, and I need to damn well stay centered if we are to make heads or tails of this whole night. And of what may come. I suddenly remember my own copy of *Magnificent Vibration* and head toward my bedroom to retrieve it. I'm now finally itching to make a certain phone call.

There's a loud hammering at the front door.

"Oh, crap," I say under my breath as I switch direction to answer the intrusive knocking because Lexington Vargas has started with the zoo noises again. Damn apartment living. I open the door with a bunch of ready explanations for the L.V. post-nasal-drip disturbances, but it's not a complaining neighbor. It's my friend Doug. He invites himself in and is immediately off and running.

"Dude, I've been calling you all morning. Everything cool? Did you hear about the plane crash on the freeway? Un-fucking-believable. It's a mess out there, I had to . . ." He stops as he takes in the company I'm keeping. His gaze comes off Alice, wearing a bathrobe and sitting comfortably on her knees at my computer, and lands back on me. His single raised eyebrow and crude smile immediately communicate that he is misreading the situation. "All right, bro!" he says with a smirk.

"No, she's a nun," I blurt out extraneously. Doug's smile only widens.

"Hey, whatever dress-up you want to play is between you. Consenting adults and all."

I interrupt him.

"No, I mean she's really a nun. We're just friends. This is Alice Young and the large lump on the couch is Lexington Vargas."

L.V., with his broad back to us, has been reawakened by Doug's arrival. He waves a meaty hand from his prone position but makes no further movement.

"Whoa, how did I miss him?" quips Doug.

"This is Doug Donald," I announce to the room as I motion to my invasive friend.

"You had a slumber party and you didn't invite your bestie?' Doug continues, walking over to Alice and shaking her hand unnecessarily.

He's standing a bit too close for comfort and I can tell he's making her uneasy, as he does most women, which is probably why we never get laid.

"Did Bobby say your name is Duck Donald?" Alice asks.

I laugh because I sometimes call him that. And Donald Duck.

"Shut up, Cottonballs," retorts Doug. Then to Alice, "Sorry for swearing, especially if you are really a nun, but honestly, I'm not buying it. Sorry." This is turning into a bad sitcom right before my eyes.

"We're kind of in the middle of something right now Dougie. Can I take a rain check on this visit?"

"Hey, man, my bad. Obviously everything's cooking along nicely and I will hit you up on the morrow. Nice to meet you, 'Dude on the couch.'" He motions to Lexington Vargas, then turns to Alice. "And you, my dear, are blistering. I only hope that robe is fireproof. No wonder Bobby wants to kick my ass outta here." Jesus!

Thankfully Doug walks himself to the door without any further prodding from me.

"I'll call you later, DD," I say as we high-five out of habit like a couple of carefree teenagers when in fact we are a couple of stressed out middle-aged misfits. Doug turns at the door and gives me a knowing wink.

"If the 'Sister' has a sister, I am SO in," he whispers loud enough for all concerned to hear. He heads down a hallway already filling with the fragrances of breakfast being prepared in fifty isolated apartments as a bunch of divorced, contrite, and lonely guys get ready for a new day.

Doug's halfway to the elevator, as I'm closing the door, when he stops and turns. "Hey," he says. "Is there a famous actor lives in this building?"

"I don't think so," I answer, further shutting the door in hopes of ending the uncomfortable stream of dialog from my friend's yap.

" 'Cause I just passed this guy standing by the entrance to this place and he looked kind of familiar. At least I think he did. If he's not an actor or a model, he *should* be."

"Yeah, I don't think there's any famous people in this building. It's mostly lawyers and accountants on their way to their second and third marriages," I toss out. The door is almost shut.

"A black guy, with long hair and really pale green eyes. Fucking unbelievably great-looking, if I can say that without sounding like a fruitcake." He just will not stop. But now he has my attention.

"This guy—was he wearing a brown leather jacket?" I hear myself ask.

"Yeah I think he was. Maybe. Dude, if I looked like he does, I'd need restraining orders against half the women of the world. Pretty wild. How come some guys look like *that* and the rest of us look like . . . us?" he sends this parting shot across my bow as he disappears around a corner, oblivious to the turmoil he has just ignited inside me.

I close the paper-thin, highly breachable apartment door and lean against it to catch the breath that seems to have escaped me all of a sudden. I decide not to say anything yet to Alice. I think I should tell L.V.

I walk back into the living room full of apologies for Doug and the extremely large and obnoxious footprint he's just left in our fragile ecosystem, but Lexington Vargas is already playing a prelude to his Sinus Symphony in E flat, and Alice is back on the spank-a-tron computer. Apparently they are more resilient than I'd given them credit for.

"I'm just going to check my email," says Alice.

"Nuns have email?" I ask, one ear trained for any odd noises that might suggest we're in peril from the extremely attractive Angel of Death, Merikh, who seems to have found us again despite our best evasive efforts.

"We nuns live in the twenty-first century just like you do, y'know," she replies.

"I just . . . I don't know, I have this vision of a stony convent in the middle of the French countryside where you all make wine and grow your own food and the only guy you ever see is a photo of the pope on the mother superior's bedroom wall." I obviously haven't updated this view since the late 1400s.

Alice smiles indulgently.

I raise my voice so she can hear me over the mighty and sonorous Lexington Vargas.

"I'm going to place that call! I think it's time."

Alice doesn't respond.

I walk over to where L.V.'s open book is lying on the coffee table. "You've got mail!" I hear the AOL guy say, with the same slightly thrilled tone he's been using for over twenty years now. How can he still be that excited about email?

"Oh, my Lord!" Alice exclaims She sounds amazingly like Julie Andrews in *The Sound of Music* when she talks like that. Another piping-hot point in her favor. "What?" I ask as I open Fred Flintstone's flip-phone.

"I just inherited a house," is the unexpected answer. She stands suddenly, pushing the chair away as her (my) robe falls open just a fraction and seems to confirm that she really isn't wearing anything underneath. Woody makes a mental note never to wash that robe again.

I close the phone. Is she purposely trying to distract me?

"I just got an email from a law firm in . . . In-ver-ness," she carefully pronounces the name of a city that, to me, is very familiar. "My father was from Scotland and I guess he had a brother back there, although he never talked about his family to us."

An image of the poster on the travel agent's window from last night's fruitless search for the bookstore flashes into my mind—"Come to Scotland!"

"Really?" I say.

"Take a look," she says, and I lean down as close to her as I dare to read what's on the spank-a-tron:

Dear Miss Young,

It is our regrettable duty to inform you that your uncle, Mr. Ronan Young, passed away on the 14th of January of this year, leaving no immediate descendants. We have been trying to contact you to apprise you of the fact that you are the beneficiary, being his sole living relative, of the property and effects from Mr. Young's estate. There is a house as well as a small bank account and a fishing boat with various accouterments that remain to be claimed once proof of identity is confirmed. By Scottish law, any beneficiary must present himself or herself in person to claim their inheritance. Please contact us at our offices here in Inverness so that we may proceed with the arrangements for the execution and completion of the disbursement of the aforementioned Mr. Young's estate.

We look forward to hearing from you.

I remain

Yours sincerely

Clive McGivney

of

McGivney, McGivney, and McGivney Law Offices
41 Church Street, Inverness, Highlands, Scotland, IV1 1EH

"I know Inverness," I say. "It's near Loch Ness."

"How do you know that?" asks Alice.

"Long story. Started when I was a kid."

Alice glances at the email again and notices that her robe is showing more Alice than she intended. She closes it, but shows no overt modesty in the action. She is a quirky girl for sure. And her skin looked flawless, what I could see of it, and believe me, I was trying really hard not to look.

"You have to go there," I continue excitedly. "You know, to present physical proof that you're you, so you can claim your inheritance. This isn't something you can settle over the Internet."

"What? I'm not going to Scotland right now. I'm trying to figure out my life. As well as understand what last night was all about."

"Well . . . maybe this could be part of it," I suggest.

"How could this be part of it?"

I am stumped for damn sure. No idea how this could have any-thing to do with whatever it is we're experiencing but . . . Scotland?? Land of the superb and possibly real Loch Ness Monster? C'mon! says twelve-year-old Horatio.

"I think I need to make a call," I finally say. "Wake Lexington—he should be in on this, too."

"Not yet," is all Alice says.

"Yes, yet," I answer. "I need to see if we can glean any more clues from whoever is on the other end of this number."

I motion to L.V.

"Wake him up." I open the phone, I open the book, and I start dialing.

———

"Tsk, tsk," clucks the Omnipotent Supreme Being, as more not-so-good news filters back from The Beautiful Blu . . . from "Earth." The one-hundred-million-ton, continental-United-States-sized heap of pelagic plastic-and-chemical sludge, known as the Pacific Trash Vortex or the Great Pacific Garbage Patch, that is cur-rently adrift in the Pacific Ocean has begun to turn more toxic due to the combination of harmful ingredients and in-creased ocean temperatures to the degree that it is killing all of the animal life that ingests it. Fish and birds that feed in the thousands-of-miles-wide collection of human detritus are dying irreplaceably at an alarming rate. How is Earth supposed to clean herself when these humans keep dumping more and more of their garbage into her oceans? Why don't they get it? Their planet will die if all seven billion of them don't stop using her as their personal toilet, flushing every man-made poison and all their biological refuse into her fragile, living system.

Dumb-asses!

"Horatio? I'm selling the house."

Mom has met me at the front door as I return from the hunt. I've been out on safari, exploring the wilds in search of the extremely rare and highly endangered American Job.

Like a couple in a bad marriage, my mother and I have been drifting apart and doing nothing to rectify it, so this thing about the house is not a completely unforeseen event.

"Okay," I say.

"I'm moving into a condominium in Sherman Oaks." It's clear she doesn't plan on having me join her.

"What'll I do with all my stuff?" I sound like a lost, loser of a kid all of a sudden.

"I expect you could throw half of it out and wouldn't miss it. All those silly plastic monster figurines (figurines?), and you don't even wear most of the clothes in your closet. The furniture is mine, but I need a fresh start so I'm going to have a garage sale and sell everything." She seems to have been thinking this through for some time now. I'm starting to feel a little blindsided the more she talks at me, even though she's hinted at this sort of me-less future before.

"You'll have to find yourself an apartment somewhere. And get a job."

"What about Josie's ashes?" I ask. They still sit on the dining room table where I first set them down, over a month ago.

"I don't want those. That's not my daughter in that box," she answers.

"I'll take them," I say, and I realize, apart from the two outfits I always wear, some underwear, socks, and a few toiletry items, the only thing of meaning and value I will take from my twenty years in this house is that black plastic box. All that's left of my sister's earthly form.

I am given twenty-eight days to get my shit together and vacate the premises.

And miracles of miracles, three months later I get a job delivering pizza and my financial security is assured. Except that I don't have a car. And I still don't have a license. And I haven't told Ernie's Pizza that I don't have a car or a license.

Mother has caved and let me sleep on the couch in her new condo after the sale of the house and the expiration of my mandatory twenty-eight-day "get-your-own-apartment" time limit. But now that I have a job and am flush with cash, I'm instructed to get the hell out and find *my own damn place. So I have the damn job, now to find the damn place. And the damn car and the damn driver's license. I settle for a damn motor scooter. I skip the damn license for now and figure I'll get it when I'm damn ready. I have to borrow money from my mother to get the apartment thing going, but I suspect she's only too happy to lend it to me and to finally see the last of my heathen, nihilistic, licentious male Cotton backside as I exit her life forever.*

I move into a closet masquerading as an apartment in Burbank and begin to hit the nine-to-five (although in reality it's more like eight a.m. to midnight) delivering pizza for the renowned Ernie's Pizza Di Napoli. Who knew "Ernie" was Italian? And from Napoli, no less. Because he sounds like he's from Redondo Beach. I begin my illustrious career as a courier of the heart attack-inducing halos of white flour, cheese, mon-key-meat and tomato paste from Ernie's of Napoli, via SoCal.

Everything goes swimmingly until a dissatisfied customer calls Ernie and complains about one of my deliveries. They want to know if the little pieces of freeway gravel are an extra topping or just part of the unique ingredients in Ernie's extra-large cheese and pepperoni. Have you ever tried to balance an oversized and extremely hot pizza on a scooter's handlebars while zooming along the freeway at forty-five MPH with trucks and cars whizzing dangerously close making wild wind vortexes that shake and wobble the crap out of you and your little bike, too? The pizzas fall off occasionally, and I do my best to pick the road-kill out of them if I'm unlucky enough that the box opens up on impact, but so far there hasn't been a problem. The people who've called to complain about the added pebbly roughage in their order say they thought they heard the sound of a small motorbike pulling away from their house post-delivery. So Ernie wants to see my car. I show him my scooter instead. He takes a swing at me but my reactions have been honed from dodging my mother's flailing fists through the years, and he misses by a mile. Correctly assuming I am fired, I jump on my scooter, flip Ernie off, and ride away with my dignity intact, as Ernie hurls unkind epithet after unkind epithet at yours unemployedly's retreating ass-end. My dreams of a pizza delivery monopoly are shot to hell, however.

I'm only on my second girlfriend (unfortunately this tally includes the Reverend's wife), so obviously the gigolo career isn't going to happen either, damnit. My second girlfriend gives me the boot once the weather starts to turn colder and she gets fed up arriving at our destinations with her eyes tearing, her nose red and dripping, and an ill-behaved case of helmet hair. I get it, though, and am now seriously motivated to purchase a car (with the all-important backseat, wink, wink). Honestly, what a clueless goober I was.

But first I have to find another job so I can actually afford the car. And somewhere along the way I'll need a driver's license.

A year or two into the serious job search, with more pizza delivering (still on the scooter, I'm afraid), busboying, and Starbucks trash-

emptying to help pay the rent and feed myself, I actually land a real adult job! I walk out of the interview at Apex Audio/Video Dubbing Sound Stages with the news that I start the following Monday still spinning around in my head. How did I fool them so completely? Why can't I do that all the time? I am absolutely giddy with success. And also extremely concerned that they'll find out I'm just a kid, even though my license, yes, license, says I am now twenty-three. When does the "man" thing kick in, I wonder? I thought it was at twenty-one, but nothing happened inside me at twenty-one. Perhaps I'm a late bloomer and I just have to handle the kid business longer than most. I do miss my monster "figurines," though. They would have looked super-cool in my cupboard/apartment.

The new gig has me starting in the "mail room," of course, and though I'm not actually delivering mail, I am sweeping floors, fetching coffee, and generally bearing the brunt of the working stiffs' frustrations in this video-dubbing house in North Hollywood. It's the very same workplace I've mentioned earlier that has, for some ungodly reason, decided that its best chance of survival in the cutthroat world of audio/video dubbing is to corner the much-maligned (mainly by me) Cambodian gangster-movie market, because someone somewhere wants to see these dreadful films in English! The way the work is described to me when I first apply for the job makes it sound waaaaay cooler than it really is, and I imagine myself eventually working on major motion pictures and rubbing elbows with Leonardo and Harrison, Scarlett and Meryl. But as it turns out, I will at best be working on movies starring Pheakdel and Samnang, Kola and Darareaksmay. This video house is many, many light years from the Hollywood silver screen. But I am on board and locked in. Starting at the bottom. Actually, come to think of it, I was much happier running out for Starbucks and emptying trash bins than I ever have been sitting in front of a video monitor watching

RICK SPRINGFIELD

the same ass-sucking scene over and over to make sure the English-speaking voice-over actors (most of whom sound like William Shatner if he'd never taken an acting lesson or Paris Hilton if she had) dub their lines in relative synch with the Cambodian dudes and babes on the screen.

And this is all before the Right Whale joins the festivities. It's still a couple of years before he belly-flops into my working life and turns it from dreary ennui to a complete and utter living hell. But right now everything is comparatively copacetic.

There's a saying the Buddhists have that's something along the lines of, "With every terrible event comes the seed of something wonderful: and vice versa."

One morning the "vice versa" of that noble saying walks her perky ass into my place of employ. My future ex-wife has just careened into my life. She's pretty and mouthy and has a sense of humor that sets her apart from most of the dour folks working in this place. She tells me she's going to be answering phones and getting coffee. These video-editing people drink more coffee than dance marathoners and long-haul truckers combined. Her name is Charlotte and she seems to like me right away (?) and I her. Since I have been working at Apex Audio/Video Dubbing Sound Stages for a while now, I offer to show her around. She says she's excited to be working in the movie business and wants to see all these "sound stages." Like me, she's made the mistake of thinking that this place is somehow connected to the exciting and glamorous world of Hollywood. I guide her to the tiny dubbing rooms, the barren, sterile office cubicles, and break the bad news to her that Chet Chong Cham is about as close as she'll ever get to Gone with the Wind.

So we begin dating, and she becomes the fourth person I have ever had sex with. (And I am including my faithful right hand in that count

160

of four.) Reflecting on this fact, I conclude that living with my mother for so long was a bad idea all round. Now that I have my very own "shaggin' shack," I anticipate a lot more action from the many, many, many, many, many hot women I see every day on the street.

But Charlotte has other plans for Woody, and she keeps him pretty busy and fairly sapped of his life-giving cocktails, if I may use that phrase in the context of discussing my penis.

Matt, a guy I have befriended at work, has an odd reaction when I tell him that Charlotte and I are an item.

"Ooh, dude. Bad idea, dating someone from work. Could get ugly."

"Poppycock," I say and wish I hadn't. Sometimes my mother just leaps right out of my mouth at the most inopportune moments. "I don't see a problem with it," I continue, not really understanding what this simple phrase portends.

Another workmate named Ned, who considers himself the resident Lothario but who I would only charitably describe as moderately good-looking and pleasantly plump, says he thinks Charlotte is "a damn fine chick." I don't really take offense because Ned is one of those guys who always has his sleeves rolled up and his shirt front undone to display the flab he sadly misreads as well-toned muscle. He also considers his beer belly muy macho. *I tell Charlotte to steer clear of Ned because he thinks she's a "damn fine chick," and I laugh. She wants to know which one is Ned, I assume so she can avoid the poor guy. Sorry, Ned.*

I move in with Charlotte—into her apartment, because there just isn't physically any room for two people to both lie down at the same time in mine. I am actually living with a woman who is not my mother! It's kind of grown-up, kind of fun, kind of weird. She cooks real food, we watch movies together, we have regular sex in our own bed, and when I wake up in the morning I don't have to get dressed and go home or feel shame from porking a theologian's missus. We even have our own computers in the kitchen just like a real couple. She's on hers a lot.

One day she tells me she's Catholic and we should have a Catholic wedding!! "Whoa, wait, what? Slow down, babe! Who said anything about marriage?" is what I want to say but I don't and instead mutter, "Hmm," thoughtfully, hoping it sounds fairly noncommittal. But she has made up her mind that it's time. Isn't that what they say in the movies to the guy on death row just before he's led to Old Sparky and cooked to perfection? "It's time?"

"Okay, Louie, it's time."

Well, it's time, Horatio. And without further ado I say, "I do."

My mother doesn't show up for the ceremony because when I call and tell her, she says "She's a Catholic, this girl you're marrying," like I'd somehow missed this point during the mass and all the frigging Latin that goes on forever and ever at the couple of Eucharists she's dragged me to in preparation for our upcoming wedding.

"Mom, she's a Catholic, not a Satanist," I try.

"It's close," answers Mommy the Presbyterian.

Accursed religious intolerance.

"I guess she won't be babysitting for us," I joke to Charlotte the Catholic.

Charlotte grabs my arm with her G.I. Joe kung-fu grip.

"Ouch," I squeal like a wussy.

"I'm not into having children," she says firmly.

"Shouldn't we have discussed that before saying our vows, renting the band, and prepping the toilet for the three a.m. hurling session because we both drank way too many vodka tonics and glasses of champagne on an empty stomach?" I want to say but again do not. It's too *late, anyway. Maybe there's a dog in my future, and as if she's reading my mind she adds, "And I'm not a dog person, either."*

Damnit! Oh well, no kids, no dogs. Maybe she'll be okay with a cat if I can just get a handle on my cat allergies that cause my eyes to redden and swell shut, my throat to close up enough to be life-threatening, and my skin to break out into angry red hives. On Google I look up "What is the third most popular pet in the United States?" figuring correctly that the first two are dogs and cats. Ferrets! Ferrets come in third. I wonder if I'm allergic to ferret fur? They sound like a tough sell: "Darling, how about a ferret or two?"

Onward!

I marry her.

Yep. I do.

That's pretty much it.

And I remind myself of a guy I met on a plane once, after I'd begun taking the odd flight here and there for my work. I start chatting lightly as one occasionally does with a fellow traveler who isn't trying to steal both armrests, doesn't smell like spoiled milk mixed with urine, and isn't coughing, sneezing, and loogie-hawking all over you. He's an older man, and he starts talking about his life. He goes on and on about the year and a half he spent in the army, serving in the Vietnam War when he was twenty-one. And he still seems really charged up about it. There are stories of dangerous missions and anecdotes about wild nights spent with war buddies and hookers during R & R in Nah Trang and Sydney. Amazingly vivid recollections and memories that seem to be burned right into his brain cells.

He doesn't stop talking for most of the three-hour flight about his time in " 'Nam." Finally the conversation slows, and I ask him what he's done since leaving the army. He sums it up in three words: "I'm in insurance."

And that's it. That's all he has to say about the following forty years.

I think I may be in a similar situation with the whole marriage bit. Three words: "I got married."

And I don't even have anything as cool as going to war (though I've never been to war to see if it's cool or not) to compare with the rest of my dull life. Okay, there is a little more to my married life than those three words, but it often doesn't feel like it.

I move up in the "firm" and actually start working on the "movies" if I may use that word in connection with the on-screen feculence we have to deal with. Sorry, I know I sound bitter.

Charlotte and I do the honeymoon thing, going only as far as San Diego and our finances will allow. A week and a half at The Shores Hotel, which isn't actually on the shores, but set a few blocks back from them, so that's a bit of false advertising on their part. I get such a great deal on the room, however, that I decide not to moan about it. The time goes fairly slowly (never a good sign on a vacation and possibly even less so on a honeymoon), and we eventually arrive home eager to get back to our separate routines. We are kind of relieved to be done honeymooning because, with the whole day and night free, once the "dance with the swollen pickle" was done, there really wasn't a whole hell of a lot to talk about, which leads me to believe that we may not actually have a lot in common as a post-coital couple.

But we are married, and I assume we're both committed to making it work, whatever that means. We'll come up with something else to take the place of actual conversation. Possibly we can take a class together. Juggling, maybe. Or macramé.

Head down, move forward.

We eventually buy a small house that's beyond both our means, as is the American way, and I, after many attempts, succeed in talking Charlotte into getting a dog. I think I threaten her with a ferret, which she believes is a type of large rat. In the end this wins the battle for me. It's a big battle, the dog battle. And I do win it, but I definitely lose the war.

The memory of barbecued Bob still lingers at the edges of my memory, along with the need to heal the wound of losing him. Or maybe I just like dogs. We see a man selling puppies in a shopping mall parking lot one Sunday and I look at Charlotte, who rolls her eyes, which I take as a fully enthusiastic acceptance of the plan. Full steam ahead on acquiring the dog. And away we go.

The conversation with the owner of the puppies goes something like this.

Me: *"Oh my god, they're so cute. What kind of dogs are they?"*

Him: *"They're Red Golden Retrievers. They're purebred, but my dogs breed like rabbits so I'm selling 'em at a discount."*

Me: *" 'Red' Golden Retrievers?"*

Him: *"Red Golden Retrievers."*

Me: *"That's two colors."*

Him: *"No, one. They're Red Golden Retrievers."*

Me: *"But isn't that like saying Black Yellow Labs?"*

Him: *"I don't know what you mean."*

Me: *"You said that they're Red Golden Retrievers. Two colors. Red and gold. But they're only red."*

Him: *"They're Red Golden Retrievers."*

Me: *"But they're really just Red Retrievers."*

Him: *"They're Red Golden Retrievers."*

Me: "Okay, I get it that's the official name but they're not golden. They're red. So doesn't that make them just Red Retrievers?"

The world-famous lonely cricket chirps in the moonlight somewhere on a cold and windy mesa in Taos, New Mexico. There is an uncomfortable silence that lasts for a second or two or three. Then . . .

Him: "They're Red Golden Retrievers."

I buy the cutest one. Actually he's the one that seems to like me the most, and I name him Murray and he is fully awesome. Charlotte thinks he's a filthy, hair-shedding varmint, bred only to chew her good shoes and the crotches out of her underwear.

I give him the thumbs-up on all three activities.

I keep Josie's little wooden box on the mantel over the fake fireplace of our new home.

Charlotte thinks it's "creepy."

My girl Josie is most certainly not creepy.

We have a brief summer of love, my new wife and I, and then we both hunker down for the remaining long winter of her discontent.

She gets fired (for reasons I'm not clear on) and I get promoted at the video-dubbing house of crap movies. It creates the beginnings of a tension that slowly grows with an argument here, a screaming match there, over the next few years as we both start to realize we have made a horrible mistake by heedlessly jumping into the whole wedlock business, so ill-suited are we as a couple. I begin to want the marriage to work for Murray's sake. He doesn't need the baggage of coming from a broken home. Okay, I may be anthropomorphically projecting onto our dog a little here, but really, he hates it when we argue so I assume he would *be devastated if we got an actual divorce. Unfortunately, he is already a damaged child. I love Murray. Murray loves me. Murray loves Charlotte. Charlotte doesn't love Murray. It seems my dog is having the same luck with women I had when I was his age. Must be hereditary.*

Charlotte finally finds work as a vehicle inspector at Enterprise Rent-a-Car in Thousand Oaks. This means she checks the returning cars for "door dings." The job doesn't have a very healthy, corporate ladder-ascending future, but it does add a little something to the weekly pot. The arguments continue nonetheless.

And just when the video-dubbing house from hell has become the only place where I can get any kind of peace and freedom from the anxiety and squabbles at home . . .

Enter The Right Whale.

He takes an instant dislike to me for some reason, and his first action is to ban Murray (who I have been bringing to work with me since things at home have gotten so tense) from the premises.

Then he bans coffee from the dubbing rooms, although no one has ever dumped coffee anywhere but down their caffeine addicted pie-holes. This is almost as bad as banning Murray, such a coffee ho have I become. And with good reason.

Hour after hour of these siesta-inducing films bestow on the unlucky viewer the need for serious stimulants. I briefly consider amphetamines but decide against it after seeing some frightening "before and after" photos of meth addicts on AOL.

The Right Whale begins out-and-out abuse and name-calling. It's very stressful for yours ass-wipedly (one of his favorite sayings). Not so much as a result of the mistreatment but because if he's talking to you, you can't miss seeing those little white milky curd balls in the corners of his mouth. And if you try to look away he gives you the "Look at me when I'm talking to you" line. Really? Do I have to? I sometimes wonder if he's married and there's some poor woman out there who has to see those cheese-clotted lips coming in for a goodnight kiss. Eeeeuuuuuuww-wwwww! He focuses his wrath on others, too, but I seem to be his favorite. Lucky teacher's pet.

One morning, we're all ordered to crowd into the lunchroom for a "bulletin." The Right Whale waddles in and grandly announces to everyone that we are moving offices. To a bigger and better facility. In Valencia. Everyone moans, because our cool new digs are now a three-hour car ride in peak traffic. The Right Whale goes apeshit in response to our mild discontent, and when he's done yelling he tells us that because of his gifted and brilliant stewardship, this firm has landed another huge account and we should all be goddamn grateful that he's keeping us out of the poorhouse. And we had better stop our whining and bitching.

"Please, please let it be a real movie studio with real watchable movies," I whisper a prayer to the Hollywood film gods.

"We will be working on films supplied by a firm called "La Société de Cinema," he announces proudly.

"Hey, that's French," I think to myself. "The French make some great movies. Fairly uninspired name, but it is in a language other than Khmer. This is promising."

What I don't know is that French is spoken by a significant minority in a certain Eastern country that's about to surprise me. And not in a good way.

"La Société de Cinema is in Laos. Right next-door to Cambodia. We'll now be dubbing a crapload of Laotian movies as well," he finishes.

"Fuckit!" I accidentally say out loud.

"You have a problem with this, Cotton?" the Right Whale shouts across the room at me.

"No, sorry, I . . . ah . . . got my finger caught in the chair," I fib.

"You sure it wasn't your dick?" he cracks and then guffaws at his own joke. Others laugh to humor and/or suck up to him, but most of them give me the pathetic sideways "You poor dude" look.

So everything is humming along superbly both at work and at home. I have my dream job and my dream boss, my dream wife and my dream home and the only one I would truly take a bullet for at this point is Murray. I think Charlotte and I need to have a child to glue us back together. A little girl like her or a little dude like me (okay, not completely like me: a better version of me—with normal-sized ears) that we can worship, idolize, and fawn over and who will unite us through our mutual love of this perfect baby trinket. Of course this is possibly the worst reason in the world to procreate: to save a marriage. Shouldn't there be a book or a video or some type of tutorial that helps ignorant doofuses like us, with young, highly fertile wombs and testicles, to steer clear of making appalling choices like this?

Luckily for everyone involved and the as-yet-unconceived baby, my wife is just as adamant now as she was when we first got hitched that she is not going to screw up her life, her body, and her wonderfully healthy narcissism by having a "fucking kid."

As it turns out, thank God. But right now, I am heartbroken about it. Good-bye, little girl in pink that will never be. Who will never call me "Daddy" or look at me like I am perfect. Good-bye, little Horatio Jr., son of mine. We will not be flying kites on the beach together in this life or playing catch on the front lawn after school. I'm kidding about the name, of course. I would never have done that to the little guy. But my biological clock's alarm must have rung loud and clear at some point, because I actually get misty-eyed when I think of the kids we will never have. I guess I really wanted kids. Who knew? I get depressed about it.

That is, until I come home really late one evening from work, having had a terrible day trying to get the American voice-over guy to say "I'm diabetic" so that it fits the Cambodian actor on screen as he mouths "K'nyom mee-un chum ngoo dteuk nom pha-em." The "actor" on screen also has a gun to his head and he's supposed to be scared (which he is faking badly), so he's saying this phrase really slowly and nervously. We try and drag the English version out to make it match, you know, "Iiiiiiiii'mmmmm diiiiiiaaaabeeeetiiiiic"—but it just looks and sounds stupid, and for all my misgivings and shame about it, I do have some pride in my work. Obviously it's an impossible task, but we do our best. I arrive home wondering at what point I will, by osmosis, be able to speak fluent Khmer. Tonight I certainly know how to say "I'm diabetic," should I ever find myself in need of insulin while vacationing in Phnom Penh.

Charlotte is already in bed and there is an empty bottle of Grey Goose vodka in the trash. Murray, of course, greets me like I've just come back from five years in Afghanistan.

"Holy shit, it's YOU!!! Oh man, I've missed you so much. I thought you weren't coming back! Have you been gone for days or weeks or years? I can't tell! Will you magically produce some food for me like you always do? I want to lick! Can I lick? Let me claw your face nearer so I can swipe my stinky tongue across it. Wow, you had CLAMS for lunch? I LOVE clams!!! Can you create clams for me right now? Oh, okay, kibble will be great! Yep, just pour it into my bowl that no one has bothered to wash in the three years I've lived here. Twenty-one years in dog time! But who's counting? I LOVE kibble in a dirty bowl!! I want us to spend more time together. How come you always smell like food? I found an old French fry with dust stuck to it, under the kitchen counter today, and I was saving it for you but then I remembered that you usually throw food out when it lands on the floor so I ate it. Boy this kibble tastes

GREAT! Can we cuddle? I love you, sir." He goes on and on like this for about ten minutes, and when he's done I feel valued once again. What an outstanding piece of work is the family dog.

On the kitchen counter I see, by the small green power light, that Charlotte has left her computer up and running, so I go to close it down. I touch the keyboard to "wake it up," and what I see as the screen lights up, wakes me up. She's left her Twitter account open. She has a Twitter account?! I didn't even know she "twitted" or whatever the hell it's called. It's a "direct message." Again this lingo is completely alien to me. But what I'm seeing is very much of this earth! The image on the monitor leaps to life in full color and as bright as a thousand suns. It takes a while for what I'm seeing to register, so out-and-out weird, unexpected, seriously fucked-up, and shocking is this thing I see on my wife's computer.

(Beep, blippity, beep, beep, blippity, beep, blip, beep, blippity, beep, beep!)

"Glad you kids found each other!"

"God?"

"Please. Don't start that again. You're not still wondering, are you?"

"No, not really. No."

"Anyway, the word 'God' has so much baggage attached to it with you people. I'd prefer if you called me 'the Omnipotent Supreme Being,' OSB for short. Or you can call me 'Arthur.' "

"What?"

"There you go with your famous 'What' again."

Alice has unexpectedly run for the bathroom and locked the door. Lexington Vargas is sitting up on the couch, hugging his blanket, looking for all the world like an enormous kid at a sleep-over. But he is listening intently to my side of the conversation.

"Sorry. Did you just say I should call you 'Arthur'?"

"Yep."

"Why?"

"It's a nice name. And hearing 'God Almighty' and 'My Lord' and 'Holy Father' with the attendant scraping and bowing all the time just gets annoying."

"You're doing this on purpose. I have some real questions now and you're trying to throw me."

"Throw you. I couldn't even lift you. Hahaha."

"Please, God . . . Arthur, can you stop acting like a freak? It's just . . . I don't know . . . kind of unseemly."

"What, I'm not supposed to have fun or a sense of humor? Do you want me to repeat the flaming-sink thing? I will if it'll make you feel better."

"No! No, I'm . . . no, please."

" 'kay."

"See, that. Just saying ' 'kay' . . . it makes you sound kind of im-mature, like some dopey teenager."

"Thanks for the pat on the back."

"I don't mean to offend you, I just want to . . ."

"It's okay. I took it as a compliment. Love kids."

Momentarily lost thanks to another bizarre dialog with the maker of Heaven and Earth, and possibly aided and abetted by my ADD, I look down at the phone number in L.V.'s open book on my lap. I'm trying to get my bearings. It's not an easy task, considering. The silence is getting uncomfortable. I blurt out . . .

"So why is the area code for the phone number in Lexington's book West Virginia? Do you live in West Virginia?"

"Ah, no, I don't live in West Virginia. That's a joke."

"How is it a joke?"

"On the cars. The license plates. They say 'West Virginia, Almost Heaven.' So do they think when they die they go to a place that's just a little bit better than West Virginia?"

"That's funny?"

"I thought so. Actually, I stole it from a guy named Jim Gaffigan. He's a comedian."

"Yeah, I know who he is."

"Your comedians are some of your smartest people."

"You steal jokes from guys who do stand-up?"

"It's okay. I'm responsible for their having a universe to do stand-up *in*, so I think it's a fair exchange, don't you? Anyway, I didn't expect you to bother looking up the area code. Must be something to do with your OCD."

"That was my sister who had the OCD."

"I know, but you have a little of it, too."

"No, I don't."

"Yeah, you do."

"I do?"

"What do you think has you so hooked on this sexual/religious obsession thing?"

"Shit . . . sorry, didn't mean to swear. You know about *that*, too?"

"One LAST time: I'm—"

"Omniscient, right. I remember you said that before."

"I did, yes."

A sudden lump appears in my throat and a shiver runs down my back.

"So how *is* my sister? Is she up there?"

"Up where?"

"In Heaven."

"(A), Why do you believe there's a heaven? (B), If there is, what makes you think it's 'up'? and (C), Why would I tell you what happens when you die and leave the rest of the universe to figure it out for themselves?"

"I thought since you gave us your phone number you were open to answering some questions."

"Look, Horatio, I do not get involved in the universe's path. I may move a few chess pieces now and then, but the outcome is always up to personal choice."

"So there's no great overall plan? No grand design? For mankind, womankind, whatever?"

"If you're asking if there's an 'end game,' well, of course there is, but it's probably not what you imagine. There will be an 'outcome,' if you'll allow me a degree of nebulousness. Seriously, what would be the point of life if I controlled things? Y'know? It's your choices, your decisions, and even your momentary lapses of reason that make your lives what they are."

"That's not what a lot of us believe."

"I know what a lot of you believe. But why would I hand a young musician or athlete fame, wealth, and success and then turn around and give an eight-year-old kid terminal cancer? Would that make any sense to anyone?"

"No, I guess not."

"So why do all those celebs keep publicly thanking me every time they make a million dollars or win some stupid award? And why does the broken-hearted mother of the eight-year-old cancer patient have moments where she curses me for not protecting her child? How is there any logic—and you people pride yourself on your logic—in that?"

"So we're on our own?"

"Like I said, I move chess pieces occasionally but it's up to all of you which path you take. What do you think is the most profound saying that you've come up with, you human beings?"

" 'You human beings?' That's. . . . really . . . odd. I think we all think you're one of us. But a perfect version. And that you're on our side."

"I know."

"Okay. Profound saying? The only one I can think of right now is 'The love you take is equal to the love you make.' "

"That's good, I'll grant you, but mainly because it rhymes. The truest and most profound saying you have is *'Shit happens.'* "

"You just said 'shit.' "

"Come on, Horatio, put on your big-boy pants."

"Okay, why 'shit happens'?"

"Because it's a universal truth. Good, bad, wonderful, and terrible random events occur, and those events, and how you react to them as individuals, define and shape who you are."

"I think there are people here who believe that, too."

"Yep."

"What about *Magnificent Vibration*?"

"Okay, I may have overstepped my own rules of non-

involvement with the books. I haven't done anything that blatant in a few thousand years. It was kind of old-school. But, if you are to be involved in . . . this whole thing . . ."

"What whole thing?"

"That's still up in the air. As I was saying before you rudely interrupted . . ."

"Sorry."

". . . I thought you should all have an honest look at your past lives. A reckoning of sorts. But then it was still your choice what you did with the books and whether you found each other or not and where it goes from this point. All I *really* did was move a chess piece."

"That's a pretty big chess piece. It's closer to a miracle than a chess move, I'd say."

"Maybe so. Maybe so."

"But there are no miracles, right?"

"I could turn you all into eight-legged transvestite goats if I wanted to, so don't mouth off, Sonny."

"I wasn't. I'm just trying to get some kind of handle on what's going on, is all."

"Well, you won't be able to do that. It's too big. Your Earth is at a tipping point. Like the Vee-Nung were."

"What's a Vee-Nung?"

"Look, I've already said too much. Let's change the subject."

"What's a Vee-Nung?"

"Hey, how about those Dodgers?"

"What?"

"Hello, it's the 'What' guy again?"

"Well then, what's your plan for the three of us?"

"Who said I had a plan?"

"But you're guiding us in some direction."

"No, I'm not. I'm presenting you with options. Which way you move will always be your choice. You humans think you're the only intelligent beings on your planet?"

"Who else is here?"

"Here endeth the lesson."

"Okay . . . well if there is a Heaven and you see Josie, tell her I love her and I'll never forget her."

There are tears in my eyes as I finish this last sentence, and sweet, giant Lexington Vargas gets up from the couch and puts an understanding and quite weighty hand on my shoulder. An idea pops into my mind that L.V. is actually more like I thought God would be than God is.

"Yes, he is a good man."

"Who?"

"You had a thought that your friend Lexington is kind of how you imagined I should be. And I agree with you that he is a good human. He *has* been through his fair share of self-induced, self-created shit, though."

"You read my mind!"

"And once more . . . I'm omniscient."

"Right."

"Right."

"So why are you helping us?"

"Trust me, when this is all done, whatever direction it goes, you won't think I was 'helping' you."

"What's that mean?"

"Nothing I'm willing to tell you at this point."

"Well, it sounds pretty ominous."

"There are some hard choices ahead to be made."

"By you?"

"By you."

"What's going to happen?"

"I'd like to talk to Sister Alice."

"You're not telling me any more?"

"Already said waaaaaay more than I meant to. Can you get her to come out of the bathroom and take the call?"

"You know she's hiding in the bathroom, huh?"

"You're not going to make me say the 'O' word *again,* are you?"

"What? . . . Oh, yeah, 'omniscient,' right. Will I ever get to talk to you again?"

"You sound very needy right now, Horatio."

"I've got a million questions."

"I'll bet you do."

"Okay, I'll get Alice."

I walk to the bathroom door and knock. Then I say the strangest and most unbelievable thing I have ever said and ever expect to say to another human being in my lifetime.

"Alice. God's on the phone."

I hear her dry-retching, and the toilet flushes. There is movement inside and then very slowly the bathroom door opens and a wan face peers out. I almost don't recognize her at first, so ghostly white and wide-eyed is she. She walks out like a guilty schoolgirl entering the principal's office. I hand her the cell phone. She hesitates, and then takes it as though it were a hand grenade. I watch as Alice drops to her knees and bows her head (oh my God, that is so frickin' hot! Woody—

Don't!), then raises the phone to her ear. Her voice is tremulous, faint, and filled with a life I know nothing about.

"Holy Father, my Lord God. I am your most unworthy serv . . ."

She stops talking as though she's been interrupted and looks up with a quizzical expression on her pale face. Then . . .

"Arthur?!"

I would give anything to be listening in to the other end of this conversation. But she rises, walks back into the bathroom, and closes the door. I do hear her parting words, though.

"Forgive me for I have sinned in word and deed, and against your decree and my faith have taken a lover . . ."

Her last three words are not lost on me or my dear friend and tormentor the Woodman. In fact, they bounce around my brain like they're on "repeat." *"Taken a lover . . . taken a lover . . . taken a lover . . ."* But as the door completes its path, the conversation is silenced. How come the *front* door to my apartment is made out of cardboard but the *bathroom* door is built like a safe? I briefly contemplate putting my ear to this door that Alice and her secrets are behind, but I stop myself. For once the big brain overrides the little brain. Thank Heaven for small favors—and the possible threat that L.V. might pound me into my shag carpeting for breaching Alice's personal space.

Lexington Vargas and I regard each other. I think we're both wearing the old "deer in the headlights" look. This is all so freaking unbelievable, yet part of me has begun to accept it as perfectly rational and routine.

The bathroom door finally opens and Alice, eyes red from crying, hands the phone to me as if it now were a priceless holy relic. Obviously she's had a very different conversation than I did. She mutters, hoarsely, "Lexington," before closing the door again and shutting us out. In the brief glimpse, I couldn't miss the silver streak in her hair starting at her temple. God's sense of humor at work, I assume.

I walk the phone over to Lexington Vargas, who takes it matter-of-factly and launches into Spanish. At one point there is a phrase I recognize.

"Realmente no entiendo el termino 'yin y yang.'"

I know the term "yin and yang"—it's a Chinese "balance" type of thing—but I don't understand the context. Now I wish I'd paid more attention in Spanish class.

L.V. shuts my phone before I can say anything, and the call is over. Right now all I want to do is talk to that slightly crazy, weird, very real, powerful voice. It's the father who never spoke to me, the mother whose decrees made no sense, and the only possible connection to my beloved, lost sister. As well as proof that I may not be the total dead-end kid I thought I was.

I hear the bathroom door open once again as Alice enters the living room. No one says anything. We square off, face each other, and just . . . stare. She brushes a hand through her hair where the new "Chuck Heston" stripe has appeared . . . she smiles . . . I smile . . . L.V. smiles. Then we all start to chuckle, and then laugh. And laugh. It's a release, it's gratitude, it's amazement. And we are awestruck, dumbfounded—and united. It's just the three of us. Four if you count Merikh, which I am hoping we don't have to.

M*y wife's computer screen force-feeds me a shocking image as I stare at it in utter disbelief and stupefaction. It's a photo. Of a* guy. *That I recognize. It's fucking Ned!!! The chubby Lothario from my work at the audio/video dubbing House from Hell, who thought my future wife was "a damn fine chick." And in this photo, he's naked! With a boner! In his hand!! On my wife's Twitter page!!! The caption reads: "Hey, Babe. Remember this big guy? He's lonely and wants to pound your pee-hole again. Love and lust, Ned the Head."*

This mind-numbing self-portrait looks like it was taken with an iPhone in his bathroom mirror. I can even make out Ned's fucking toothbrush on the sink in this unlovely photograph.

WHAT!! IS!!! THIS??!!

I'm trying to grasp the possibilities here, and they are scary and endless. First Ned, then the boner, then the words "pound your pee-hole AGAIN!" So this fairly unattractive human being has been sticking that misshapen pink mushroom into my faithless wife? Murray senses a change in my demeanor and whimpers, softly pressing his nose into my crotch. It is misdirected comfort, considering the awful image I am looking at right now.

"Murray. What's been going on?" I whisper breathlessly to him as I pat his soft head in some kind of unconscious need for solace. I am cold with the realization that I have been cuckolded. And suddenly the Reverend's tortured face leaps into my mind and I finally know exactly how the poor bastard felt. So THIS is karma!

It's more than I can physically and mentally absorb.

In complete shock I click around the "direct message" section of her Twitter page and find more brain-bursting photos of more guys with more tumescent phalluses and more lewd comments to my dear Charlotte that make my hair curl and my stomach drop like an elevator cut loose from its moorings. As was the Reverend from my past lustful youth, I have been unwittingly cuckolded many times over. There's

Freddy from the dry cleaners; I recognize him even without *his clothes on. And Gabriel, our fricking gardener!! And some young dude wearing an Enterprise Rent-a-Car shirt and nothing else—obviously work-related. Plus some guy named Henrik who lives in Finland. (??) And what's with them all sending photos of their naked asses to a married woman? MY married woman! This time an image from the past of the Reverend's strumpet launches into my fevered brain!! Oh, the calamity! Oh, the torment! What vile, unfettered retribution is this? Unkind fate, thou hast sent the hounds of hell to bang my wife and cause their balls to slap against her naked ass-cheeks, provoking them to send her pictures of their quite prodigious erections. And most of them look like "rough boys." Obviously the slightly-nerdy-yet-funny, self-deprecating, bright-though-doofusy, warm, loving man I thought I was is NOT her cup of tea. These guys all look like they need a bath, a shave, and a good delousing. Has she been hopping into the sack with any guy who swings a dick her way? Holy faithless fornicator, Batman!!!*

I walk like a mortally wounded namby-pamby (I was going to say "warrior," but that would be a serious misnomer) into our bedroom, wondering if any of this wayward action ever happened in the bed I sleep in. I wake her up. She is groggy from the vodka and irritated to have been roused.

"So you're screwing other guys?" is what I say.

"What?" is what she says.

"You left your Twitter page up," is what I say.

"Twitter page?" is what she says.

"You've been fucking Ned, that fat idiot from my work?"

"Shit!" spits out the lovely Charlotte.

"And he's not the only one? I just saw a bunch of photos of strange naked men all over your Twitter page."

"You asshole!" she replies. Like it's my fault. And maybe it is in the long run. I knew this union was broken the moment I realized we had nothing to say to each other post-nookie.

"Why am I the asshole?" and not for the first time it is the whiny little boy answering in my stead.

"What are you doing snooping around on my computer?"

"I wasn't snooping around. You left your Twitter page open. I want you to get out of bed, because we need to talk about this," is my stunningly lame, white-bread, and incredibly sensible rejoinder.

"Godamnit!" she yells as she throws the covers off and rises drunkenly and unsteadily to her feet.

"I need to deal with this now. I can't just go to sleep having seen all . . . that!" I think it's a fair response considering my other option is to go completely bat-shit and end up on a future episode of Cops.

We head to the kitchen with Murray inappropriately jumping for joy, excited beyond belief that we are both awake at this late hour. Sorry, Murray, but I don't think there'll be any snacks on this trip. Unless plates are thrown that still have old food stuck to them.

Charlotte slumps down into the bar stool by her computer, which has gone to sleep again. How it can sleep with all this shit going on I have no idea. "You're having sex with Ned?" I say as I hit a "wake up" key and Ned's unflattering physique appears on screen again, hard-on in hand. It's a rough image to digest at this hour.

"I want a divorce," is Charlotte's somewhat evasive response. She is obviously no stranger to the concept that the best defense is a strong offense.

"Why? It looks like you've been acting as if we aren't married anyway. How would a divorce change that?" I think in an odd way I am pleading for our marriage.

"*I should never have married you.*" Another punch to the gut from my purported partner for life.

"*Can we at least talk about this first?*" I try.

"*I'll see you in court. And I want everything,*" she says as she struggles to her feet, grabs her car keys, and walks out the front door wearing nothing but an over-sized T shirt. And you are correct, no underwear.

"*Wait, Char!*" I throw out a bone, but the only one ready to grab it is Murray.

"*I'll be sleeping at my boyfriend's apartment. My lawyer (she has a boyfriend and a lawyer, too?) will call you.*" And once again the door of my life slams shut, painfully catching the tip of my flaccid penis in it. Not literally, of course, but equally as traumatic and painful.

I suddenly remember the empty vodka bottle I saw in the trash.

"*You've been drinking. Drive safely,*" I squeak. "*Drive safely?*" Am I the moron of all morons? Drive safely on your way to Ned the Head's house or Nick the Dick's apartment or Cole the A-Hole's place or Kirk the Jerk's townhouse or Billy Bob the Knob Job's double-wide. And thanks so much for the eight wasted years. Truly, what a simpleton I am.

I walk back into the kitchen and sit on the bar stool near her cheating, lying tramp of a computer. I want to smash it, like it's somehow the computer's fault. But I don't. These things cost money. So instead I use it to dial up some free porn and whittle Woody so I can at least get a good night's sleep. Images of Charlotte, legs akimbo, being driven to ecstasy by the naked ass and slapping ball-sack of some roughneck, randy dude keep flitting in and out of my mental vision along with the matching and unwanted sound effects. It's a serious anger wank, to be sure! And I have Ned the Head to deal with tomorrow, which I am not looking forward to, such is my dislike for confrontation. But he has *been bonking my wife, so I think I need to address it with him in person. What should a man do? What would my father do? No fucking idea.*

In an act I will possibly regret later when the divorce kicks into full and legal gear, I send, to each and every guy, each and every OTHER guy's naked photo and their inebriated messages, with the added note that they are all weenies and are hung like field mice. Such is the power of the Internet!

The good news is that we are almost up to speed with the present and will soon have no more of this backtracking, historically pertinent, yet extremely painful narrative shit.

The bad news is that other dudes have been shafting my significant other.

Cold-hearted karma! If only I'd known what I had sown in my salad days. And can we fast-forward to the present so I don't have to relive this awful stuff AGAIN!!! . . . Thank you.

The email begins:

Dear Miss Young,

In order to claim your inheritance as sole surviving heir to Mr. Ronan Bon Young's bequeathed estate, we will respectfully require you to present yourself here for probate along with full and necessary documentation including birth certificate, passport, a bank account number in your name, and VAT identification number (or its U.S. equivalent). We regret the imposition and understand you do not live locally but it is part and parcel of our legal system that you must be physically present in order for us to execute the will of your uncle.

I remain

Your faithful servant
Clive McGivney

of

McGivney, McGivney, & McGivney Law Offices
41 Church Street, Inverness, Highlands, Scotland, IV1 1EH

Three days into the world's most bizarre sleep-over, Alice has received this response from the lawyers in Inverness on her antediluvian AOL server—"Thou hast a dispatch by electronic post, M'lady." The containers of takeout food delivered from the Fook Hing Chinese Restaurant are piled a mile high in my kitchen and I'm sure we're all getting a little sick of MSG and its headaches. It's been like one of those high school "self-discovery" trips where the counselors take a bunch of kids away for a week and they all become sleep-deprived and end up revealing very personal stuff—fears, home-life issues, doubts about themselves—and then connect on a deeper level than they would have by just hanging out on the playground or going from class to class. Only we all think God—sorry, Arthur—is somehow on this sleep-over with us. This is about considerably more than just getting to know your fellow human being. The three of us understand that something big is afoot—something momentous. But what?

We have gotten very close in the intervening days and nights, even taken to reading some of the darker sections of our respective copies of *Magnificent Vibration* to one another. And, yes, I read the explicit account of my adulterous interlude with the Reverend's wife to Alice and Lexington Vargas—all of it—the unvarnished, unflattering truth. And how I neglected my sweet girl Josie as a result of my relentlessly lustful horn-dogging.

Alice reads us the story of her tortuous journey through her adolescence. She cries as she reads the account of the car accident that killed both her drunken father and her much-loved mother when Alice was seventeen. And Lexington Vargas translates pieces of his journey in and out of the criminal justice system as a very young *cholo* while he was struggling to find his way. There's nothing *current* from Alice's readings that might shed some clarity on her mind-blowingly stimulating "taken a lover" remark, however. I am keeping Woody on serious lockdown for now while we work our way through this craziness. No sign of Merikh, although Doug's sighting has me on edge. I've walked the apartment complex's halls occasionally, looking for the beautiful bastard, but have seen no sign of his perfectly cleft chin nor his (damn him) exquisitely formed ears.

Alice may be on sabbatical and L.V. doesn't appear to work every day at the high school, but I need to put in some face time at the dubbing house for monumentally mind-sucking movies if I have any hope of getting a little time off so I can try to understand where all this may be leading us. I'm already late.

Alice wants to be dropped off at her place so she can grab some clean clothes and take a little time to pray and meditate on all that's happened, so that will make me even later but I'm cool with it. I haven't told her or Lexington Vargas about Doug's Merikh sighting and I don't actually know if she'd be any safer at my place, since he's apparently already cased it. L.V. is good with remaining at the apartment (and squeezing in and out of some of the more forgiving articles of my wardrobe), as the freeway plane-crash site is still cordoned off, seriously screwing up traffic throughout the greater Los Angeles area.

I drive Alice to the Oakwood Apartments (Really? Isn't that place full of divorced guys, too?) and then aim the Oriental Batmobile for my office.

I enter the Whale's den with misgivings and my videophone on "record" and peeking out of the top of my T-shirt pocket (yes, I wear T-shirts with pockets). I'm anticipating a megaton outburst the instant I ask for holiday leave—and I am not disappointed.

"You little sucking asswipe," is his opening salvo after I apologize for showing up late for work, citing the snarled traffic. And then I ask for my due days off. Maybe I could have broached the subject a little more diplomatically, but I am highly stressed from the previous night's crazy-assed goings-on, so I say, "I haven't had a vacation since my honeymoon! I know you don't like me, but I actually couldn't care less. I would like some days off so I can deal with . . . ah . . . certain issues at home," I improvise.

He tells me to close his door, and then he turns on me. I think I'm seeing weeks of paid vacation flying through the air every time he opens the biomass infecting his lips.

"I think you and your whore of a goddamn wife are the worst pieces of shit I have ever encountered. I fired her because she wouldn't fuck me even though she fucked just about every other guy in this goddamned building. And YOU were totally clueless!! Hahaha! It was fuckin' hilarious."

He is definitely on a roll. This has obviously been building in him, and although it hurts, I bear it, keeping the Human Resources folks in mind. And I have done my best to keep out of this guy's way, but he has zeroed in on me like a heat-seeking missile on a camel fart in the desert.

I'm sure there is a cussword limit to what the human mind can comprehend and mine is certainly breached during his fifteen-minute tirade. All of which is being filmed from my handy-dandy top pocket. At the end of it, baleen spewing from his lactose-tolerant lips, I exit with my hat in my hand, bowing and apologizing, and then, as a parting shot (once I've switched the video off), I say, "Got it all on film. Really appreciate the award-winning performance, dickface."

A dumbstruck look twists his features for a fraction of a second, and then he charges at me as if he means to crush my narrow frame in his gaping, curd-laced maw. I slam the door shut and run for the Human Resources office AFAP (as fast as possible), pretty sure he isn't running after me. But he does call, as I am playing the video for the older and apparently very by-the-book HR lady who looks on in absolute horror, her mouth hanging open in disbelief. There are cuss phrases I'm sure neither of us has ever heard before, and I have to hand it to him, the guy has a gift. What the hell is a "twatwaffle"?

She answers the HR phone and I hear her say, "Yes, Mr. Cotton is sitting in my office right now." And then in a delightful piece of theater, she holds the earpiece to my cell phone so the Right Whale can listen back to his own rant as he hits one of his many, many crescendos. His voice is tinny and thin coming through the minuscule phone speaker, but his words are crystal-clear:

"You, you fucking bumblefuck and your ball-gargling douche-canoe of a wife can kiss my Captain Craptastic and his Brown Dirt Butthairs if you think you're getting any rat-fucking vacation time outta me so you can go holiday on Gayboy Island and suck the love-snot out of young boys' blue-veined skin-monkeys all day long while your cum-sucking slut of a wife blows the local natives!" Obviously he hasn't heard that my wife and I are no longer vacationing together.

I must say, this moment is almost worth the years of abuse I have had to put up with. Why didn't I think of this video thing before? The look on Ms. Human Resources' face tells me I am most certainly getting my paid vacation days. And that the Right Whale will be appropriately chastised and could even be forced to abdicate his self-vaunted position as sovereign of shitty cinema. And I thought putting cameras in cell phones was a dumb idea when they first came up with it. What do I know?

On my way home in the amazing life-saving Kia, the amazing paid-vacation-giving cell phone chimes to alert me to an incoming message. I grab the superb invention and check it. There is no return or identifying number of any kind and the message simply says, *"Trobhad gu Caledonia."* Is that even English? And what's a "Trobhad"?

I look up to see that the cars twenty feet in front of me have stopped at a red light and I absolutely cannot brake in time. I had promised myself I'd never read or write texts while driving! Well, now I know why. But it's a bit fucking late. The only opening I can see is between the two stationary vehicles at the crosswalk, so I steer wildly in that direction and careen through the gap with a half-inch to spare on either side. A truck, pulling out into the opposing intersection in perceived safety, screeches to a halt as I accelerate and whip the mighty Lamborghini in cheap Asiatic clothing around the front end of said truck, missing it by an easy half-millimeter or so, and roar to the other side, running two sets of red lights, thank you very much. Miraculously there is no police car nearby to monitor my lucky idiocy, only the blaring horns of fellow motorists eager to tell me what a butt-plug I am. I drive like a stunned mullet for a minute or two, trying to grasp the awful mess I have just avoided.

I say out loud, "Wow, Arthur, was that you?"

My cell phone, still clutched in a death-grip in my sweaty hand, remains silent.

"And what the hell does *Trobhad gu Caledonia* mean?" I add to no one in particular as I speed away, highly embarrassed, from the almost-tragic-accident scene. But there is obviously someone in particular listening because suddenly words appear on the "heads up" display across my windshield, which is strange because there is no "heads-up" display on this model Kia. Nor any model Kia, for that matter. The words read: NO, THAT WAS JUST YOUR DUMB LUCK, AND I DID NOT SEND THAT LAST MESSAGE. KEEP YOUR EYES ON THE ROAD, IDIOT.

Great, now God thinks I'm an idiot. And who sent the first message?

I drop the phone onto the seat beside me and swear anew never to drive and text again. Unless it's Arthur. But he seems to have the means to bypass the technology anyway.

I'm still shaking from the near-possibly-fatal car crash, especially given that the front end of the great Kia appears to be constructed of tin foil.

Again, shit happens. Or in some cases, thankfully, doesn't.

I swing by the Oakwood and pick up Alice and her overnight bag. She looks fresh and revitalized, but I thought she looked pretty great before too, with her red-rimmed eyes and bed hair. Am I falling in love? Does it happen this quickly? No, it's probably just Woody messing with me.

She climbs into the car and without a word shows me her cell phone. The screen says *"Trobhad gu Caledonia."*

"Is it from . . ." she doesn't finish the sentence.

"No, I already asked. Arthur said it wasn't from him/her," I answer as if it's an everyday occurrence, God directly responding to my petty questions. And I have a vague feeling that my life will never be the same after this inconceivable experience we three are involved in.

At this point I don't know just how prophetic I am.

We speed on, working our way through the discombobulated traffic. The 101 is still closed in the aftermath of the plane crash and now it's rush hour (whoever named it "rush" hour should be found and whipped). We maneuver our way around it all.

"What's a *Trobhad*?" is the first thing out of Lexington Vargas's mouth as we enter my now-crowded bachelor pad. Obviously he got the same message on his cell phone, too, although he never said he *had* a cell phone.

"Is it . . . ?"

"No, it's not from Arthur," I say anticipating that his question is the same one Alice had.

And her pale, delicate fingers are already working the keys on my computer looking for the phrase *"Trobhad gu Caledonia"* as I struggle to push away the image of myself, late at night on the very same laptop, searching for free porn to ease my heat. Honestly I can't wait till I'm seventy and—as Willie Nelson says—I finally outlive my dick, such are the constant interruptions to my life that Woody causes. Focus Cotton, focus.

"It's Scottish Gaelic. A language that peaked in the ninth to eleventh centuries," says Alice.

"Can you translate it?" I ask. I've often used the English-to-Spanish translator on the spank-a-tron PC to talk to that cuckolding bastard Gabriel, my ex-gardener, who is no longer mowing my lawn but probably still mowing my ex-wife. Again, focus, Cotton, focus.

"I seriously doubt there's an English-to-Scottish-Gaelic translator," I venture.

"There're translators for pretty much any language on the Internet. Latin, Zulu, Yupik, Khmer," replies Alice.

Okay, I don't need an English-to-Khmer translator, since I already know how to say "I'm diabetic" in that language, so I am fully good, I think to myself. Honestly, how fucking lame is my job? But how amazing have become its paid vacations!! [First-pumping action inserted here.]

I hear Alice tap, tap, tapping around on the keyboard, and we huddle in to see what she comes up with. Finally, after some false starts and links that take us to weight-loss programs and (blush) porn sites, we strike gold.

"It means 'Come to Caledonia,' " she says at last.

"Where's Caledonia?" Lexington Vargas speaks for us all.

Alice dives back into the computer and brings up the world-famous and highly informative, though often mistaken, Wikipedia.

Alice and I both exhale in wonder at what we see.

Caledonia, unless Wikipedia is lying to us, is an old Roman name (were the Romans *everywhere*, for crying out loud?) for Scotland.

Come to Scotland. The awesome Urquhart Castle on the banks of Loch Ness poster on the travel agent/magic bookstore's window leaps into my brain in a sharp mental image. *Come to Scotland.*

I ask them if they saw the same poster I did in the travel agent/bookseller's window last night. They don't remember.

But it is another call to come to the land of ice, snow, and vast deposits of North Sea oil.

"So, are we all going to Scotland?" asks L.V., sounding almost childlike.

"How can we all go to Scotland? It's on the other side of the world," says Alice. "I don't have that kind of money."

Having, I imagine, just come off a vow of poverty, I would guess she wouldn't be exactly rolling in assets. Apart from her stunning looks and burning body, that is. (Wooooodyyyy!!!)

"Wait, wait, let's think here for a minute," I say, trying to be rational in this very irrational situation.

"A lot of signs are pointing us toward making this trip to Scotland. And Inverness in particular," I begin, with some degree of understatement. I look to the inheritance-worthy nun.

"You've already had emails from 'Your faithful servants Mac-Gyver, MacGyver, and MacGyver—about having to show up in person to claim some house and a bunch of fishing tackle or whatever, right?"

"But we don't know who sent that last text to us. It could have been anybody. Totally unrelated." Alice is unconvinced. And Arthur's disavowed it.

"No one in my small circle of friends speaks Scottish Gaelic . . . or Old Roman. No return sender on the text, either. It seems to be from 'somewhere else,' though where that is I have no clue, which makes it part and parcel of this whole freaking freak show, wouldn't you say?" I counter.

Lexington Vargas nods his assent. Alice is staring at the computer screen, both hands to her face. It's as if she was contemplating a trip to Pluto.

"I just don't know," she whispers. "How would we get there? It just seems so . . . impossible."

"Haven't we already gone a little north of 'impossible'?" says Lexington Vargas with one of his brief, self-restrained moments of clarity and insight.

"How would we get there?" repeats Alice, almost whispering.

We all sit in silence, running all the probabilities through our collective minds. Could I really live the rest of my life in peace without seeing this thing through? I make a decision, grab my wallet, and whip out my MasterCard. I think I hear it whimper like a gutless weasel.

"Let's max this baby out," I say with the bravado of someone who is okay with taking on more mountainous debt than he can ever repay and being charged 21 percent interest for the privilege. My credit is totally screwed anyway, thanks to the divorce.

"Something's going on, and we need to follow it through," I say decisively, though I'm actually not as convinced as I sound.

"Won't we all need passports and visas and things?" Alice is resisting with some fair and honest questions.

"I still have my Mexican passport from when my family moved here in the 'nineties. I renew it just in case anything goes down in the States and I need to get out of Dodge," says L.V.

"You came here legally?" I ask. Really, is there no end to my prejudice? Lexington Vargas again takes no issue with my ignorance, but he does smile.

"My father was a pretty famous guy," is all he says.

"I have mine too," answers Sister Alice. "We needed to be ready in case of missionary work. I think it's still good."

Mr. Gung-ho-let's-all-go-to-Scotland-tomorrow is the only one without a passport.

"Okay, I guess I'll have to get one," I say meekly.

I hear Alice's flying fingers again as she pulls up a government website. She is SLAMMIN' on this thing. And I thought its main function was to help lonely guys get a restful night's sleep.

"You can get one in five to seven days, according to the Department of State's website," says Alice.

I want to go sit in the Kia and ask Arthur if this is the right move or not. Pretty sure the "heads up" display no longer exists in my rent-a-car.

I pull out my cell and hit "redial" on the West Virginia number. It rings twice and a smarmy voice recording says, "Sorry, Charlie," and disconnects. We are on our own again.

"Looks like we're going to Scotland," I announce like a dad to his kids on spring break.

"I'm spending way too much time with this planet," thinks the OSB. "I shouldn't be playing favorites." But it is a magnificent piece of work, if the OSB does think so him/herself. "And then along they come pissing and pooping all over it, needlessly slaughtering its elegant and beautiful flora and fauna, again if I do say so myself."

Mid-reverie, a sudden thousand-light-years-wide supernova (waaaay on the other side of the universe) catches the OSB's attention, as thousands of inhabited planets are deep-fried with radiation in half a Plank-unit, killing all life forms.

"Shit . . . ," says the OSB, ". . . happens," then turns his/her attention back to the Beautiful Blue, Green/White Majest . . . "<u>Earth</u>."

The morning following my horrific discovery of all those mind-melting images of naked, hairy, unwashed men hiding under the bed of my wife's lying, cheating Twitter page, I drive to work, angry and scared at the same time. There were so many guys—where do I start? Do I go around exacting physical revenge on them all like a true bad-ass and probably end up in the hospital myself with major breakages, lacerations, and contusions, or do I tell them how much they've all hurt and saddened me, like a little wussy-baby? Either way it's a daunting prospect. I have no model for this, as far as how I ought to behave. But then I realize I actually do. I'm my mother, and my wife is my father if he had access to a Twitter page. And I am stunned by the unfortunate synchronicity of my life. Am I done with women now, the way my mother was finished with men after all my father's crap? I don't think so. I'm too young. And Woody is too needy. All I want to do right now is go home and curl up in the fetal position in a corner with Murray. But I have to face Ned the Head. I take the long, scenic route to work. I tell myself I'm doing this to figure out how best to address this frightful situation, but honestly I think I'm trying to avoid it altogether. Maybe he'll call in sick.

Alice and I stare from the car, our mouths open in shock. I have piloted the Kia through traffic so thick and tangled that from the air it must all look like an earthworm orgy. I've just had the world's worst-ever photo taken so that for the next fifteen years my passport will show everyone that I am actually an eighty-five-year-old, inbred, fat-faced pig-fucker. Alice and Lexington Vargas both laughed out loud and unkindly when, disenchanted, I dropped it on the dashboard of the car after a hasty and embarrassed exit from the local Mail Boxes Etc. It sits there mocking the kind of mildly good-looking thirty-two-year-old I thought I was.

Now, as L.V. hauls his substantial frame out of the groaning Kia, it is his house we are staring at, thunderstruck. It's in the *hills* of La Crescenta, and it's a magnificent, beautifully groomed hacienda that would fit three or four of my little ex-houses inside it.

"Dude!" is all I can say as he walks around to my window.

"Oh, yeah," he answers, as if my reaction isn't the first of its kind that he's encountered. He leans against the hood of the Kia, and I think there will be a Lexington Vargas–sized ass-dent in the body-work when he is done telling the story he looks like he's about to tell.

"That's a pretty cool house," I tell him unnecessarily.

"My dad left it to me," is his explanation.

"Wow, what did your father do?" asks Alice through the window opening.

"He was a doctor. UCLA recruited him from the hospital he was working at in Mexico City and brought us all here because he'd invented a new heart surgery technique and they wanted him to teach it to their doctors," answers L.V. who has just received a very large upgrade in my judgmental and easily-impressed-by-money mind.

"Then what are you doing groundskeeping at a high school?" I don't *think* that's an offensive question. I check. No, he doesn't look offended, but he has shown himself to be pretty resilient to my some-times-rash, clueless-white-boy assumptions based on his ethnicity.

"I was the 'bad' kid of all my brothers. I ditched school and then had some trouble with the cops. Messed with drugs and stuff, y'know," he answers, and although he's read to us about this life from his copy of *Magnificent Vibration*, I don't really know, but I nod my head like I do.

"My father gave me this place in his will and set up a trust fund that only takes care of the upkeep of the house and grounds. I can't touch the money for anything else, and I can't sell the house or raid the trust until I'm sixty-five. He made it so I *have* to work. He thought it would be good for me and teach me to be self-sufficient. He covered all the bases. Tough and from the Old Country, but whip-smart." He finishes his story and stands, leaving as I suspected, an ass-dent in the paper-thin bodywork of the rent-a-Kia.

"I'll catch you guys later," he says, waving casually, and walks up the impressive pepper-tree-lined driveway.

The decision to spend the week or so it will take me to get my passport in our separate digs and do some heavy contemplating and evaluating on our own was not an easy one to reach. We have become intensely and deeply connected, dependent and protective of one another in the short time we've been together. It's amazing to me. Other than to Josie, I've never felt this connected to anyone. Arthur has been noticeably silent, so we are just moving ahead based on our own best guesses. The round-trip tickets to Scotland have already been purchased via my whining bitch of a MasterCard, so I wouldn't really call them *paid for*, but we are booked and committed to this very odd trip. We're all wondering, "Why Scotland?" but I am secretly as excited as a Loch-Ness-Monster-obsessed twelve-year-old boy to be getting this close to the Magical Mystery Lake. We both watch as Lexington Vargas unlocks the front door and enters his spec-freaking-tacular house.

"I hope the one you're inheriting in Inverness looks like this," I joke to Alice.

"I don't think the Spanish ever made it that far north," she says with a tired smile. I fire up the Kia-hamster.

With misgivings I drop her off at the Oakwood. I tell her I'll miss her. She kisses me on the cheek. I blush. She gets out and is gone.

Now for the difficult part of the day. I begrudgingly turn the reluctant auto toward my ex-house and my ex-wife. The good news is, I will see Murray, if only briefly, *and* tonight I'll get to sleep in my own bed—the one that Alice has recently vacated. Pretty sure I won't be washing the sheets. It smells like her. I already checked.

I sit parked outside my little ex-house for a while. Damn, it looks even smaller after seeing the Spanish castle Lexington Vargas lives in. And I don't even live in this one anymore. I stay in the car 'til Murray senses my presence (how do they do that?) and stands up at the living room window, smiling. As I walk toward the old homestead, he jumps down and runs to where I know he is waiting behind the front door. I ring the doorbell to my own house as a visitor for the first time. It's a strange, disorienting feeling. Murray barks. I hear a muffled but definitely male voice yell, "Shut up, Murray." How dare some dude talk to my boy like that? This is already not going well. Charlotte finally cracks the door and Murray shoves his nose through it to get to me.

"Hey Mur-mur." I choose to say hello to my dog first because he is the only faithful one in the entire building.

"Bob?" questions Charlotte with a disagreeable look on her face.

"Hi," I answer, but it's not the answer she's looking for.

"What are you doing here?" she is certainly not at all huggy-buggy as Murray finally gets enough of the door open and bolts out to me, jumping, whimpering, and barking.

"Jesus, Murray. That dog's a pain in the ass since you left," she says.

I want to remind her that I didn't leave, I was kicked out. But it's just semantics.

"Who is it, babe?" says some guy who's been sleeping in my bed.

"It's Bob, my ex," she calls back to whoever is sitting in my chair.

"What do you want?" she asks.

"I need to borrow one of our . . . one of the suitcases," I tell her while trying to stop Murray from clawing at my crotch.

"Frank and I are flying to Hawaii in a week. We're going to need both of them," she answers matter-of-factly.

"Who the fuck is fucking Frank, and tell him to buy his own fucking suitcase!" is what I (again) want to say, but instead I say, "Oh." And silently wonder if I'm paying for this fabulous vacation to Hawaii while I drag my ass and two new friends to the sub-zero, bone-chilling Highlands of Scotland.

Murray bounces around me like Tigger, oblivious to my pain.

I hear Frank get up out of my fucking chair finally and I listen to his footsteps on the wooden floor that I laid down with these two bare hands, thank you very much, as he comes to the door. He's not at all what I expect. He's not a big, tough, hardcore, Harley-riding bro like the half-naked and mostly tumescent guys on Charlotte's Twitter page—he's kind of a weeny nerd like me. He even has horn-rimmed glasses that make him look like friggin' Poindexter. What the hell? She dumped me and went out and shacked up with another guy just like me? What happened to Ned the Head and Rob the Knob, Jake the Trouser Snake, and Russell the Love Muscle?

"Hello, Bob," says Frank. He is so much like me. Completely non-combative and agreeable. Why didn't she just stick with me?

"This is my boyfriend, Frank," says Charlotte needlessly. I think to myself, Isn't a "boyfriend" something a sixteen-year-old has?

"I strongly suggest that you get your skinny cracker ass out of this nightmare before she fucks your life up and starts screwing around on you, too!" Yep, of course it's my inner voice, but I suck it down and instead say, "Hi, Frank. Nice to meet you."

Nice to meet you? Really? *Nice* to *meet* you? I figure maybe when I'm ninety years old and no longer give a shit what people think and don't care whether I offend anyone or not, I'll finally have the *cojones* to say what I mean. Or in another life, maybe.

"Wow, Murray seems to have missed you," says Frank cluelessly.

"Yeah. He's actually *my* dog," I say, and I guess when it comes to my dog I have no problem standing up for him or me.

"Why don't you take him?" Charlotte throws me a bone. "He's not really fitting in well with us."

I am ecstatic and pissed at the same time. I think (but don't say) "He's not 'fitting in' well with you? He's not a secondhand couch you bought at a swap meet, he's a DOG!!!"

But I really want him so instead I say, "Wow, that'd be great!"

I came to get a suitcase and I leave with Murray. That's what I call a seriously good deal.

Charlotte heads to the kitchen to get his food and dish. Frank and I look at the floor in uncomfortable silence. She seems to be taking forever.

"It's turning out to be a beautiful day," says Dopey.

"Yes, it is," answers Bashful.

Thankfully the Wicked Queen arrives back with the goods before any more of this banal drivel can be uttered.

When Murray sees his only possessions being handed to me across the threshold, he suddenly gets it and bolts for my car. I think he's as happy as I am.

"Thanks," I yell back as I follow him to the Kia.

"*That's* the *car* you're driving?" throws out my ex in a derisive tone. But she doesn't know what this common but awesome automobile has been privy to. Some pretty wild shit. And I don't feel bad the way she probably intended me to feel.

"It's the best car I've ever rented," I toss back as I open the door and Murray jumps into the back seat with a look that says "Please, let's just go!"

I step on the hamster pedal and we zoom away from the House of Heartbreak forever. Together.

I am so happy that I break into song. It's *The Murray Song*. I've sung it to him all of his short life.

> *Murray's got a bum it's kind of stinky,*
> *And a little tiny wiener it's a pinky.*
> *But when nature calls, you can see he's got no balls*
> *When he lifts his little leg to do a tinkie.*

And that goes straight into:

> *Murray, Murray, bo Burray*
> *Banana fana fo Furray*
> *Fee fi mo Murray . . .*

"Oh crap, we almost made it, Mur. Too bad your name starts with an M, huh, because that last line busts us every time."

And he thinks this dopey song is as funny as the first time he heard it four years ago. I look in the rearview mirror and he is smiling at me with his chestnut-colored eyes.

I sneak him into Heartbreak Hotel under the cover of darkness because we aren't allowed to have pets in the apartments. Great, just what every guy needs after a brutal divorce (and this place is truly *filled* with divorcés)—some frosty, impersonal, residential corporation telling us we can't have a warm mutt to cuddle up with and ease our torment. I smuggle my fuzzy bro, wrapped in a blanket, through the Gestapo lights, barbed-wire, and roadblocks, holding him like a baby so if I run into the manager, Murray could perhaps be mistaken for an exceptionally ugly child with a severe case of hypertrichosis (werewolf's disease). But we run the gauntlet with no hindrance and Mur-mur is soon ensconced in the Lonely Guys' Villa with yours cynophilistically.

Now that I'm alone and hanging with Murray, things seem fairly normal again and I'm beginning to wonder if Lexington Vargas, the simmering would-be Christ-bride, and I have somehow gotten things a little muddled or been under some weird collective spell. Maybe we just didn't get enough sleep over the three days we were together. I am having a "cold-light-of-dawn" reflection on it all, and it's beginning to seem like a dream or an hallucination. Could all this have really happened? I am leaning toward being less and less committed to this nutty trip to Scotland. If it weren't for the fact that it's a paid vacation and the Loch Ness Monster from my childhood lives there, I'd probably bail right now.

The three of us have agreed not to contact one another unless we hear from Arthur or have a Merikh sighting. Another hard decision. Especially for me. The "no call" policy was Alice's idea and we all consented, though why, I have no idea. I'd love to talk to her, damnit. I'm missing her more than I even thought I would. L.V. too, but although he is a charming fellow, not quite as much. Now that I'm not getting up at three o'clock in the morning to make the mind-numbing trek to Siberia—I mean, Valencia, where the "Frightfully Faulty Films

Dubbing Stages" are now located, I have had time to read more of my copy of *Magnificent Vibration*. I discover in it that my father died from colon cancer last year in Philadelphia (?), and I actually cry over this. Why didn't he ever want to see me again? It's another of the irreparable rents in the fabric of my life that has no restitution and no way back home. I know the phrase "Get over it," and I try my best, but guilt and pain hang on me and screw with me like a bad girlfriend. There is so much I regret in my life, and I wish I could have a do-over. Was I that much of a disappointment as a son to him? Did he never even want me in the first place? Why didn't he fall in love with me like a dad is supposed to? I have photos of me as a little kid, and even *I* think I was kind of adorable. What was missing for him? Why did he not connect with me? He was my dad. It's a broken piece, now he's gone, that I can never repair. As Arthur said: Shit happens.

My mother was a slightly different story, and even according to my book, we healed a few things before her passing. I stayed by her side until she died from emphysema. She was a lifelong smoker and hid it from us so well that even if I saw evidence of it as a kid, I never really got it. She was numbed up under a morphine blanket for the last few days, but I sat with her and told her I loved her and, of course, asked her to give my sweet girl a kiss when they met on the other side. I said over and over to her, "Josie is waiting for you, Mom." I know in moments like these we revert to the basic, core beliefs and teachings of our youth, and I most certainly did. As Mother was dying there was, for me, most certainly a Heaven where we would all recognize one another and all be healed of our human illnesses, and failings, and sweet forgiveness would reign over us. We would actually be able to hug and kiss everyone who'd gone before us. Even my dad would hold me tightly and say he was sorry. We would be friends. Hmm.

Part of me still believes that, but I don't know if it's conditioning, blind hope, truth, or the whole there-are-no-atheists-on-a-crashing-plane syndrome.

My passport arrives finally with the "guy who has sex with goats" photo permanently embedded in its pages, as does the email with all our plane tickets to the Land of the Awesome Loch Ness Monster. My misgivings about this journey have grown. If someone were to relate back to me this whole scenario, I would force a smile, be kind of weirded out, and slowly back away to a safe blast-distance in case the bomb they had strapped around their chest went off.

Then Alice calls my cell phone, crying hysterically.

S*orry, but we are not done with the painful flashbacks quite yet.*
I arrive at my work a little late because of the scenic route taken, still no clearer on how this should be handled vis-à-vis me, Ned the Dickhead, and his bone-chilling boner photo on my wife's computer. Seeing him will be like rubbing salt into the tiny pee-hole at the end of my todger that, I am told, has more nerve endings than any other part of the body. Of course it does. That's why Woody continues to have such a hold over me. As luck would have it, Ned is late, too, and is just getting out of his Chevy truck that he thinks is so friggin' macho. And honestly, it is. I am driving my "Hey look everyone. I'm earning more money than you are," C-class Mercedes that I am struggling to make the lease payments on, and I feel totally phony and pretentious right at this mo-ment. Ned gives me a wave. Is he saying "Good morning," or "Thanks for the use of your wife's vagina"? I don't know. I can't tell.

As he walks to the door into the Cambodian Cinema Underworld,

I call to him, "Ned, can I talk to you for a second?" He stops, and a look of concern or possibly irritation flits briefly across his face, because we never, ever talk, Ned and I. This, to me, just compounds his guilt, and I feel the anger rise in me like a great leopard seal breaching for the kill as a fat and juicy penguin swims heedlessly through the frigid waves above.

I suddenly lose all self-control and scream, like a man dishonored, outraged, and abused, across the parking lot and loud enough for the entire building to hear: "Get ready, asshole, because I am about to open up the biggest, most painful can of whoopass that you or anyone else has ever experienced. And if you ever touch my wife again or even so much as 'Twit' with her or send her another badly lit photo of your pudgy, aging, naked body, I will tear you a new ass-opening so substantial you'll become the eighth and ninth wonders of the fucking world and people will drive their cars through you so their kids can gawk, take snapshots, and admire my handiwork!!!!!"

In my head I scream this. In reality I non-confrontationally waddle over and say: "I just found out that Charlotte, my wife, has been unfaithful. And I saw your photo on her laptop. I guess you're one of the men she's been seeing."

That is my best shot? "I guess you're one of the men she's been seeing????" Been SEEING??" As in, throwing her legs over your shoulders while you mercilessly pound her pee-hole, "been seeing"?? Jesus, next life bless me with balls, please.

"Oh man, sorry, dude. I don't think I'm the only one, though," is his reply, and he walks in to work as if this is all that needs to be said.

I think to myself, "That's a fair response to my ball-less enquiry. I deserve no more, considering I broached the subject as though it were a minor complaint. A mere annoyance. Something bothersome but not really worth getting all tense and worked-up over." You get what you give.

I then remember that I sent Ned's photo to everyone else and everyone else's photo to Ned. I guess he hasn't checked his Twitter page yet. I suddenly feel like I'm the one who's been the immoral cheating bastard. I avoid Ned from then on as though it's my fault. We have no further conversation, Ned and I, and anytime we accidentally meet, it's a quick embarrassed nod of recognition and we move on, eyes to the floor. Why am I such a weed? Where's the Charles Bronson in me with his vigilante justice and the six-shot revolver that can kill twenty-seven bad guys without reloading? Where are truth and balance and fairness? Maybe that's it. Life just isn't fucking fair.

After this first, distressing day at work, I climb back into my pretentious "economy" Mercedes and drive myself to the dry cleaners. Obviously and unfortunately I am not done yet. I walk in and Freddy the wife-fucker says "Hello, Mr. Cotton. Your lady was in earlier and picked everything up." I think he has a slightly nervous look about him that tells me she may have mentioned the bust or maybe he's already logged on to his computer. It must be a bit disconcerting to suddenly find thirty-five anonymous photos of naked and emotionally/erotically charged men on your home page with quotes like, "Please, ma'am. I want some more?" and "I'm still jacking off to your ass, baby!!!!" or "I know you must have a million guys but that one night was INSANE!!!!!!!" And if they could add more exclamation points I would insist on disqualifying them from ever touching a keyboard again. I am having trouble focusing, of course, given the circumstances and the amount of hooch I have just consumed.

"So, Freddy," I begin with an unpracticed and possibly misinterpreted leer. Unfortunately, to numb the pain I have stopped off at a local tavern on the way home from work and treated myself to several glasses of something severely alcoholic, so I am wearing a courage coat that normally is not mine. "You've been a-messin' where you shouldn't a-been a-messin,' " I start out, quoting Nancy Sinatra. The lyrics are from her 1966 song "These Boots Are Made for Walkin'," which is a pop quote so dumb and inappropriate, considering the very real and extremely painful circumstances I find myself in, that I will never, ever cop to it even if someone reads this back to me.

"What do you mean?" says flustered Freddy, his Asian features coloring slightly. To be honest, although he has the "rough boy" tattooed look about him that my wife seems to find so irresistible and humpable, he is a smallish guy, and given my state of inebriation I think I'd probably best him in an exchange of blows, mainly because I am feeling no pain and could probably absorb a punch to the nose and continue unabated. It doesn't come to that, of course. Fights are actually difficult to start once you pass the age of twenty-five.

"You fucked my wife," I uncharacteristically say.

Mrs. Chang, the owner of Chang's Dry Cleaning Service, overhears my lewd comment to her employee and takes me to task.

"You no talk to my man like that. Not say bad words in here," she admonishes me in a heavy Chinese accent.

"Your employee here has been having sexual relations with my significant other," I counter. In my dizzy state, I think this is a fair and reasonable approach.

"I call police," says Mrs. Chang, and she leaves in a huff.

"I've been coming to this dry cleaners for three years," I yell after her, sure she will understand and concede my point.

I think she's bluffing, so I continue my one-sided conversation with Freddy the Fornicating Fuck-Face. Powered by the mighty forces of firewater, I proceed to question and berate him. He is sweating lightly but saying nothing in return.

"How would you like it if I was cheating on you?" I try, making no sense to anyone, as the alcohol I don't usually consume begins to have a serious effect on the cognitive areas of my brain.

"My wife's computer is full of guys. Naked guys. With lots of hair all over their bodies and with . . . with boners. I saw your dick, man! I now know you're not circumcised!" I am actually embarrassing myself, such are the lack of a cohesive argument and the painful detail I am allowing myself to divulge.

"I trusted you with my clothes!" I plead. It's pathetic. Someone shut me the hell up. People are entering the establishment, hearing me having a one-sided argument with dear Freddy, then turning around and walking right out, uncleaned clothes still in hand. I peripherally understand that my presence is not very good for Mrs. Chang's dry-cleaning business. I arrive at that awful drunken point where I know I am off the rails but am powerless to do anything to correct the path of the crashing train I am on. If only I had a good friend with me right now to lead me outside, stick his fingers down my throat, and then take me home and put me to bed so I could sleep it off, no harm, no foul. But it only gets worse.

"I've probably worked on films that actors you admire are starring in," I wail, monumentally confusing the Chinese with the Cambodians.

Eventually, and to my utter surprise, the police do arrive. And arrest me. And book me. Drunk in public. Me? Who doesn't drink! I am caught so completely off-guard that I point at a mortified Freddy the Copulating Cleaner and start shouting stupid and highly arrest-worthy shit like, "You should be arresting this idiot. Don't you people read your Bible? 'Thou shalt not commit adultery!' " Oh my God, my mother is now spouting words out of my own mouth! And I am one of those guilty adulterers, let's be honest. The police add "resisting arrest" to the charges and then, thankfully for my own dignity's sake, handcuff me and shove me into the back of their black-and-white while shoppers gawk. I even tell the *two cops as they are driving me to the local lockup for the night that my wife has been screwing her way through my phone book. They have no sympathy or words of consolation for yours hammeredly. The universe sucks balls. I spend some time in a holding cell next-door to a guy who wants me to make a call to his wife for him and tell her to get rid of the "stuff" because the cops are on their way over. Since I am in for a lesser offense I get more access to the phone. He makes the "rocking a baby" motion to signify to me he has a little one at home. It's a sympathy ploy that unfortunately wins me over, such is my current state, and I make the call for him. But the back office, or wherever, is monitoring all this and I am summarily pulled out of the holding cell and placed in a dark, isolated interior dungeon consisting of a locked door, no windows, and a stainless steel toilet without a seat. Welcome to the joint, MF! Okay, it's not really "the joint." It's only the local jail, but I feel castrated, castigated, and completely at their mercy. Could I get raped in here? I'm beginning to think it's a possibility. They could throw any crackhead in with me. I lie down on the rock-hard bench that has probably seen the likes of murderers, drug dealers, drunks who threw up everywhere, and homeless weirdos who peed all over the very place where I am currently laying my head and trying to cry myself to sleep. Jail is not for pansies like me.*

I now have to pay for two lawyers. One is handling the divorce that Charlotte is still adamant about and refuses to discuss any further, plus I have a different, criminal lawyer for the arrest and consequent court appearances relating to my mortifying performance at Live at Mrs. Chang's Improv and Dry Cleaners, *co-starring Freddy the Spouse Shagger. I am going downhill fast, folks.*

Compared to the arrest, the divorce proceedings are a cakewalk. A fairly heartbreaking and bleak cakewalk, but there is nothing that compares with being ensnared in the criminal justice system. I wish I'd read my horoscope for those two days; I could have skipped a lot of this and just stayed in bed. Maybe.

The divorce is cut (my throat) and dried (my carcass), and then I spend what little money I end up with on the two lawyers. I now have fines to pay as well as AA meetings to attend, and my criminal attorney tells me that I'm lucky to have avoided prison time. I tell him my idea of lucky is winning a gazillion dollars on a five-cent slot machine in Las Vegas while a twenty-year-old hooker hangs off each of my arms and Siegfried and Roy and their white tigers guard my winnings in their penthouse at the top of Caesar's fucking Palace. My legal counsel doesn't even begin to crack a smile. And I'm pretty sure he says that thing about the prison time I just missed out on to scare me into forking over the exorbitant fee he's charging me without complaining.

I decide (actually I'm ordered by the court) not to contact any of Charlotte's hedonistic, sybaritic Twitter lovers, and thankfully the mass mailing I did of everyone's skin-flutes is not brought up in either the divorce case or the drunk-in-public arrest. I think each recipient was shocked into submission and didn't want it publicly known that he had posted in-the-cold-light-of-day fairly unflattering photos of his imperfect and moderately endowed self to a married woman whose crazy husband might be tossing lawsuits at any Tom, Dick, or Dick who might have exposed his genitals in this very public forum.

I go into a serious funk once I am alone and the lawyers and the judges and the D.A. and the police and the AA folks are all done with me. I move my meager possessions into the Divorcés' Domicile for Deadbeats. The only photo I take with me from our home is of Murray, smiling with his whole face. I put it by my new bed along with Josie's ashes. Depression lands like a dark angel on the footboard and takes up residence. I begin to think about dying. Really soon. Then I steal a book.

can't even understand what she's saying, so convulsive is her sobbing on the other end of the line.

"Alice? What the hell?" I've always been good with words of comfort in time of need.

"Can . . . (sob) . . . you . . . (sob) . . . come . . . (sob) . . . over?" she
finally manages. I can get no more from her but these few choked
words.

"I'll be right there," I say and am already mentally in the powerful but neutral-colored Kia and on my way. Woody steps on the gas.
"Down, boy!"

I drive as fast as the Hamster allows, watching out for cops
because a speeding ticket would definitely be counterproductive
right now. I'm stressing as I drive, so out-of-the-blue and desperate-
sounding was her call. I begin to fear that Merikh is somehow involved. Could he have found out where Alice lives? He apparently
had no problem locating me. I berate myself for not keeping a more
watchful eye on her, for even letting her go off by herself. None of us
knows what pretty-boy Merikh's intentions are, but they seem to be
counter to anything regarding our safety and well-being. I think about
calling 911 as I speed on. Maybe the police should meet me at Alice's
apartment, just in case. I open my cell and begin dialing her number
instead, looking back and forth from the traffic to the fricking teeny-
tiny goddamn numbers on this ridiculously small phone, cognizant of
my promise never to use it again while driving after the near-death experience at the Intersection of Idiots. But this could be an emergency.
Her line rings and rings and then goes to voice-mail. I don't even
have the mild comfort of hearing her recorded voice on the outgoing

message. In fact, it sounds like that same smarmy chick that I think called me an "asshole" when I tried redialing Arthur back, the very first night. I'm sweating with anxiety thinking of all the possible scenarios that could be unfolding at Alice's apartment, and when I arrive, I sprint like Usain Bolt for her door. I knock loudly and call her name.

The front door finally swings open and she collapses into my arms. She is a mess, but alive, and she doesn't seem to be physically injured. And I'm thinking, "Thank God. Oh, thank God she's not hurt."

"My girl is dead," she weeps into my neck as I hold her.

I wait, while she clings to me, for her to continue but she does not, cannot, so hard is she crying.

"Who? What girl?" I'm trying to play catch-up.

"Genevieve killed herself last night," is the unexpected reply.

And I have to ask, "Who's Genevieve?" but she can't answer. The name alone brings wracking sobs from her core, so deep that I can feel them as they roll in waves up through her body, and I think, "*I'm* the one she called in her darkest hour?"

I wait patiently for her brokenhearted wailing to ease enough so she is able to speak. I make her tea, rub her back, and tell her I am here for her, whatever she needs—and honestly, I mean it. I would kill for her. Something in this woman brings out the protector, the sword and shield; the guardian that I knew was inside me all this time, although neither Charlotte's deceit nor Ned the Head's casual attitude toward destroying my marriage had this effect. It seems as though every step we have taken, Alice and I, has brought us closer and closer, and she has just allowed me in one step farther.

Finally, as we sit cross-legged on the floor together, she reveals the source of her pain. She begins, through her tears, a box of almost empty tissues in her lap: "Genevieve was a novice like me. She was from a wealthy family in Brussels who'd collectively agreed that she would join a convent as soon as she came of age. By the time we met, she was already twenty-one and had been a postulant for three years. I was in my fourth year, and we were both several years away from taking our final vows."

Alice takes a breath and looks at me with puffy eyes. Is she gauging me? "I'm here," I listen to myself say, and it has so much meaning as I utter it that I know she feels the truth in my words. She smiles at me weakly through her pain and continues.

"We both were young, insecure, each with our own doubts and fears, unsure of our vocation. The older sisters around us mothered us, chastised us, helped us and hindered us. Then we found each other. And in our uncertainty and loneliness, we fell in love . . . and became lovers."

I inhale audibly. She looks at me as if I am judging, but I am most definitely not. "You think that's wrong?" she questions. There is a deep hurt in her eyes. I am holding my breath. I can't speak. All I can do is shake my head "no."

"We both knew it was against our commitment to our celibacy and everything the Catholic sisterhood stood for, but it was so . . . natural . . . felt so normal. We both needed to be loved and although we came from totally different backgrounds, we'd both missed out on any kind of warmth and affection. Never experienced it . . ."

I find my voice and interrupt, eager to explain myself. It's my turn to reveal my past.

"No. No, I don't think it's wrong at all. I would never judge you like that," I fumble, trying to guide Woody to his happy place.

"But that sound you made. It sounded like a judgment," she challenges.

I take a very deep breath and then proceed to lay out my obses-sion with the female of the species and the whole, odd tie to orga-nized religion. I tell her in the most basic of terms, as though Woody himself had the floor. I even mention my young self being turned on by a vibrant and youthful Julie Andrews in the musical *The Sound of Religious Hotness.* She actually smiles wanly at this. I feel like I have given her a moment away from her pain. And, for the life of me, I have never been more articulate.

"Forgive me for being insensitive when you're in this much pain, but it just . . . hit me where I live. It was the forbidden, sexual-fantasy aspect of your confession that kind of caught me off-guard. I'm sorry; it was totally inappropriate, but also completely involuntary. There was no criticism or condemnation in what you heard. I'm telling you the truth, at the expense of you now seeing me as some creepy weirdo with a giant hole in his marble bag, but I would never want you to think I thought any less of you about . . . anything. I lo—" I stop my-self from saying the "L" word, just in time. That's something I could never take back, and it would change the whole dynamic of whatever is happening with us all in this strange moment in time. Sitting on the floor of her apartment, she leans in and hugs me. I hug her back.

With her head on my shoulder she whispers: "Genevieve jumped from her fourth-floor window last night and died while I was sleep-ing." Again a shudder runs through her and she weeps breathlessly.

"She'd talked about doing something like this. She was so un-happy, I know, but she believed if God wanted her to live, and she jumped, He would catch her." She breaks down again and begins to cry anew.

I could have told her that God would not catch her.

I hug her, trying to make it feel as platonic as I possibly can.

"I really don't want to be alone tonight. Will you stay with me?" She asks the question so tenderly and with such intense vulnerability in her voice that I understand there are no sexual undertones (damnit) in her request. I would never try to take advantage of this situation anyway, as much as I would love to, and although Woody is ready to kick my ass for being such a mensch, he can just suck it up. Plus now, after her sad confession, I'm not sure which team she's batting for. It adds another level of intrigue to this fascinating girl/woman and, yes, an added layer of sexuality, as if she needs it! Christ on a crutch! I am waist-deep in the waters of the unknown.

I have a brief mental picture of Murray crossing his legs by the front door of my bachelor pad, but I think he can handle it for one night. I did have the good fortune to take him out "walkies" before Alice's emotional phone call came in, and he promptly got in a brief scuffle with a Chow, before he eventually did "get busy," as Charlotte insisted we euphemistically call his peeing-and-pooping ritual, so I think he's good for the night. If not, there's always Formula 409. Hey, it's not *my* house.

Ever the gentleman, I choose the outer sheet to lie on top of, giving Alice some personal space and myself a set of bright and shiny blue balls by three a.m., but it is the right thing to do and I think she feels safer and more comfortable to hug me when she has the need if there is a "modesty barrier" between us. And she does cuddle in, often, through the night as she cries and sniffles. I on the other hand wake up at one point to find with some mortification that I am humping my pillow in my sleep. I hope that Alice is dozing and didn't pick up on the rhythm I was unconsciously laying down. It is a familiar beat! I'm sure in my dream she was supposed to be the pillow, but I am so embarrassed that I toss it to the floor and try sleeping without it.

When the morning finally arrives, neither of us is particularly well rested. From all her crying, Alice's eyes look like she's gone a few rounds with Junior dos Santos. (Sorry, that's a guy thing. He's a champion UFC fighter.) I limp to the bathroom, trying my best to hide my painful testicles. (Again, a guy thing. Google "blue balls.")

"Are you hurt?" asks Alice, seeing me hobbling slightly.

"No, I'm good. I think I pulled something," I answer euphemistically.

The long night of mourning seems to have settled her pain a little, and I'm glad for that and for whatever small comfort I've offered. I look at her over the tea she has just brewed. With her puffy eyes, red nose, and tangled hair, she is still beyond beautiful and SO hot to me. I realize I am in love with this woman. Completely and fully in love, and will go to the ends of the earth with her if that is where she needs me to go.

"Thank you, Bobby," she says softly, as if reading my mind.

Why I'm not sure, but it comes out of my mouth before I can weigh the reasons: "Call me Tio."

"Tio?"

"It's my real name. Well, part of my real name. My name is actually Horatio."

This is the first time I've told another human being my ball-sucking birth name since I was ten years old.

She stifles a laugh, which under the circumstances, I am glad to hear.

"Horatio? Really?" she asks.

"Really," I answer.

"Okay. Tio it is," she replies with a soft smile.

One step closer.

"If you're good, I should get home and let Murray out."

"You got Murray back?"

"Yeah, it just kind of happened. I have to find someone to watch him while we're away. I'm hoping maybe Doug will do it."

She kisses my cheek at the door, and I use the willpower of Saint Jerome not to turn my head and kiss her full on her lips. I smile like a goofus and run like a rabbit.

Poor Murray has indeed embarrassed himself and I step in it, so close to the inside of the front door is his little pile of poop, as I enter. He looks chagrined.

"Sorry, Murray. It's okay, no big deal. When you gotta go you gotta go, buddy," and other phrases I hope will ease his ignominy.

"Come on, Mur, let's 'get busy,' " I shout, hoping to distract him from his self-imposed mortification. He jumps all over me as I get his leash, so happy is he that I'm okay with wearing his crap on my shoes.

"We'll clean that up later, dude. Don't worry," and we sneak out into the Great Wide Open so he can sniff the many fine deposits left by earlier dogs.

Murray is a happy boy. Maybe he got blamed for his mistakes in his "other home." It's all good.

"You're here now, Mur-mur," I say as I rub his squishy head and slap his haunches playfully, and he leaps up on me with a slobbery smile. We are buds, he and I. He sniffs the grass in front of the Lodging House for Losers and is obviously looking for the perfect spot to pee on. The grass must be just right, the scent ideal, no one looking, and zero distractions, or urine will not flow. He does like to take his time. I think dogs enjoy the whole preamble to peeing as much as the act itself. He is getting ready to squat, I can tell by the moves. Yes,

Murray, my "boy" dog squats like a girl. Must be something to do with the loss of the valuable "twins" that make his sad, shriveled scrotum look like an old lady's wrinkled empty leather coin purse. Suddenly his head shoots up. Something has caught the attention of the two billion olfactory receptors in his prodigious sniffer: a nose that is approximately one hundred thousand times more sensitive than mine. Across the street, a squirrel is frozen in place, hoping he doesn't get ID'd by the big red mutt with the amazing nasal aptitude. I smile at the funny animal tableau, Murray staring, front leg raised as though he's some kind of professional hunting dog (which he most certainly is not) and the squirrel, eyes unblinking, pretending to be a small gray rock. I take a step away to move him along when Murray suddenly launches for the rodent and yanks the leash out of my hands. He's halfway across the street before I can even yell for him to stop.

"Murray!! Come here!!" I shout at his retreating fuzzy red-golden butt. The squirrel is long gone. But the car is not.

It hits him so hard that I hear his sweet noggin crack against the car's fender. The squeal of tires drowns out my howl of pain and Murray's yelp of shock. "Murray!!" is all I can scream as I run to him. He's lying on the black asphalt, his legs kicking spasmodically, his back broken, blood running from his nose and mouth. I fall to my knees at his side. A kid runs up to us professing his innocence and begging forgiveness. I barely hear him as I lay my face on my dying boy's side.

"Murray, no, no," is all I can say.

His breathing is belabored and clearly painful as his lungs fill with blood. I cradle his shattered head in my hands as he leaves this earth.

I think he looks at me once with a sad sideways glance. We see all the years we will not be spending together. Then his eyes defocus and he is gone.

The driver is beside me talking nervously.

"I didn't see him. Honestly. I'm so sorry. Let me take him to a vet."

But there is no need. I stare hopelessly at his broken, lifeless form.

"*Murray, Murray, bo Burray, Banana fana fo Furray . . .*" runs through my head.

I couldn't protect him. I couldn't save him. I couldn't stop what was about to happen from happening.

Murray is gone to where all good dogs go. And at this point I don't even know where that is.

My final words to him replay themselves in my head:

"Murray!! Come here!!"

How I wish.

Shit happens.

Dear Miss Young,

We are in receipt of your most recent email dated 3/21/14 and are pleased to hear of your imminent arrival in Inverness so that we may settle the estate of your uncle, Ronan Bon Young.

Once you sign the necessary documentation you are within your legal rights to take up residence at Mr. Young's house, although there are still some formalities remaining in order to complete execution and distribution of the estate. Please stop by our offices when you reach Inverness—the address is included at the bottom of this email with our company hallmark—and we will have the appropriate legal papers ready for you to sign and shall supply you with keys and directions. Or I would be happy to drive you to the house myself.

Provided you have all the correct documentation noted in the previous email, this matter should be resolved fairly quickly.

Please call my cellular phone when you arrive. The number from your U.S. device is: 011 44 1463 3789 131.

Looking forward to meeting you. Your uncle was quite a fixture around this part of the Highlands.

Your faithful servant,

Clive McGivney

of

McGivney, McGivney, & McGivney Law Offices, Inverness, Scotland
41 Church Street, Inverness, Highlands, IV1 1EH

Los Angeles International is so crowded at 7:30 in the evening that there's not even enough room to change your mind. And we are all thinking about doing just that as the three of us head to Security on our way to Immigration (where I will be forced to display my inhuman, zombie passport photo) that will then take us to the gate that will take us to the plane that will take us to London and then Glasgow, where we will rent a car that will take us to McGivney, McGivney, and McGivney of Inverness. And who knows where else? We're all at the point of thinking this could really just be just some wild, stoned-goose chase. Or maybe not. I guess at the very least, Alice gets a new house and I get to dip my imagination into the cold and awesome Loch Ness, "home of the world's coolest creature," to quote twelve-year-old Horatio Cotton. Not sure what Lexington Vargas's hopes for this trip would be. He doesn't say much.

All this excitement, however, is tempered by the brick of pain that sits on my chest. Murray died on my watch. I'm heartsick to have lost him like that. We made a deal a long time ago, we humans and dogs. They would give up their wild, wandering ways to idolize us and keep us good company, and we would love them and protect them from harm. Murray lived up to his part of the bargain; I did not. I'm still so mad at God for not looking out for us. I know it's ironic, given my recent conversations with the entity, that I still seem to be able to blame him/her for shit happening, but old habits die hard and my boy Murray just . . . died.

I am glad to be going somewhere new and away from the scene of my pain, if not from the pain itself. It's welcomingly distracting to consider what we might find at the end of this wild-ass rainbow, although a big part of me is dreading flying twelve-plus hours sitting next to a traveler's worst nightmare, the very large and space-consuming Lexington Vargas. I got the best price I could on the round-trip fares, and the best price was, unfortunately but obviously, coach. So the three of us will be squished into a space that wouldn't fit three *normal*-sized people very comfortably and certainly not for as many long hours as we will be so ensconced. But we'll endure.

Everything is going as swimmingly as I imagine it could until we get to Security and they find L.V.'s hunting knife in his backpack. I look at him in disbelief as they yank the wicked-looking man-killer out of his carry-on.

"Dude, what were you thinking?" I say, possibly in an attempt to publicly distance Alice and myself from this globetrotter's faux pas.

"What? I'm not allowed to carry a knife?" says Lexington Vargas, nonplussed.

"Sir, it's illegal to board an airplane with a weapon," says the stern young woman in the blue shirt, and every time someone in authority says "Sir" like that it sounds like what they really mean is "Hey, dip-shit." Am I the only one who picks up on this? Ms. Blue Shirt has a look on her face as though she were holding a bag of heroin, a block of C4 plastic explosive, and a certificate of transit for the eight white-slave-trade hookers we have drugged-up, bound, and stashed in our checked luggage, rather than a small hunting knife. We're all glad she is keeping the skies safe by patting down little kids and strip-searching grandmas.

"This is clearly on the list of banned carry-ons," she continues, pointing to a large sign that also contains illustrations of explosives (really?) guns, chainsaws (no way!) and fire extinguishers. "Please step over here." She points to a spot right next to the lethal-dose-emitting X-ray machines that they work beside day in and day out, and an-nounces over her walkie-talkie: "Male assist. Male assist."

"What does that mean?" I ask her.

"Are you three travelling together?" she replies sharply. It's not quite the response I'm looking for.

"Er . . . yes," I say. I guess it's pretty obvious. Ms. TSA looks at Alice and speaks again into her intercom.

"One female assist. I need two male assists and a single female assist."

We wait by the death-dealing radioactive machines in silence, thinking that this trip just got a whole lot more complicated. Eventually three more Blue Shirts approach us and signal us forward with a commanding and slightly demeaning wave of their blue-rubber-gloved hands.

"Oh, shit, are they going to body-cavity search us?" I think, seeing they are *all* wearing the same "rectal exam" rubber gloves.

But it's not *that* bad. They rummage through our carry-ons, pulling out each article and inspecting it as though they were monkeys that have never seen an iPod or a Sudafed inhaler before. Then they run everything *back* through the X-ray machines! We are subjected to a hand-search and are told they will only touch our "sensitive areas" with the backs of their gloved hands. So no rectal exam, but some strange dude rubs Woody with the back of his hand as I send mental signals to the aforementioned penis to ignore the stimulation because (a) it's coming from a man, (b) I'd be mortified if he (Woody) moved a muscle, and (c) do not, repeat, do NOT look over at Alice as the lucky female Blue Shirt rubs the back of *her* hands over Alice's "sensitive areas."

Soon, after much wiping of rubber gloves with strips of cloth and consequent processing of those strips, we are free to go. Lexington Vargas wants to know if he can have his knife back.

"Tell me the address of the rock you've been living under since the whole 9/11 thing, and I'll have them mail the knife to you," I say, maybe a bit heatedly, but honestly . . . "Can I have my knife back"? Fuck!

Lexington Vargas's response is an expectedly low-key "I don't know, I thought we might need it."

Which actually may have more truth to it than I'd like to admit to myself.

We're herded with the other cattle and board the aircraft inch by inch, bit by bit, as people mindlessly whack us with luggage, take forever to stow their bags, sit in the wrong seats, and generally make me wish I wasn't a part of the same human race. Jesus, some of them smell bad already! What's it going to be like after twelve or so hours with them all snoring and farting and generally causing me to yearn for Lexington Vargas's hunting knife to put either them or me out of our misery?

The aircraft takes off with an explosive and thundering noise, jolting the three of us into fearful flashbacks of the plane crash on the 101 that will probably never leave our fear receptors.

Alice grips my hand until her knuckles show white. On the other side of me (yep, I got the middle seat), L.V. does the same. His giant hand engulfs and crushes my little mitt in his panic. He gives me a furtive look that speaks volumes. It says "Sorry, man. I'm totally freaked out about flying, and that whole plane-crash thing the other night didn't help any. Hold me, Daddy." Wow, when did I become the rock in this weird partnership?

We do not crash in a fiery ball of boiling jet fuel on takeoff, and eventually the whole aircraft settles into the strange and restless lethargy that is part and parcel of flying across continents and time zones.

Alice has the window seat and the interior wall of the fuselage to sleep against. Lexington Vargas has the aisle and can stretch out to some degree, with his heavy head lolling into the walkway, although sporadic collisions with drink carts steered by aggressive flight attendants occasionally smack him into wakefulness. I have the choice of either Alice's or L.V.'s shoulder. And although L.V. is more padded and would provide a fairly comfortable pillow (given the fact that his body also takes up half of my seat's real estate already), I'm more than happy to lean my head on the fragile surface of Alice's shoulder, even though I know it will leave me with a neck-ache for days. I think it's a fair exchange. She is the only person on the whole airplane who smells good. She smells more than good. I slowly drift off.

"Wake up! Bobby, wake up!!" someone is prodding and poking me and yelling in my ear. Where am I? Is it raining? I hear thunder. And it's really stinky. Suddenly I am awake and trying to grasp *why* I am awake. The thunder is the jet noise, the awful smell is my fellow passengers, the shoulder I have been drooling, yes drooling on, is Alice's, and the face in my face is large and looks like a giant about to eat me, but I quickly realize it's Lexington Vargas. I'm immediately on high alert. Something is going on. Are we crashing? "Bobby, wake up!!!" L.V. keeps yelling, although he's not really yelling, but it sure feels like it. My neck hurts.

"What? What is it? I'm awake. Stop yelling. What's the matter?"

"I just went to the bathroom," L.V. begins.

"You woke me up to tell me you just went to the bathroom?"

"No, no, listen to me."

"Stop shouting at me," I plead.

"I'm not shouting," whispers Lexington Vargas.

He sits up straight in his seat. The seat groans audibly. So do I as he leans in.

"The coach bathrooms were all busy or clogged up or something, and I really had to go, man . . ."

"Please, I don't need to hear this."

He continues anyway.

"So I walked down to the business-class toilets and one of the flight attendants asked me which section I was sitting in. I pointed to the back of the bus, so she said I had to use those bathrooms, but I told her they were full or out of service, and she said that the business-class restrooms were for business-class passengers only, and I said that I really needed to go and that it was "turtle-headin'," and she said she didn't understand what I meant by that and should she get one of the male flight attendants and did we have a problem here? and I said "*Oye, hermana*, I've got a brick knocking at the back door and—"

I stop him with an actual hand over his mouth, so close is he.

"Okay, stop. I need to sleep."

"Merikh is on the plane!" says Lexington Vargas with some force, though muffled, through my hand.

"What?" I remove my hand and wipe it on my pant leg.

"He's sitting in business class."

"What?" Why does this seem to be my "go-to" word of choice?

"I saw him just as I was turning to come back here. He's kind of unmistakable."

I am awake!

"*Our* Merikh?" is all I can muster.

"He's on the plane, man. With us!" says L.V.

"No fucking way," I return.

"Come on. I'll show you."

He leads me to the business-class/cheap-seats barrier where the really fortunate upper class is sleeping luxuriously in exotic modular chairs that look incredibly comfortable.

"Are they sleeping in *pods*?" I ask, momentarily distracted by the opulence of business class.

L.V. ignores me and points to a profile that I have only seen once but recognize in an instant. It is perfect, flawless, beautiful, and it chills my heart. Sitting in the section we are not allowed to enter, even if the *Titanic* hits an iceberg and the only lifeboats are in business class, is the Angel of Death himself.

"Is he going to crash this plane?" asks Lexington Vargas, like I friggin' know. "Should we tell a flight attendant?"

"Tell them what?" I reason. "That we saw this guy jump from a burning plane crash that no one was supposed to have survived and that he held us up with a gun right out of *Pirates of the Caribbean* and we think he might be the Angel of Death but we're not really sure?"

"Okay," answers L.V., like a little kid who's been told by Mommy that there will be no trip to the zoo this Saturday because of his bad grades.

How did Merikh find us? Why is he following us? What's with the long hair? All questions that need to be answered.

L.V. and I walk back to our seats on the lower decks with the rest of the Irish immigrants and wait for the possible collision with an ice mountain.

"We need some protection," says Lexington Vargas. "Damn, I wish they hadn't taken my knife."

Okay, now I agree.

We decide not to tell Alice, but like a dopey kid who can't keep a secret from his sister, I end up letting the nervous cat out of the bag and then wishing I hadn't. She looks stricken.

My thinking is that if Merikh is going to bring this plane down, then Alice should know ahead of time so she can prepare for the afterlife or whatever. She sneaks up to take a look for herself.

"It's him," she confirms, squeezing past both of us to reclaim her seat, just as the plane starts to shake violently.

Again Alice and L.V. crush my hands into submission as the giant aircraft pitches and yaws. Is this it? Is Merikh about to turn another plane and its occupants into ash and embers?

The intercom clicks on and a casual voice says, "Sorry, folks. We seem to have hit a little bit of rough air. Please make sure your seat belts are fastened. We should be clear of this is a few minutes."

So we're good for now. But we're on high alert, condition red! *Danger, Will Robinson, danger!*

We take turns at checking on Merikh to see if he looks like he's planning some kind of sabotage, but all he seems to be doing is sleeping. And the militant flight attendant who first accosted Lexington Vargas is getting pretty upset with our cavalier attitude towards her God Almighty authority.

"Get back to the sardine-packed seats and the plugged up crappers where you peasants belong!" she says with her eyes and her demeanor every time one of us ventures toward business class on recon.

"That guy sitting over there brought down the plane on the 101 freeway. We think he may be the Angel of Death, and we're all in great peril, including you and your little area of sovereignty here by the business-class toilets," is what I want to tell her, but instead I say: "Sorry, I thought these bathrooms were for everyone."

After seeing the awesome pods the upper-class passengers sleep in, what must their *bathrooms* be like? Do they have gilt-edged wall-to-wall mirrors? Attendants that hand out mints? Automatic butt-wipers?

The flight seems interminable, but eventually we land at Heathrow Airport in Jolly Olde England unscathed and in one piece, and the Angel of Death can bite me.

We watch for Merikh all through immigration (where I'm pretty sure the young British admissions officer smirks at the photograph of the incestuous chicken-rapist masquerading as me in my passport— but I may be projecting) and the Angel of Death is nowhere to be seen. Nor is he on the flight from London to Glasgow. Believe me, we check. Often.

"I need to get us some protection," says L.V.

Unfortunately, Woody thinks he means condoms because we'll be shagging our brains out here in the Highlands with many of the fine young Scottish lassies. But I know what L.V. is referring to.

"Like what?" I ask as I hand over my eunuch of a MasterCard to the Hertz guy, who has no idea I could never pay the bill I've run up if I lived to be 150. "I need to get us a gun, I think," says Lexington Vargas quietly and ominously to me.

"How?" This is way out of my very small area of expertise.

"Don't worry about it. I know how to do that," answers L.V. reassuringly, and I believe him. "I think they still get weapons smuggled in here from old IRA stashes. I'll go digging for something when we get to where we're going."

I have absolutely zero idea how to do what he is suggesting, so I do what I know how to do and pay for the rent-a-car. Oh my God, it's a Kia!! Yes! I think this is a very good sign. Alice is still anxiously looking for Merikh in every person she sees and doesn't join in my Kia joy.

L.V. and I have decided not to tell Alice about the weapon he is going to attempt to procure, and I *do* manage to keep that secret. We are all famished (when did they stop serving real meals on airplanes?) so I ease the McKia into a restaurant parking lot just up the street from Europe Cars-for-Hire. We head inside the ultramodern glass-and-steel building and order up some traditional old Scottish fare: haggis, neeps, and tatties (not really—we settle for a basket of soggy French fries and something resembling a hot dog). I am kind of disturbed by L.V.'s insistence that he get us some protection, and I wonder if he really will return from the dark streets of Inverness with the condoms—shut up Woody, Jesus!—gun.

"There are only two choices for opposing sides: force or reason. Why do they always seem to choose force?" thinks the OSB. "All force has ever done is inspire more force and more anger, never any lasting and true peace. Just ask the Vee-Nung. Well, you can't, since sadly, the aforementioned organisms no longer exist. The dominant species is the dominant species because of the dominant weapons created by their dominant brains: that is, until these top-of-the-food-chain geniuses self-destruct. Weapons always provide the initial advantage, but then they become the genie that can't be put back in the bottle. No principal life form has ever been able to avoid this. The ruling class on any planet always seems to fall into the same trap. And once they are in power, they think it's their right to do whatever they want and take whatever they desire from their world and expect not to have a balancing of the books, a reckoning, an equilibrium to be reached at some point. And the longer they insist on their "free lunch," the more dramatic and painful the counterbalance. The greater the yin, the greater the yang."

The OSB is just riffing right now because, with the

whole Universe to watch over, it sometimes helps to orga-
nize your thoughts.

"How is it that the ascendant class of a world like
Earth never seems to understand that their planet is alive
and made of the same stuff they are? If I weren't perfect,
I'd be pissed off!"

We wedge ourselves back into the mighty, midget motorcar,
accompanied by our queasy hot-dog-filled stomachs. I think
that haggis might have been the better choice for lunch. I mean, tradi-
tionally, the Scottish know how to whip up this meal of sheep entrails
and other minced internal organs boiled inside the animal's stomach
bag, yes? Yummy!

I gun the Scottish hamster, we jump onto the A82, and we're on
our way as we settle back for the three-hour-plus drive through some

magnificently craggy, stunningly brutal, and highly alien countryside. We are all exhausted and finally both Alice and Lexington Vargas fall asleep. Unfortunately so do I, which is not a particularly good move if you're the actual driver of the vehicle. Thank God for those yellow bumpy things between the lanes, because the rhythmic *thump, thump, thump* wakes me up every time. Yep, I fall asleep more than once. You try flying from L.A. to Glasgow while keeping an eye open for the possible Angel of Death. It's a little taxing on the system, to put it mildly. At least I'm not dialing or texting. And we do make it to Inverness in one piece.

As Alice and I take the stairs up to the law offices of McGivney, McGivney, and McGivney, Lexington Vargas quietly slips away from this civilized quarter and out into a world that only he knows how to navigate. When Alice notices he's missing, I tell her he's gone to get "the lay of the land," and when she asks me what I mean by that, I say I don't know; it's all he told me. That he'll be back in a while. She frowns and sighs but accepts it as some "L.V. thing" and asks no more questions. We get down to the business of her inheritance once we are introduced and settled.

After some extremely polite document-signing at McGivney, McGivney, and McGivney, as well as several increasingly embarrassing "I'm sorry, could you repeat that, please?" from us because of our untrained ear and the younger McGivney's heavy Highland brogue, we get directions to 5 Holm Dell Park, Alice's new house. And just like that, she's a homeowner. It took me a lot more blood, sweat, and tears of torment dubbing crap movies like the staggeringly awful *Ghost Banana Hitman* to get *my* house, and even then it was snatched away from me as suddenly as if I were the proverbial Job. But I'm happy for Alice, and she is giddy with the reality of what, up until now, has appeared to be something of an abstract lark, a secondary reason to come to this cold, beautiful, and forbidding place.

Alice's "vow of poverty" notwithstanding, I pay her modest lawyer's bill with my ass-helmet of a credit card and wonder why it isn't bursting into flames as Miss McGivney (yep, the secretary's in the family, too) hands it back to me after she's run it. Unbelievably, the transaction goes through with no red flags, no over-the-limit messages, and no fraud early warnings screaming at her to call the cops! I momentarily wonder if Arthur's hand is in this deception and if, like an irresponsible parent, he/she is encouraging me to live beyond my means.

Brand-spanking-new house keys in hand, we reboard the Kia and wait for L.V., who eventually joins us and gives me the curt nod that any down-with-it, hardcore homeboy like me understands to mean, "I got the goods, man. Let's blow this taco stand." Alice regards him but says nothing.

I somehow manage to maneuver the subcompact sedan through the maze of streets that eventually lead us to 5 Holm Dell Park. The house is a charming (yes, I said "charming," which is not a word I would normally use, but it leaps out at me as we enter this place), fairly old (and by that I mean "ancient" in American terms), two-bedroom ("Hey, looks like one of us will be sleeping on the couch again"), quite cozy (okay, tiny) cottage (or "house," but it has the general appearance of something you would call a "cottage") backed up against trees that I believe should be referred to as a "wood" in this part of the world if I'm not confusing the Scottish with the English (which I understand is a *huge* friggin' faux pas). We wander through the interior of Alice's new digs, the three of us, in a kind of jet-lagged daze. Merikh is momentarily forgotten, phone calls to Arthur on the back burner, along with whatever greater purpose may have brought us here. We are all sleep-deprived and completely enervated, and I feel like we're adolescents left alone in the house with Mom and Dad gone off to Miami for the weekend.

The place is fully furnished in the eminently timeless "old grandma" style, with daring hints of Highland tchotchkes in the many nooks and crannies. It's appealingly quaint, but the whole place smells musty and needs a good cleaning as well as a serious airing-out. No one's going to do that right now, so Alice lights the gas fire in the living room—her living room—as we all huddle into the warmth and just stare through the blue-yellow flames, amazed that we have actually made this journey together.

"What do we do now?" asks Alice.

"Wait?" suggests L.V.

"For what?" Alice again.

No one replies, because no one has an answer for that.

There is an unexpressed, shared feeling that something will happen here: that we have somehow been summoned to this rough-hewn place, but none of us has even an inkling as to what that might be. We are the blind sheep looking for our shepherd.

What we have opened ourselves up to by coming here is both exhilarating and daunting. It's a very scary feeling. Is it a waste of time, or something truly transformative? Again, no clue. We will have to wait and see. The brief phone calls with Arthur still do not sit well in the rational areas of my brain. Were they something real and a part of this universe we're living in, or were they just our fertile imaginations struggling to create meaning in our pointless lives? I think we are either three very deluded fuckers, or we are all Moses. Or is there something in between that I'm missing?

"We probably should get some sleep," I say. It's only four in the afternoon but my scratchy eyeballs are screaming at me to close their eyelids and give them a break. I don't even want to try to figure out what time it is back home.

There are nods of assent, but nobody moves. We feel like we're all alone on this Earth right now. No one (we hope) knows we're here, and the "why" is so big that it can't fit in this small room with us right now. So none of us is willing to further broach that subject.

"Well, I for one am not coming all this way to miss out on a possible Loch Ness Monster sighting," I say, tempering the comment with a chuckle. But, secretly, I mean it. Or at least the kid in me does.

Alice laughs.

"Maybe that's the whole point of this journey. To fulfill your childhood fantasy."

She smiles at me.

"What's a Lock whatever-you-said monster?" asks L.V.

"Loch Ness Monster."

"Lock-nuts monster?"

"You've never heard of the Loch Ness Monster?" I ask incredulously.

"I don't know what you're saying," is his staggeringly uninformed (to me) reply.

"Dude! It's the most famous monster in the world!" I assure him.

"Frankenstein is the most famous monster in the world," he answers deadpan.

"I mean *real* monster," I reply, and I may be pushing the envelope on the meaning of the term "real" here.

"What is that? Some white-boy folklore thing?" he asks with a smirk.

"We are going out on the Loch tomorrow, and five bucks says

you will see for yourself whether it's folklore or not," I challenge him, pretty sure it's a bet I'll lose.

"What?" laughs Alice. "That's crazy."

"I'll have to take your word for it," answers Lexington Vargas. "I'm not a water guy. You know how I'm not an airplane guy? Well, I'm twice as much not a boat guy."

"I don't think my hands could deal with the pain," I tell him as he scowls at me amiably.

After some rooting-around in the kitchen, I make my way back to the fireplace gathering with three fairly clean but water-spotted glasses and a bottle of newly breached port.

"What the heck is 'port,' anyway?" I ask, sitting down on the hearth and filling the tumblers. It's blood-red and seems to have more body and weight than wine as it flows from the thick neck of the bottle.

"I don't know if either of you is up for a nightcap, but I'm pretty certain I could use one," I say, smiling, as I raise my glass in a toast.

Lexington Vargas picks his glass up and tips it to mine with a hail-fellow-well-met nod of his sizeable head. Alice hesitates, and then with a shrug joins the group. We clink in salute to whatever is to come.

"I don't know what's going to happen or if anything is, but whatever is coming down the pike, I hope it comes soon because I'm running out of paid vacation days and my credit card is in traction," I announce and wish I hadn't. Both Alice and L.V. seem disappointed with my toast. So I say what I meant to say in the first place.

"You both have become my friends, and I couldn't imagine going on this wild ride with anyone else. Here's to a positive outcome!" I say, not knowing of what I speak.

"I love you," I toast to them both but dare not look at Alice as I utter these heartfelt words disguised as bonhomie. We tap our glasses and down the slightly cherry-cough-syrup-flavored and exceedingly sweet salute.

"It tastes like communion wine," says Alice. "But not as good." She smiles as the warmth envelops her tired frame.

"The blood of our Lord Jesus Christ, which was shed for you, preserve your soul and body unto everlasting life," I say from the dark recesses of my memory.

Alice gives me a quick, sharp look.

"Just reciting a little liturgy from a long time ago," I say. So many communions with my mother that I never understood and that were never explained to the young boy I was. Nor did I seek any explanation once I became a man. Who's to blame? The teacher or the young scholar?

Her look turns softer as she regards me, understanding that I mean no offense to her years under the veil. I think at this point she feels as lost as I do.

We drain our glasses and I refill them. We are all beyond tired but are reluctant to leave one another's company. We are three vagabond orphans with no ties to home. There is nothing we pine for that would cause us to wish we were anywhere but where we are right now. And I can't think of any other people I would rather be sitting by the fire with than Alice and Lexington Vargas. I have a suspicion that both of them share my view.

We bed down eventually, exhausted, excited, and a little afraid. Sleep comes. And I dream. I dream of the Loch Ness Monster. He is male and carries a gift in his dark blood.

Someone else has found his way to 5 Holm Dell Park. A raw wind blows off the wintry lake and pushes its way into this old town, as a figure stands motionless, across from the darkened house. He feels no cold. No enmity. No indecision. He is merely watching. More has been revealed to him, the one they know as Merikh, and although he is unsure of when or where or even what the outcome may be, he understands that he may soon have to be ready.

I surface slowly from my dream with an uneasy feeling. It's still night, and in my jet lag I have no idea what time it is, but I am heavy with an emotion I can't quite name. It feels like guilt and depression, but for the life of me I can't figure out why I'm feeling this. I haven't had a dream about the Loch Ness Monster since I was a boy and they always used to excite me, leave me breathless. Now I just feel sad. I turn over in the creaky, complaining bed and try to shake the sensation.

Since meeting Alice and getting involved in whatever the hell this journey is, my spirits have been pretty high. Considering where they were, it's been a godsend. Okay, that's an odd choice of words . . . considering. My eyes are gradually adjusting to the lightless bedroom and I think about getting up to pee. Holy shit! Somebody's in my room. I can see a dark form standing in the corner just away from the door. I'm freaking. It's a ghost! Crap! These old British houses are crawling with 'em. Some crazy old lady who murdered the hapless family that lived here centuries ago, then tucked them all into bed and read stories to the dead children until they found her days later, insane, frothing at the mouth and eating the bloody flesh off her own fingers. She was publicly beheaded in the town square and now the ghost of her body is looking for the ghost of her severed head that was probably stuck on a pike in the center of the village . . . stop, stop, STOP!!! This is not helping. Jesus, it just moved! It's really not a coat or a shadow or something. I want to call out for Lexington Vargas to come and save me but that will only reveal my location to the wraith, and if I open my mouth to scream the ghost will enter my body through that offending orifice and steal my soul. I read that somewhere in *Tales from the Crypt* when I was an impressionable dickweed. Hoping it is benevolent and only looking for its head, I slooowly reach up and fumble, trying to locate the switch through the ruffles of the Grandma-designed bedside lamp. I find it and the room explodes with light.

"Alice?" I croak in surprise.

She is standing in the corner shivering, wearing a way-too-thin-for-this-climate nightdress. Her eyes grow owl-big as they adjust to the sudden intrusion of light.

"I don't know why I'm here," she says, and she seems so fragile.

I'm in shock. I was more prepared for the headless ghost of the crazy lady. Alice is *totally* unexpected. I push the covers back and sit up on the edge of the bed, looking for some kind of answer for her. I say softly,

"Well . . . you're here to claim your inheritance and because we believe we were somehow . . . called here."

"No. I mean, I don't know why I'm here in your room," is her answer. My heart is beating so loud that I'm sure she can hear it. She moves to me and I rise to take her willowy frame in my arms. She buries her face in my "Loch Ness Lives" T-shirt (which has a very snappy drawing of my favorite monster beneath the caption) that I'm wearing for the occasion. The occasion of being at Loch Ness, I mean, not the occasion of Alice appearing unannounced in my room.

"Can you just hold me?" she asks.

"Here?" I'm cold now, too.

"In bed," are the words she says to me. I step aside and let her enter Woody's playground, but Woody will be a good boy, hang tough, mind his fucking manners, and not screw this moment up.

I climb in after her and she snuggles into me for warmth and comfort, without the "modesty sheet," as I pull the thick covers over both of us.

My heart is a hammer in my chest. I have to say it. I can't stop myself as Woody steps up to the podium, taps the microphone, and says "Hello? Is this thing on?" I take a deep breath and inhale her. She is beautiful. I tell her from my soul:

"I want you."

"I know," she says.

That pregnant phrase hangs in the chilly, still night air.

"Thank you for not pushing me," she adds and kisses me on the cheek. Woody asks why the cheek again. "We do have other parts of our anatomy that are smooch-worthy, y'know."

I ignore him and hold this incredible human being close to me until her steady, rhythmic breathing tells me she is asleep.

We don't know it, but this is the last restful night we will ever spend together.

When morning breaks, chill and bright, Merikh is standing on the shore of the great Loch, communing. His long sleek hair trails behind him in the wind like some ritual headdress as spirit voices come and go through the ether and across the surface of the dark and ancient water.

Now he understands why he is here.

I blast through the front door of 5 Holm Dell Park at a serious clip, head for the much needed bathroom, and enter without knocking, thinking Alice is still asleep in my bed just as I left her more than an hour ago. Lexington Vargas, God bless him, has taken the couch again even though, as I see while I sprint by, he is almost bent double, trying to fit his full frame on the small country sofa. I have had a staggeringly productive morning on my walk around this town, but apparently the Scots don't believe in public bathrooms, or at least I couldn't find any on my travels and had to hold it all the way back home. Woody is howling as I burst into the "privy" (the local term) just as Alice is stepping out of her bath. She gasps in surprise and clutches the towel to her breasts as the door swings open and I roar in.

"Oh, shit! Sorry. Oh my God!" I can't believe she's standing there naked. I back out, pulling the door shut with more apologies and professions of ignorance and "What an idiot I am for not knocking, sorry, sorry. I thought you were still asleep . . ."

She smiles warmly as I slam it into reverse.

"It's okay, Tio," she says through the closing door, and I lean against the outside wall struggling to catch my breath, such is the intensity of the sight I just stumbled in on.

Her face rosy and flushed from the heat of the bath, the tips of her hair wet at her slender neck, her skin dripping and unblemished, and a large, brilliantly executed half-sleeve tattoo that is totally unexpected. So surprising is the ink on her right arm that it burns itself into my brain as I walk out to the kitchen trying to push the image of her naked body from my reptile brain. The symbols on her skin were both beautiful and bleak. Complex and intertwined images that seemed to be centered around a death's-head skull with a cross on its forehead. She fills my senses. All of her. All of me. But first I *must* pee! I make my way out to the back garden so I can do a little watering, which has now become exceedingly difficult because Woody also caught sight of the stunning and naked Alice-of-the-Cloth and he is refusing to go flaccid, the little bastard. The male of the species simply cannot take a whiz with an erection. So I hang outside with my great Loch Ness news and wait for the Woodman to relax his crack so I can take a leak. Eventually he does and I do. I wait for Alice, with trepidation, in the kitchen.

She finally strolls out in a robe and a smile. I am all apologies again as I diligently brew tea, but she hugs me from behind and whispers her okay.

One step closer.

"I like your tattoo," I say, much more casually than I feel.

"It's from my wilder, younger days," she explains.

"It's beautiful," I reply and want to add more but don't dare, so close am I to mentally going AWOL when I rerun the vision of her, naked, flushed, and branded in her rebellious youth.

"I'm not the only sister with a tattoo, believe it or not," she continues. "We don't all come from devoted, God-fearing households. A lot of us are damaged goods looking for personal healing, too."

"I get that," is all I will allow myself, even though I want to say, "Please can I see you naked again? I'll pay ya!" but even Woody isn't that stupid. I obviously need to change the subject before he makes me say something we'll both regret, so I turn to her and begin to run off at the mouth about my amazing morning. I tell her of the old guy I met who said he has a boat and will take us out on the Loch this afternoon for free!!! AND he says he knows where Nessie hunts! Okay, maybe some wily local is just pranking me, but I want to have the chance to be on the great Loch Ness. I'm just like all those kids who looked up at the moon when they were little and wished they could go there and then Neil Armstrong grew up and did it. Well, I am the Neil Armstrong of Loch Ness, mofo, so get used to it. Of course I say none of this to Alice, mainly because she's begun to giggle.

"Stop it, I'm serious," I try, but it doesn't help and I actually begin to laugh, too. "He said we should meet him at the little jetty just south of Urquhart castle at four this afternoon. It's a small boat with room for no more than two passengers, which is perfect, right?"

"You're a nut," is all Alice says to me. And I like it when she calls me a nut like that. This journey has been good for both of us and has eased some of the pain we have both left behind.

Lexington Vargas hears none of this, as he is busy with the snoring farm noises again. The guy could sleep though an earthquake.

And an earthquake it is.

The fracture in the world that is known as the Great Glen Fault, which runs directly under Loch Ness, decides to make itself known at 10:33 in the morning, and Alice's new home starts to shake for the first time since 1901.

"Is that an earthquake?" asks Alice in alarm.

We grab hold of each other and the kitchen counter as teacups slosh their contents out over our hands.

"Ow!" I yell in pain as the hot brew scalds my fingers.

"What the heck's goin' on?" Lexington Vargas shouts in his morning voice from the sofa. I guess he *doesn't* sleep through earthquakes.

"I think it's an earthquake," I yell to him. I thought we escaped this type of natural disaster when we left L.A.

It lasts for an interminable thirty seconds, and when the house stops rolling, the world is still. Until every parked car's alarm begins bleating and honking like a good, angry day in New York City.

I run outside to shut the McKia's wimpy horn up as, unknown to us, sightseeing cruise boats and pleasure craft are leaving the Loch and heading for the safety of their respective berths. Today's outings are cancelled until the water's surface calms itself and any danger of rockslides is assessed. Local radio and TV stations announce the closure of the Loch, but we are aware of none of it.

L.V. is on his feet and helping Alice straighten lamps, sweep up broken china, and mop up spilled tea as I enter and happen to glance over at his sofa/bed. Sticking out in plain sight from under his pillow (?) is the very ugly, very dangerous-looking revolver that he has, in his street wisdom, seen fit to procure. The menacing thing looks like it was made in someone's backyard shed. Even to my untrained eye it appears to be a semi-professional piece of gunsmithing; it is, I would imagine, what they call a "Saturday-night special."

"He sleeps with it under his pillow?" I ask myself silently, rhetorically, and incredulously. Isn't that just something they do in old gangster movies? Real people don't actually put loaded weapons under their pillows, right? He could shoot his own ear off. Or one of us in the next room. These interior walls look solid enough, but who knows?

I silently grab his attention as Alice continues to clean, and give him the old "head-jerk toward the sofa" gesture with the old "What the fuck?" look on my face until he notices the old "gun under the pillow" thing.

He grimaces and heads into the living room to make the old "conceal the dangerous fricking gun from the little woman" move.

I make a mental note to tell him to stash it somewhere else when I get the chance. I still can't figure out how he managed to get his hands on a weapon in the first place. Pretty savvy in the old "ways of the street" is Lexington Vargas. But then, I bet he doesn't know how to do the old "rent-the-Kia-with-the-over-the-limit-credit-card" thing, so I guess we're a well-matched pair.

Loch Ness is now, and for the first time in a long while, completely free of all water traffic. Unaware of this, I'm looking forward to our trip on the legendary lake of my prepubescent fantasy.

Throughout the day, and without a word to one another about why we are even doing it, we take turns stepping outside and staring up at the heavy, gray sky. I think we're looking for a sign—but a sign in the old biblical sense, which is crazy because this whole thing has hardly followed regulation biblical procedure. At least I don't believe so, although I've never actually *read* the Bible. Maybe it's time I did. I need to do *something* with these hours until we hit the mighty Loch, so I head on into the house and start rummaging around for a Bible. A home like this has to have a Bible.

In my search I open a cupboard and see a few framed pictures stacked on a shelf. A couple of them reveal an older woman with soft eyes and a good smile. There's about a half dozen lovingly framed photos of two dogs, who look like Toto's brothers from another mother, as they both journey through their lives from puppyhood to old age.

A sad memory of Murray, who never got to grow old with me, surfaces. My lungs suddenly reach for oxygen as though the air has thinned, but I choose not to succumb and instead pick up a photo of an older couple. The woman is the kind face from the first shot, and with her is an old man in fishing gear, his features mostly obscured by a long billed cap, sunglasses, and a thick white beard. Someone from McGivney, McGivney, and McGivney must have shelved them prior to our arrival, thinking perhaps that photos of complete strangers all over the house might weird us out. It felt like there was something missing, and now I know what that something is. It's a family house without family photos. I close the cupboard door and see a frame I've missed, lying facedown on the floor. It must have fallen in the earthquake. Another photograph of the deceased and beneficent couple. It's a good shot of the two of them, and they both look content in a way I think I have never experienced. I like the shot, so I walk it out into the living room and set it on a side table. It feels like it belongs there.

I'm waiting anxiously for the afternoon to roll around, thoughts of my beloved monster, Nessie, running round and about my inner twelve-year-old. Back on the Bible hunt, I eventually locate one and begin reading it for the first time in my life. The verses I scan conjure up visions of an Old Testament God who is remote, harsh, unforgiving, and demanding. Sounds like my mother.

I flip to the New Testament, where I believe there is a kinder, gentler God, and I am trying to reconcile the teachings of Jesus with the very human and flippant attitude that "Arthur" displayed on the phone. I guess humor was not a big prerequisite in the minds of the Gospel writers, because whether I like it or not, Arthur does have a rather incongruous and off-putting sense of humor. Jesus, in this biography called the New Testament, seems very loving and pure-natured (except for the bit where he throws a wobbly in the temple), and he exhorts us all to follow his example, so why did Arthur seem so, well, odd? And with all the talk of peace and love and treating thy neighbor as thyself, why does he/she create something as naturally brutal as the Australian hunting wasp, which lays its eggs on a spider's abdomen so that when they are born, the little hatchlings can eat their way into their living host, causing considerable distress and, eventually, considerable death to the spider? I guess that's filed under "Shit happens." I don't know. I never was good at *reconciling*.

I think I should have done a bit more biblical research before we left on this trip, but then I realize that we have our resident expert, the lovely and beguiling Alice of the Good Book, who might be able to answer some questions for me, although, since the death of her friend Genevieve, she has seemed to be slightly spiritually adrift. And I think Arthur is done playing chess and that we are now officially on our own with this one, boys and girls, whatever *it* is.

"Something is coming," says Merikh to the one he is guiding along the path less traveled. It is an unusual journey for both of them.

"What is it?" asks the other.

"I'm not sure," Merikh answers.

"Will it be good or bad?"

"There is no good *or* bad. There is only both: good *and* bad together," says Merikh.

"I see," says the other, but Merikh doubts that.

"The ones who call themselves 'zhongguo ren,' and who the world know as the Chinese, have a symbol for 'crisis' that is actually *two* symbols: Danger and Opportunity, which is quite correct."

"I'm not sure I follow you," replies the other.

"It doesn't matter," says Merikh. He is done conversing and must now watch and wait for his moment.

Alice and I leave the severely aquaphobic Lexington Vargas to his own devices and motor to the meeting place by the legendary Urquhart Castle. I am beyond excited, Alice not so much, but she seems happy to be out in the fresh, biting air. There really *is* a newly constructed oak jetty by the castle where the old guy said it would be, so I have high hopes that the rest of his spiel will be equally on the money. Yes, I'm referring to an actual encounter with the great beast of the Loch. Alice can't even keep a straight face when I bring it up. But as we stand on the small wooden pier in the brisk breeze, I say to her that she believes in certain things I find fanciful, so why shouldn't I believe in the possibility of a Loch Ness Monster?

"What exactly are you referring to?" she answers with mild amusement.

"Well," I waffle, "There are some things in the Bible that stretch the credulity of the reader, if I may be blunt." I could be skating on thin ice here, so I keep my tone light—even though I think I may have a pretty good argument.

"Are you actually comparing stories of this Loch Ness Monster to the Word of God?" she answers, accompanied by the very annoying "WTF" look.

"Er . . . possibly?" I try. "At least we have *photos!*"

"That's like me saying I have proof of God's existence because there's a photograph of what looks like the face of Jesus on a burned taco shell," she says, dive-bombing my "pretty good argument" and strafing the hell out of it. Alice laughs, and she sounds like a girl making fun of a boy at school who maybe she likes just a little.

This is the last time I will ever hear her laugh. I don't know this, of course, but in retrospect I will wish I had known. I would have savored it and locked it safely within my memory for the rest of my life.

We are distracted from our debate by the sound of an approaching engine. The two of us turn to see a small fishing boat headed our way. At the helm is the old guy I met earlier this morning. Yes! My twelve-year-old claps his hands with glee, jumps up and down, and does a white-boy butt-dance of joy and excitement. The grown-up me says, "Okay, here's our guy."

"Well, well. Off we go, I guess," replies Doubting Alice.

As we climb aboard the compact but apparently well-loved vessel, I introduce Alice to the old man, who announces that we should call him "Skipper." It's a good name and it suits him. He has an old salt's lined, rough-hewn face that seems to echo the surrounding Highlands in its furrows, contours, and age.

"You look a lot like your grandmother, lass," says the Skipper to Alice as we settle in.

"You knew my father's mother?" she asks in surprise.

The Skipper smiles fondly as he turns the small craft out into deeper water.

"I did," he answers. "Quite well."

The boat jostles and bounces on the rough surface.

"You're as bonnie and beautiful as she was in her youth," he offers.

"What a sweet thing to say," says Alice. Then she hesitates.

"Did you know my father at all? Devin Young?"

The water is calmer now that we are farther out into the Loch. I'm amazed at the serendipity of this meeting, but I'm also scanning the renowned lake for any signs of a mythical aquatic beast. Any ruffles on the surface that don't resemble the natural wave patterns. I am walking on the moon, yessir. Me and Neil!

"I did know Devin," answers the Skipper.

That seems to be the end of the conversation, as no one is picking up the ball. It appears that Alice doesn't really want to know any more and the Skipper is reluctant to continue. I guess we had similar fathers in some ways, Alice and I.

"It's pretty crazy that you knew Alice's family," I tell him.

"Inverness is a wee town, really. We're all in and out of each other's business fairly regularly," acknowledges the Skipper with a chuckle.

I scan the horizon of the twenty-one-square-mile body of very famous water.

"Wow, it seems like we're the only ones out here. How come? I don't see anybody else driving a boat," I say, sounding very un-nautical even to myself.

"I think perhaps you're right, lad," the Skipper answers, not really answering.

We chug on around the headlands in silence and I finally get to see for myself how impressive this glacially scoured ten-thousand-year-old lake really is, its size aided and abetted by the fault line it sits directly over. The old sailor seems to know where he's headed and I am really, really happy about that. Although it hasn't been officially stated since I was a boy, I do still believe there is a creature living here in these cold, deep waters, and I don't mean a fish. I wobble to a standing position and yell at the top of my lungs, "NESSIE!!!" It bounces and reverberates off the surrounding crags. My awestruck grin is like that of a child who's hearing his own echo for the first time.

"I wouldn't do that, son," cautions the Skipper.

"Oh, okay, sorry." I sit back down, chastised by the old mariner and smirked at by the young proselyte.

"We don't want to frighten the old girl away," he continues, and I think I catch a covert and conspiratorial wink to Alice.

Let them laugh. They laughed at Columbus, too. I man the gunwale and scan the waters, knowing full well that the odds of a chance meeting are slim to nonexistent, even if I *am* one of the faithful believers. There are people (Charlotte, my ex, called them "fucking nutjobs") who have dedicated their whole lives to catching a glimpse of the acclaimed and elusive creature of the Loch and still come up empty-handed. But for me, just walking on the moon like this is joy and distraction enough from whatever has called us here. For whatever unknown purpose. I definitely needed the break. We cruise on past partially sunken logs, dead fish, and other detritus that could conceivably, through serious wishful thinking, be mistaken for a fabled leviathan. The journey is certainly taking its time, as the old vessel toots along at a mild meander. I am starting to wonder, "Where is this hotspot?" Suddenly I see a disturbance in the water that looks like no wave action I am familiar with. "No way," I think to myself. "I just saw something," I say out loud.

Everyone is alert, no matter his or her level of belief in the disrespected and highly maligned Loch denizen.

We crane our necks instinctively.

"Come on," admonishes Alice. "Really?" and there is actual disbelief in her tone. Oh ye of little faith.

The sunless water has folded in on itself and back-filled over what

I thought I might have seen. The Skipper kills the engine. I take note of this. I'm pretty sure they only stop the prop so as not to scare away any local aquatic life, yes, no, maybe?

We are all standing as the boat jostles us slightly but not uncomfortably. With the motor silenced, the air is suddenly still.

"Of course you're going to *think* you see a shape of some sort." Is Alice trying to pop my balloon? I am staring at a point twenty yards away and to the right of the gently bobbing craft. I don't blink. I hold my breath. I think maybe my heart has stopped. No, it's thumping like a jackrabbit who's being chased by a coyote. No one is moving. Time stands still for a kid from the San Fernando Valley as he bobs like a cork on the great Loch Ness here in the Scottish Highlands. All is quiet. All is still.

Then a dark flipper flashes quickly amidst the frothy wake it causes and is gone.

"Shit!! Did you see that?" I am beside myself. "That was too big to be an otter, right?"

"I didn't see anything," replies Alice the wet blanket.

"Seriously? You didn't just see that thing like a dorsal fin or whatever it was?" I shout in my excitement, "Damn, I wish I'd brought my cell phone," I think out loud, as crappy as the camera on it is. Again there is still water. I am about to turn to the Skipper for some kind of confirmation on the object I thought I saw when, Jesus help me, a long serpentine neck pokes itself up, through and out of the surface of the lake as the snakelike head opens its jaws to yawn or breathe or whatever it is this astonishing creature does. Wet, slick, smooth-skinned. Dark gray to black in hue with subtle mottlings of greens and lighter grays. Its neck is muscular and as thick as a small redwood but with the sinuous grace of a boa constrictor. Its eye is the color of midnight with a tiny star burning in its depths. It's everything I ever imagined it would be, this beast. Large, reptilian and super-cool. I shriek out loud like a little girl at a boy-band concert as the neck and head sink back into the gloomy depths, leaving expanding ripples that cannot be denied. They cannot!! I look at Alice, because there's no way she missed *that!* She is wearing an expression of absolute wonder on her face and is smiling a beatific smile. She looks even more entranced than I *feel*.

"My God," she whispers to herself. She isn't moving, still staring at the point where the creature broke the surface. There is an odd, silver light reflecting in her eyes and I don't understand the source. But right now I don't have time to consider it because my heart is still hammering in my breast. I am shivering but not from the cold.

And then it launches.

I turn again to the area where Alice's eyes are still fixed, and to my absolute rapture, an enormous, ancient, mottled, and mythical creature the size of a frigging city bus, with the same, previously and reverently viewed long snakelike neck and head, breaches out of the coal-black, icy waters of Loch Ness, with the approximate snarl of a tiger. It is the fucking Loch fucking Ness fucking Monster! I scream in surprise, joy, wonder, astonishment, and vindication.

"Skipper, you're seeing this, yes?" I need confirmation that I'm not just moonstruck. It feels as though I could be. I'm dizzy, faint, and hyperventilating.

"It's not meant for me," is the strange reply from the old mariner.

The brute has turned and is now heading toward our waaay-too-small craft. Alice moans, low, rasping. It's a feline growl of warning or pain from her very soul.

"No." She utters the one word with so much anguish in her voice that I turn to her. Tears are running from her eyes and she is trembling.

"Don't worry. I don't think it means to hurt us," I tell her, although now I'm not a hundred percent certain of that myself.

"Are we okay?" I ask the Skipper, turning back to this magnificent, frightful, and rapidly advancing water-dragon.

"I don't believe so," he answers. Not what I really wanted to hear.

Alice is muttering phrases and I can catch only fragments. "You can't ask this of me . . . Please, no."

It makes no sense to me, but there is a childhood fantasy come to bright, shining, and vibrant life towering over me right at this moment and I am starting to believe it means us harm, so I am a little preoccupied.

The beast smells dank and wet as its mouth opens to reveal rows of needle-like tooth cones. But this is not an attack. Instead it dives under our craft, the black water covering it and healing the tear in the surface of the inland sea, leaving it as though a great and fabled creature has not just rent the barrier.

"We should probably get out of here," I strongly suggest, and I think I'm going into some form of shock as the Skipper guns the engine. I drop into a sitting position on the floor of the vessel and wipe at my nose, which feels wet and is running from all the excitement. What comes away on the back of my hand is blood. I hear Alice weeping and still whispering, "No, no. I will not be a part of this . . ." She is distraught and crying beyond ordinary fear. She is bleeding profusely from her nose as well, and still looking out at the water although the great beast is long gone. I wrap my arm around her as we turn tail and run, but she pushes me away like a petulant child might. We are having two very different experiences out here on the Loch, I think. Blood flows, my mind reels, the small vessel purrs, and the Skipper remains silent. I exist in a dream as I begin to feel light-headed, seated on the floor of the boat amid Alice's crying and moaning, "No, no this can't be happening. God help me. God help me. God help me." She repeats it over and over as though it were a liturgy while I quietly lose consciousness on the decking of the small ark.

The OSB thinks about putting one more teeny, tiny call in to the three apostles but this is not the time, and the OSB is really starting to think He/She has overstepped His/Her self-imposed boundaries already regarding omnipotent interference in this whole scenario. It must go how it must go, or there is no reason for any of this. And by "any of this" the OSB means more than one small species on one floating rock could even <u>begin</u> to imagine. The OSB is strengthened in the understanding that life is resilient and will eventually do what it must for its own survival, although the goddamned Vee-Nung certainly disproved that thesis, thank you very effing much!

No more is said as the Skipper unloads his shell-shocked cargo back at the Urquhart castle jetty. I have peppered him with questions once I returned to the land of the conscious, but he has answered me only vaguely. It seems he has no more idea what happened out there on the water than I do. I am at a complete loss as to Alice's reaction and she is refusing or unable to respond. She appears to be in some kind of stupor and is even having trouble maintaining her balance. My urgent questions, "Are you okay? What's wrong?" remain unanswered.

So I watch as the little boat with the odd name disappears into the dusk, and I guide Alice back to the car. Her face is smeared with her own blood, as I assume my face is with mine. What the hell happened out there?

Merikh is back watching 5 Holm Dell Park as the cold night rolls in. He understands much more now. And he is waiting for his role to begin in whatever is to come. But someone is approaching, and he turns to face the advancing figure. Anger and fear color the features of the one who draws near, but he is receptive, too. Merikh begins to explain as much as he can. As much as he comprehends.

I carry Alice into the house calling out for Lexington Vargas, but he appears to have gone missing. I lay her on her bed. By now she is in a swoon or asleep or somewhere in between. I carefully sponge the dried blood from her face and then make my way into the bathroom to do the same for myself. In the mirror I see my reflection. My nose, mouth, and chin are smeared with my own dark, desiccated gore; my skin is whiter than I've ever known it to be, and my eyes are pinpoints of light. I hardly recognize myself. If it weren't for the bat-ears I'd wonder who the hell this *was* looking back at me. To my uncommon reflection I say out loud, "You saw the Loch Ness Monster today, you lucky friggin' bastard! Your life will never be the same." I don't know the truth I speak. I am at this moment thinking that this whole weird trip, the phone calls with Arthur, the three books, Alice and Lexington Vargas and me meeting up, all of it, was just so I could have this day and see the creature of my boyhood dreams, in real and resplendent life. But something in the "back room" tells me that there's possibly a little more to it than that. It is enough for me right now, though. I'm ready to pack up and get back to America so I can brag to Doug about it. How limited and narrow my thinking is at this point.

I brew strong tea out in the kitchen and take two cups back into Alice's bedroom.

She is awake. Her eyes look like mine do. Bright. Almost too bright.

"Can you talk yet?" I try.

She nods an assent but says nothing as she takes the steaming cup from me and sips at it tentatively.

"This has been an unbelievable day," I say after a long moment. Understatement of all understatements.

She pulls the comforter up from the bottom of the bed and looks every bit like a little girl getting ready to have Dad read her a bedtime story as she tucks herself in. But there is no bedtime story. Still trembling, she props herself up on the pillows.

"Are you cold?" I ask. She shakes her head, no.

"I think we should talk about what happened out there today."

She nods her agreement once more but still does not speak. She looks so vulnerable lying there, her delicate and peaked face peering out from the bedding.

"I love you." The words leap out of me unexpectedly and catch me by surprise more than I imagine they do her. They are spoken almost breathlessly, so charged with emotion and longing are they. I've never said them to another human being before, except to my sweet Josie, and then only as she lay dying. I never spoke them to my ex, even in our most passionate moments. But I mean them now as though my life depended on it.

"I understand," is all she says.

"What do you understand?"

"That you're in love with me."

"What does that mean to you?"

"That God has bound you to me for some reason. And now I think I know what that reason is."

"God didn't make me fall in love with you. *You* made me fall in love with you."

"Did you not hear what she said out on the lake?"

"What who said? The monster?"

"What are you talking about?"

"What are *you* talking about?"

I'm completely lost, and what I thought was an impulsive and romantic statement has now taken a severe left turn.

"The figure standing on the water," Alice says with a quiver in her voice.

"I don't think we're talking about the same thing here. *I* saw the Loch Ness Monster. What did *you* see?" And as the words leave my mouth they sound to me like bad dialog from a 1950s horror movie. You just can't say the words "I saw the Loch Ness Monster" and not sound like you're a few fries short of a Happy Meal.

"Are you joking? How can you joke like that?"

"I saw it. And so did the Skipper, I think. Are you telling me you didn't see it?" I am suddenly swimming in a very surrealistic sea.

"I saw a woman standing on the water. And she told me why we were called here. That we were chosen."

My only reference to someone "standing" on water is Jesus. And maybe Daffy Duck before he realizes it's actually water and not the deck of a ship he's on and then sinks like a stone.

"You really didn't see the creature?" I am desperately trying to clarify what I feel is an undisputable point.

Alice locks eyes with me as though I just fell out of the "stupid tree" and hit every branch on the way down.

"There was a woman, a spirit, standing on the surface of the lake, and she spoke to me and told me I was being given a gift. And she said terrible things."

"What terrible things?" This has certainly grabbed my attention. I suspected that we were having parallel but markedly different experiences out there on the Loch, and now I am realizing how truly different they were.

"What did she say?"

"She told me the gift is from the Earth and that I am now the carrier," answers Alice, her voice breaking with emotion.

I am still in the was-it-Jesus? mode, so I think she means she's supernaturally "with child" . . . or something!!! I'm *so* lost.

"Are you pregnant?" and it sounds incongruous just saying the words.

"Pregnant?"

"What do you mean you're the 'carrier'?" I am struggling.

"I carry the death of half the world," Alice replies.

Okay, not what I was expecting *at* all.

"How could God allow this?" She begins to cry and I long to hold her but know I would be rebuffed. I have a feeling we are both in way over our heads.

I need to clarify this point even though the whole "death of half the world" thing is spinning round and round in my mind like a bird in the sky with a broken wing.

"You're saying you did *not* see the same Loch Ness Monster I saw?"

"There is no Loch Ness Monster. Other than the spirit who spoke to me," is her sure reply.

Did I hallucinate? Did she? Did we both?

"I *saw* this creature. It was right in front of me. But you're saying you saw some spirit . . . person, standing on the water. Water that's seven hundred feet deep. And that this person spoke to you?" It all sounds like lunacy to me as I put it into its most basic terms. I think there is more going on here than I can absorb.

"She didn't speak audibly. It's as if I was thinking the words—but they weren't my own thoughts," she says.

"What did this spirit say?" I'm on shaky ground here, not knowing who is the loony in the rubber room—Alice or me? Or both of us?

She regards me with her big wide eyes and takes a shallow breath.

She seems to be debating whether to say what she is about to say. "You are as much a part of this as I am, you know."

"A part of what?"

"The new beginning. A reboot. The thinning of the herd," is her answer.

"Thinning of *what* herd?" An awful idea is forming in the back of my mind. I always was a bit of a slow learner.

"The human race," is her not completely unexpected reply.

Lexington Vargas has finished his conversation with Merikh and now sees his part in this. He unsheathes the weapon from his coat pocket as he walks toward the house. Yin and yang. There can be no shadow without light. No male without female. And no life without death. He has been studying the Chinese concept of yin and yang ever since "Arthur" said he was the yang to Alice's yin. When he first heard the phrase it was meaningless to him but he is and always has been a diligent student of life (although his father thought otherwise) and he has come to understand the truth in the idea that there is no good or bad, only both. At once. Everything in balance. Yin and yang together form the whole. There are always two paths and he has been chosen. Alice is one and he, Lexington, is the other. For every path there is an alternate way, for every firm, hard choice there is an alternative possibility. And he, himself, is the second choice, the other possible outcome of this event to which they have all been summoned. He understands that God makes no choices for us. Life presents us with options and we are free to choose—good/evil, positive/negative, virtue/depravity—and the resulting outcome, whether we suffer or flourish, is always our choice. As Alice and Bobby have been given two options, so has he, Lexington, been given two options. To act and prevent this or not to act and by non-action allow it. He has chosen. Yin and yang. And these two, once his friends, cannot be allowed to do what they are contemplating. Even if it means the death of everything. If the end of the world is the natural order of things, then so be it. Yang walks toward the small house at 5 Holm Dell Park with a loaded gun in his hand.

"How are we supposed to thin the herd? And why?" This has gone so far left that I don't even know where center is anymore.

Alice has become agitated and has risen from her bed. She's now pacing in front of the fireplace, her energy contagious. She begins her terrible litany.

"She said she is an Earth spirit, the one on the Loch, and that there are others like her. They are guardians of our world and the Earth is alive—and we are made from and nurtured by her. But our Earth is dying and life can't grow from a dead thing. We are poisoning her. Killing her. Burying her under our apathy, our garbage, waste, and filth, and our self-righteous entitlement. Even a pregnant mother must abort her baby if it threatens her life. And that is the task she has given to me, to us. To save her. And save ourselves. But how can I do what is being asked of me? It's murder! Mass murder!"

She finishes her mind-blowing monologue, drops into a chair, and puts her face in her hands. And Atlas is contemplating whether she should shrug or not. At least I think she is.

"How are you supposed to accomplish this? Eliminate four billion people? Nothing on Earth can do that." This all sounds so nutty I just can't absorb it.

"It isn't something *on* Earth, it comes from *within* the earth," Alice answers as I move to sit on the arm of her chair to be closer to her. "I have been given a virus that will kill half the world in six months," she finishes, and I leap up from my almost-sitting position as though she's just said she's radioactive.

"What?" My go-to phrase again.

"It isn't viable yet," she says darkly.

"When does it become . . . viable?" I ask.

"That's where you come in."

"Me?" I yell a little too loud in the small house. How did I get involved in all this? I just wanted to see the Loch Ness effing Monster.

"I have the female component to the virus. You were given the male element, by whatever Earth spirit appeared to you out on that lake," is her bizarre answer.

"The Loch Ness Monster is an Earth spirit?" And there is disappointment in my voice.

"If that's what you saw, then yes," answers Alice the reluctant assassin.

"How long do we have?" I'm in shock.

"As the carrier, I am immune," she replies. "The symptoms start with a bloody nose. That's as far as it will go with me. The rest of the infected will die within twenty-four hours of the first sighting of blood."

"Christ almighty," I breathe.

"And some will be immune," she finishes.

"How does it become . . . operational?" I hardly have the words for this, and I think at this point I'm just using phrases again from old movies I've seen.

Alice hesitates as though she were deliberating whether to answer or not. Then she opens her mouth and says the best thing I could ever hope to hear and the worst thing I could ever hope to hear. It is the undisputed winner of the "jaw-dropping moment of the century" award.

"All life begins with the sex act. You and I must have sex to make the virus active. Then, as the carrier, it will flow from me with every breath I exhale, and it will grow exponentially through airborne contagion," she says and starts to cry again.

"Holy shit!" is my gut reaction. "That is seriously fucked-up. So if I were to have . . . make love to you, it will kill half the world's population?"

Alice nods and dabs at her eyes with the sleeve of the sweatshirt I loaned her for our trip on the Loch. It looks enormous on her and has a cartoon of a pig with the legend, "Swine flu. Bacon's revenge." I've got to stop buying clothes with slogans on them. They are way too prescient.

"She told me that the Earth has no alternatives left. We have passed the tipping point. Our breeding has run amuck and we've abused and laid waste to her. If this doesn't happen, if we choose not to activate the virus, then *everyone* and *everything* will die." It just keeps getting worse and worse as Alice speaks.

"All life on Earth?"

"Yes."

"Why us?" is all I can ask.

"She believes we'll understand what's at stake," replies Alice. "And we have no family to be concerned with. That we are bonded. Maybe you're meant to protect me."

"With *these* arms?" I try to make a joke, but I was never good with timing.

She smiles despite our dire predicament.

"Can God really want this?" she asks, and her face looks like some kid who's been told there really is no Easter Bunny and is looking for the sad confirmation from her parents.

"He's kind of been leading the charge," I answer.

"My God," responds the unluckiest woman in the world.

"So where does Lexington fit into all of this?" I ask, like she would know.

And no sooner have the words left my mouth than the aforementioned humongous human being walks into the kitchen where Alice and I are struggling to decide the fate of the world. He is sweating and looks distraught. He has something in his right hand. He raises the gun and points it at Alice's face.

"I'm so sorry," he says as tears begin to form a shimmery film over his eyes. "I love you both, like a brother and sister—but this is wrong, what you plan to do."

I am on my feet. The wimpy protector.

"Stop! Lexington, no! She isn't going to make the virus active. It's still our choice!"

I proclaim this to the crazy giant as I make a move to try to place myself between the black hole of the barrel and the person I now love most in this world. Who knew I would ever choose to take a bullet for someone other than Murray?

"Merikh told me you might say that," answers our dear old friend L.V.

"Merikh just wants everyone dead. That's what he does for a living. He's the Angel of Death!" I'm shooting from the hip.

"No. *You* are the Angels of Death. You can't be allowed to do this. *Que Dios me perdone*," replies the now lethal Lexington Vargas holding his illegally obtained weapon.

"*Click*," says the cocking gun.

"Shit," says I.

"Stop," yells someone.

There is a roaring explosion, and I actually see flames leap from the Lexington Vargas's "persuader." Someone screams in pain, but it isn't me.

"It goes the way it goes," thinks the Omnipotent Supreme Being. The OSB has His/Her fingers in many pies and is monitoring all of them. And there are 92 to the 17-trillionth-power moments all happening simultaneously around the universe. But this path the "Earth" is trying to take, as a living planet, is unique in the OSB's experience, which is prodigious and fairly complete. It might just be the radical direction all the other worlds need to follow to ensure <u>their</u> survival. Certainly there can be no more episodes like the Vee-Nung, damn their stubborn shortsightedness and flabby, amphibian limbs. The OSB is watching very closely because every Father/Mother wants to see their children live long and prosper. "Oh, crap," the OSB says to His/Her self, "I may have a little too much invested in this planet. I'm quoting <u>Star Trek</u> now?"

All I can see is blood on the walls of the kitchen as ugly gray smoke and the smell of cordite hang in the air like a bad guest that won't leave. Lexington Vargas has apparently fled. I anxiously turn to Alice to help her but she looks unharmed.

"Are you shot?" I ask desperately, checking her for signs of a wound. She is, like me, in shock.

"I . . . I don't think so," she says. "Are you?"

I pat down my own body as though I'm looking for misplaced car keys or someone has just asked me if I have change for a dollar. No entry or exit wounds on me, either.

"I guess not," I answer.

I peer at the kitchen and see blood-spatter. I hear a scuffling noise and move cautiously into the area as though it were land-mined.

Writhing there on the floor is Lexington Vargas, our would-be-assassin. He is moaning in pain, hands to his blood-covered face. I look for the revolver but see only pieces. A barrel here, half a hand-grip there, metal fragments scattered across the counter and littering the ground around the struggling behemoth. I guess not everything "handmade with pride in Scotland" is the better buy.

"I think the gun exploded," I yell to Alice as I drop to my knees to help our potential murderer and friend.

"Call an ambulance. Call the police."

"How?" asks Alice. It's a fair question.

"Isn't it nine-one-one?" I shout as I grab a towel from the refrigerator handle and dab at L.V.'s face and hands as he blindly pushes me away, howling in pain. I tell him I'm trying to help.

Alice runs to the phone and dials.

"Nine-one-one just goes to a busy signal," she yells back at me.

"The emergency number is nine-nine-nine," says someone other than Alice, me, or Lexington Vargas.

Just when I thought Hansel and Gretel might be out of the woods, the Big Bad Wolf is standing inside the front door of Grandma's house, offering up the local emergency number. Merikh now has a gun in *his* hand as well. I thought guns were really hard to *get* in the UK!!

Alice dials and gives our address, never taking her eyes off Merikh. He isn't doing anything threatening other than holding the weapon (which looks to be an exact copy of the one L.V. just tried to dispatch us with, and I think maybe this weird apparently super-natural being creates his firearms out of our imaginations) at his side, so I continue to administer to Lexington Vargas, who has what look like some seriously deep puncture wounds to his face and right hand. I see a bloody stump where one of his fingers used to be. He moans and utters Spanish phrases I don't understand.

"The situation had to play itself out. I am sorry," Merikh says. "It is not possible for me to take a life." He puts the gun inside his jacket and I assume the frigging thing just disappears again because I see no telltale bulge. He bends down near L.V. and me on the blood-speckled floor and hooks his long ebony mane behind his ears, which are *per-fect* and just how I always imagined mine would look if I'd had them surgically repaired by the best plastics guy in Beverly Hills. But he does nothing to help.

"The Angel of Death can't take a life?" I say in as perplexed a tone as I can muster.

"I am not this Angel of Death you think I am," he answers.

L.V. has stopped struggling and is now lying still. I check to make sure he has a pulse. It's racing and blood continues to leak, deep, dark, and crimson, from the many ruptures in his skin.

"But you killed everyone on that plane on the freeway," I counter, still swabbing away.

"I did not. I told you that. Most of them were already dead from a chemical leak that poisoned the atmosphere inside the cabin before the aircraft went down," he counters my counter. "I was there to help them cross through. That is what I do as an Earth spirit. That is why I was in Japan for the tsunami event. I help those who die find their way. Many are confused and don't realize they are dead. So I guide them to the next step."

Alice has joined us at L.V.'s side and is staring wide-eyed at Merikh.

"Are you sent from God?" She sounds breathless.

"I am from the Earth," answers Merikh.

"Where do you guide them? The ones that die?" I ask.

"That is not for me to say," he replies.

"Why are you here? Why did you follow us?" challenges Alice.

"To help you. Though I could not help you with this. I cannot interfere in the natural way of things." I trust the absolute honesty in his voice. It's like he's incapable of lying. "If you choose the path of initiating the virus, I will have many souls to guide on their way."

Alice stands with anger in her body. "How can I do what has been asked? My path, with God's help, has always been to heal, not harm."

"Then you will *all* die. As will the Earth," Merikh says with no judgment in his tone. "Humans have entered the time of unsustainable growth. Fifty years from now there will be total rampant disease, starvation, misery, and the end of all meaning to existence. The extinction of everything. The death of our world. The Earth is trying to save herself. Save life. You may choose to act or not to act. But non-action is *still* a choice, though it's the less desirable of the two. By doing nothing, you choose the death of all living things. And of the planet herself."

Alice drops to her knees and I catch her plaintive prayer, "Dear God, help me." I hear distant sirens. They sound alien, but the meaning of their strident wail is unmistakable. The police are on their way.

"I think we better come up with a story," I suggest to Alice, since I'm pretty sure that Merikh won't be here when the local constabulary arrive.

I walk into the living room to see if there's anything out of place that we might need to explain when the police arrive and I catch sight of the photograph of the couple that lived their lives in this house before we brought this craziness to it. It's the one I found earlier and placed on the side table not six hours ago. I recognize the man in the framed shot. It is the one who said, "Call me 'Skipper.'"

He is glad to have been with his "girl" one final time, as brief as it was. He wishes he could take her memory with him, but he knows once he crosses the barrier, she will no longer be in his mind. His *Bonnie Bradana* is for those who remain on Earth. He runs a hand along her bow and bids her good-bye. So close to the heart of his life was she. And as far as the one previously known as Ronan Bon Young can tell, she most certainly has a soul. He walks away and casts a last look back as he calls out in his native tongue, *Soraidh gu bràth.*

Farewell forever.

Merikh takes his hand to lead him home.

Of course Merikh's stunning presence is markedly absent when the police and the paramedics arrive. Alice and I, with only a toehold in reality, tell them the story we've concocted on the fly. The gun was found on the premises while we were housecleaning, and it accidentally discharged as our companion was inspecting it. No one is accused of attempted homicide, but Lexington Vargas is pretty seriously fucked-up. The paramedics are fairly sure he's lost the sight in his left eye, and he'll need surgery to remove the metal fragments that are buried deep in his face and hands. Guns are not toys, we are told. Really?

"You should be very careful if you find a weapon. Call the police and do not handle the firearm," are the words of wisdom from what look like sixteen-year-old dudes masquerading as grown-up cops while Lexington Vargas is wheeled away on a gurney and Alice and I contemplate the fate of half the world. Truly, youth *is* wasted on the young.

We both apologize for the inconvenience. And thanks for the great advice on guns. We'll visit our friend tomorrow in the local sanatorium; by the way, what are the visiting hours? Here's my credit-card information, just put it on my tab, and no we don't need an AIDS test even though copious amounts of bodily fluids are spattered all around, thanks a lot. Don't forget to wear a condom when you finally get laid, see you all tomorrow, and take good care of our friend the attempted hitman. Bye! *Cheerio andràsta!*

After the medics and the constables leave, I mop up the blood that could have been Alice's but for . . . what? A twist of fate? An act of God? A plain old "shit happens"? I am as close to a spiritual awakening as I have ever been and as far from it at the same time. What was it Alice said? "Dear God, help me."

She is sitting on the couch that, judging by the amount of wheat-colored fur still lodged deep in the corners, was also the regular haunt of Toby and Jacoby, the two little Cairn terriers who lived out their span of years here. I sit beside her and take her elegant hands in mine. I can see the edge of her tattoo peeking out from the low neck of my borrowed sweatshirt. Our minds are reeling.

Something comes to me that I read somewhere, a long, long time ago:

> *"What about the pain and sorrow?" asks the student.*
> *The Master answers, "Stay with it. The wound is the place where*
> *the light enters."*

And I have no choice but to stay with it.

"How can we do this terrible thing?" Alice finally asks.

"How can we *not*?" I answer, and believe me, Woody has no say in this conversation. I know I have portrayed myself as a dick-driven idiot through most of this narrative but my soul has been screaming for recognition. And it's time I gave my soul a voice.

"Alice," I begin, "I will go with whatever you decide. I love you more than I love my own life, and more than anyone else's, so whatever you choose is okay with me. If I can help you to make a choice then all you have to do is ask. If you choose *not* to choose, then, as Merikh said, you've made a choice anyway."

She says nothing.

"You never told me if *I* was immune to this virus, so if these are my last days, then I'm happy with that as long as I'm with you," I say from the deepest place in my soul.

Alice stands and extends her hand, I take it, and she leads me into her bedroom. I still don't know if I will die or not. And I am okay with not knowing.

She will go out into the world, the emissary of global catastrophe and savior of the planet. God help us.

THANKS TO:

My wife, Barbara, for putting up with me sitting in the shade working on my laptop during our Christmas vacation in Australia when she wanted to go and do stuff.

My editor and good friend Stacy Creamer, who encouraged me from the very beginning of our relationship to write novels, and to the team at Touchstone: Susan Moldow, David Falk, Brian Belfiglio, Sophie Vershbow, Meredith Vilarello, Cherlynne Li, and webmaster Jim Bullotta, for being, in the words of Horatio Cotton, "fully awesome."

To everyone who spent their hard-earned cash buying this book—I hope you think it was worth it—and to those who stole it (like I used to when I was a kid)—I hope you think it was worth it. :)